RIP-RAP

Fiction and Poetry from The Banff Centre for the Arts

RipRap

CAROLINE ADDERSON
KELLEY AITKEN
PAUL ANDERSON
KEN BABSTOCK
ROSEMARY BLAKE
LESLEY-ANNE BOURNE
MARC ANDRÉ BROUILLETTE
CHRIS COLLINS
MÉIRA COOK
JOHN DONLAN
IRENE GUILFORD

RACHNA MARA
JOSEPH MAVIGLIA
LORIE MISECK
LISA MOORE
SHELDON OBERMAN
JOANNE PAGE
HELEN PEREIRA
SINA QUEYRAS
CHETAN RAJANI
J. JILL ROBINSON
BARBARA SCOTT

NAOMI GUTTMAN
STEPHEN HEIGHTON
BRUCE HUNTER
MAUREEN HYNES
MICHAEL C. KENYON
RICHARD LEMM
JOHN LENT
ELISE LEVINE
LAURA LUSH
SUE MACLEOD
RANDALL MAGGS

THE BANFF CENTRE
PRESS

ANNE SIMPSON
STRUAN SINCLAIR
DOROTHY SPEAK
JOHN STEFFLER
ROYSTON TESTER
BARBARA TURNER-VESSELAGO
LIZ UKRAINETZ
SUE WHEELER

Edited by Edna Alford, Don McKay,
Rhea Tregebov, and Rachel Wyatt

CANADIAN CATALOGUING IN PUBLICATION DATA

Main entry under title:
Rip-rap
ISBN 0-920159-65-6

1. Canadian literature (English)—20th century. I. Alford, Edna, 1947– II. Banff Centre for the Arts.
PS8251.R56 1999   C810.8'0054   C99-910541-8
PR9194.9.R56 1999

Cover and book design by Alan Brownoff
Cover photography by Don Lee–The Banff Centre for the Arts
Printed and bound in Canada by Friesens, Altona, Manitoba.

We gratefully acknowledge the support of the Canada Council for the Arts for our publishing program.

THE CANADA COUNCIL | LE CONSEIL DES ARTS
FOR THE ARTS | DU CANADA
SINCE 1957 | DEPUIS 1957

BANFF CENTRE PRESS
The Banff Centre for the Arts
Box 1020-17
Banff, Alberta Canada ToL oCo
http://www.banffcentre.ab.ca/Writing/Press/

THE BANFF CENTRE
FOR THE ARTS

CONTENTS

RACHEL *Wyatt*

INTRODUCTION

TWO YEARS AGO, I was sitting at dinner in a Halifax restaurant with several writers. They had all attended the Banff Writing Program but in different years. One of them, obviously a trouble-maker, said, "Rachel, you told us we were the best group ever." Looks were exchanged and then from the others came cries of "But she said that to us." "No. We were the best!"

I had been found out. Not in a lie but in the kind of truth that can get you into trouble. And what is fiction but a kind of dangerous truth? What is fiction indeed? There is no easy definition. Fiction is. Poetry is. And for five weeks in the mountains, The Banff Centre for the Arts is alive with words. The mountains, Rundle, Cascade, Sulphur, Norquay, echo with images and visions, characters and scenes. Wandering elk and malicious magpies are witness, or would be if they cared, to a remarkable flourishing of talent.

Poets and fiction writers from Newfoundland and British Columbia and all points in between come together to complete a novel, to work on short stories, to put together a manuscript of poems. Or to be inspired by that amazing and thaumaturgic view to write something entirely different. It is not unknown for a poet in this atmosphere to take to prose or for a novelist to turn out a fine sestina or ghazal.

For nearly seven decades, writers have been gathering in the shadow of these mountains to learn from various masters. One of the first teachers was Hugh MacLennan and one of those early students was Robert Kroetsch.

In 1972, W.O. Mitchell became director of the Writing Program. It was, he insisted, to have no element of the creative writing programs being set up in universities, no formality. At Banff, writers were to write "without the pressure of performance." Like a mediaeval scholar, he gathered writers around him and talked to them and showed them ways in which to free their captive ideas.

It was a summer program then and high-school students as well as mature writers came to sit at the feet of the master and to work their way into the craft and art of writing. Poetry and prose, drama and writing for radio, all had a place and all, with variations, continue to thrive in Banff.

Adele Wiseman agreed with W.O. Mitchell's view of formal writing courses. When she took over as director in 1987, she brought her own distinct ideas and built onto what was already in place. Her vision was primarily to create a community of writers in what had become the May Studios. Working individually with editors, writers would be encouraged to be independent artists confident in their own voices. Adele had a sharp editorial eye and was often able to make invaluable suggestions to a writer but always with the admonition, *Remember, this is your work.*

When she was offered the directorship of the program, Adele called me and said, "Would you like to go to Banff?" The Banff Centre for the Arts, specifically the Writing Studio, had been till then a kind of Mecca for other writers who knew a secret password that would never be revealed to me. I had been given a ticket to the Enchanted Kingdom.

My first view of the mountains as the car passed by Lac des Arcs confirmed this. The "Welcome, Rachel" banner that Adele had hung over the balcony in Lloyd Hall was a sign of the future; my three-week assignment turned into a twelve-year relationship. Due to ill health, Adele was only present as director of the program for three alternate years out of her six-year term, but she set her mark on the program in that short time.

There were days when I felt like saying to Adele, "'This is another fine mess you've gotten me into.'" But most of the time it has been a wonderful experience and, after all, a writing program without some problems would seem to be out of touch with that reality from which we all write.

When, four years ago, due to accommodation problems, the program was moved to the fall, some feared it would wither and die. As if perhaps the long dark evenings might drive writers to mayhem and madness. So far, mayhem and madness have largely stayed away. These years have been extremely productive and many remarkable writers have been able to take time out from busy working lives, in the home or out of it, to pursue their creative goals. Of the group of twenty writers in the 1996 program, eleven have subsequently had books published or accepted for publication.

"My book has been accepted!" It is a joy to hear these words on the other end of the line. And the writer who speaks them knows that across the country many others will truly share the pleasure in that moment of triumph.

As important as the new work that is written here, the ideas that fall into place, the leaps forward, is the support from others in the group. It is easy for a writer who has till then worked alone to think that all the other writers in the program, the country, the world, come to their desks fresh each morning and produce a masterpiece a day. What a comfort then to discover that it is the same for everyone: writing is a struggle; a wastebasket full of discarded pages is nothing unusual; sweat and tears are normal.

It is impossible to praise highly enough the men and women who have given up their own writing time to come to Banff as faculty members. Without them, their honest critical work, their careful, sometimes painful-to-hear suggestions, their gentle attention to problems of all kinds, there would be no Writing Program. They have made it what it is and given the program its now international reputation.

The effect of the Banff Writing Program can't be measured in the number of books published or the acknowledgements on the first pages of those books. But it might be measured in the letters we get and in the "conversations" that continue long after the mountains are left behind.

Over time, the Banff Centre has changed. New buildings stand where once were trees. More programs and more conferences take place than ever before. One year, writers were startled by shrieks beneath their windows. Members of a management training course were jumping into one another's arms from the trees. On another occasion, I was startled to see a minotaur tethered near the theatre building. It was not a figment of an over-stimulated imagination, but a Brahma bull brought there to grace a western-style pancake breakfast. Another conference brought Stephen Hawking to Banff and we were able to sneak into the back of the room to be inspired by the man himself and the poetic language he used in his discussion of "black holes." That same evening Cleo Laine gave a concert in the theatre. Such days and nights!

Amid all this and the good sounds of musicians practising, the Writing Program goes on in its quiet and, to some, mysterious way. And writers emerging like spring bears from their rooms after a long day at the keyboard, can go to a fine concert, the opening of an art exhibition, or walk to the Sundance Canyon.

The Writing Program would be chaotic affair without the support and help of the staff and administration at the Banff Centre. Nothing seems to be beyond the capacity of the co-ordinator or the people in the Community Services office. In the past few years, cries of "Where can I get a new typewriter ribbon?" have been replaced by "The printer needs new toner" or, "I can't read my disk." All these and many other needs are responded to with due speed. For the writer used to working against the demands of ordinary life, it is like being cared for by a flock of kindly aunts—of both sexes.

All across Canada and now in England, Australia, and the United States, there are writers who met one another at the Banff Centre and who are friends for life because of those weeks in the mountains. They know that there are people out there who understand, who share their struggles and their memories of walks up Tunnel Mountain, of volleyball games, Hallowe'en goblins, and the great bargains at the downtown church rummage sale.

"It was the best experience of my life," the letters say. Or as one faculty member put it, "I came home feeling there were new worlds to conquer and I believe the writers went away with the same excitement."

And what kind of people are they who come to spend five weeks in the mountains and write? Men and women, married and single, just out of college or ready for retirement, they have one thing in common. And that mysterious *thing* is caught here between these covers: stories of family life, of travel, of other worlds; poems with visions and styles as varied as the poets themselves.

There would be no book had it not been for the generous and rapid response of these writers from the program's past twenty-five years. To all of them, whether their work is included here or not, the editors would like to express deep gratitude. It has been a true pleasure to read so much fine writing, to re-discover old friends, and to be delighted by new work.

I am writing this soon after W.O. Mitchell's death and six years after Adele Wiseman passed on. To them and to all those fine faculty members who have generously given of their time, their knowledge, and their skill to help and encourage so many writers, this book is a dedication and a tribute.

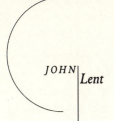

JOHN Lent

ROOFS IN THE MORNING

THERE IS AN INTIMACY about neighbourhoods early in the morning that only occurs then, when the sun is just beginning to catch the roofs and the chimneys, when the street is so quiet only non-habitual sounds, like a car driving by, or the backing-up beep of a delivery truck a couple of blocks away, draw attention to themselves and break the sense of a cocoon unfolding in the morning air, a cocoon that is a collective rather than an individual thing.

It's the collective nature of the intimacy that intrigues me and makes me wonder, for it flies in the face of the privacy that defines neighbourhoods: all the obvious grids and lines drawn round a person—the curbs, fences, garages, garbage cans, curtains, doors with latches—that defy collectivity and persist as quiet announcements of borders in the air. Maybe it's the relaxation of these borders early in the morning beneath these roofs that creates the intimacy I'm thinking of this morning. I'm not sure. It's just that this intimacy is almost physical and, in some curious ways, accessible, whatever that means. On another level, I guess, this intimacy and its collective nature redeems other things that happen to us.

We're down here in Vancouver for a few days staying in her brother's flat on the main floor of an old house on West Twelfth in Kitsilano. If you're familiar with Vancouver, his flat is just south of Broadway, a couple of blocks down from the futuristic McDonald's, west of the Hollywood theatre and east of Orestes Restaurant. You know where I am, then.

We're down here because she has an appointment with her specialist and we're trying to make the trip simple and inexpensive by staying in his flat and avoiding the West End where we'd be tempted to spend money. We put Malcolm on the plane this morning, the morning after we arrived, so we have his place to ourselves now, which is nice in another way, too. The privacy I was talking about earlier, I guess.

He's off to Ecuador for six weeks with a friend. He's excited about it and, naturally, we got caught up in the excitement. We pored over his atlas with him, browsed through his guide books, listened to the itinerary that had been set up for him by a travel agent. It was fascinating to be drawn into a landscape that I was completely unaware of except in general terms like the vague, solid shape of South America itself in my mind. Also, because this flat is new for him, we were drawn into its details for the first time and that was fun, too.

It's a small, two-bedroom flat renovated in the early eighties. The owner of the house had raised the house twelve feet, poured a basement, then finished it off as a rental to pay down the mortgage.

It's a very Kitsilano thing to do. Everywhere you look in this neighbourhood, no matter how small the house, you become aware of its division into rental flats. In some ways, these neighbourhoods have at least double, maybe triple the residents they might have had back in the twenties and thirties when they were all single-family dwellings.

After we put him on the plane this morning, we drove around the city, went for a cappuccino in a small café on West Fourth, then picked up some bagels for supper. Because her appointment is for tomorrow, we decided to stay at home tonight and go out for supper and a movie tomorrow night when the appointment is behind her and we don't feel so distracted. We're thinking of seeing a new flick called *The Crying Game*. It's supposed to be good. It's supposed to have a plot twist, like *Body Heat*. You can never tell in advance. You just hope that's true. But staying home tonight was a good move. She and I both love bagels but don't get to eat them much because nobody makes good bagels back in Vernon. We bought some cream cheese, sliced some tomatoes, and sat and talked and watched the television for a while. Both of us had trouble getting to sleep.

We had a lot on our minds, I guess. Things have built up over the past three months while she's been sick. She's in remission now, and her visit to her specialist will confirm it, we think, and allow her, both of us I guess, to breathe more easily. But you can't tell about these things in advance. We've made these trips before and both of us are drifting in and out of those memories, positive and negative. At one point, while neither of us could sleep, we talked more honestly than we ever had about sickness, and about hope and the things that interfere with it. It was a painful talk in some ways. The darkness allowed us to be more direct than we usually are, to abandon some of the protectiveness we use to shield ourselves from things. We cried and became even closer in the dark, an incredible thing considering the first trip we made like this one was in 1975, seventeen years ago. Then she fell asleep. I watched her for a while, then got up and sat on the couch in his living room. I played with his radio tuner trying to get CBC but mostly getting Seattle stations instead. Something to do with his cable channels, I guessed. That, and living so close to Seattle.

But tuning in the Seattle stations was fascinating by itself. Listening to the early deejays talk about local traffic patterns there made me feel like a voyeur, as if I was peering in on a closed, ritualized world of early morning coffee and cars in the mist and ferry schedules. It wasn't like listening to your own station. It felt like another world, another country. Finally, around six a.m. I found the CBC and lay on the couch listening to the morning show, its familiar voices and announcements. Then I showered and decided to go out for a coffee and bring her home something from a bakery for breakfast.

Out in the street in the early sun, it was cold. This was an unusual cold snap for Vancouver and you actually had to scrape the windows and let the car warm up for ten minutes before setting out. If I don't wait, my Tercel will stall. Sometimes when it stalls, it will flood itself and it can take another fifteen or twenty minutes to get it going again. It wasn't really built for weather this cold. So I scraped the window and sat in the car, watching. While I did this, other people surfaced to warm their cars and I could see still more moving in windows while dozens of lights came on.

One young man, in a blue parka with the hood up so that fur circled his head, came out on the street across from me and scraped off the windows of an old Dodge truck. Then he sat in it and turned it over, sitting there just like me. I nodded at him and he flashed a wide smile back. I could see his teeth, white in the grey haze of the window above the dash. I imagined him tuning in his favourite station on the radio or even flicking in a cassette. On the other side of the street, a woman in her late twenties was standing in her living-room window in her housecoat, holding a cup of coffee in both hands. The morning air was so clear I imagined I could see the veins moving in the hand facing me. Her head was tilted upward. She was looking at something behind and above my car. A young girl in blue pyjamas joined her, squinted out directly at me, then dragged her mother off by pulling her housecoat. They disappeared into a bright light that must have been in the kitchen at the back of the house. Two cars passed me, both gauging the ruts in the road so they wouldn't come too close to my car. I kept thinking, they do this every morning. The only thing different about this one is that I'm sitting here, a strange face, a strange car. Sitting in the dawn.

Every morning, I thought. And I wondered about their lives, the surfaces of the Arborite counters in their kitchens, the feel of their boots as they slipped into them, the brush of nylon against arms and legs as they dressed for the cold. I wondered about their coffees, their orange juice, their different breakfasts, and the dishes they left on the table or cleaned up and put away. I could almost see the different wallpaper and rugs. And each of these people, if I had eye contact with them, was open, smiling, in the strange freedom and hopefulness that faces acquire in the morning for some reason. I seemed to be slipping into the physical texture of the lives around me, fabric for fabric, flesh for flesh. And I almost wanted to be there every morning with them, be part of this breathing. I wanted everything. Love is like that, isn't it? Then I saw her standing in her brother's window, waving back at me, trying to get my attention, pointing dramatically at the mug of coffee she was holding out with one hand, and I thought this is my morning, she is my morning, here where I've found myself lost again.

SUE MacLeod

A WOMAN IS MAKING

A woman is making
herself. She is taking the lines
of her body from the hills across the water, her breath
from salty air. She is panning for tears in the deep
cold sea, and heating them up
to make them ready, warming
her hands at the stove. She wants fire, she wants wind
to burn a lifeline in-
to doughy palms like these.
A woman is frightened. Her fears rise
like curlicues of steam, they turn to mildew
on the kitchen ceiling. She is swaying
a child on her hip, and her swaying
is the *lap lap lap*
of water on a shoreline
and her swaying
is the clatter and the rumble of a subway train, cradled
in its track. A woman is meeting the eye
of a needle, she is sewing the uneasy pieces
into one. She is folding her memories into a box

small enough to slide into
an apron pocket.
A woman can make herself
small, she can slide into the pocket,
curl herself up in her memory box
until she is back in the first
of her childhood apartments, on her knees and rocking
in the platform chair. The curtains are blowing.
On the balcony, her mother is shaking a dust-mop,
banging the handle on the crusted metal rail,
backing into the room—her own
dust-mop shuffle.
"There," she says brightly
as if she had shaken
shame away.
She pulls the door shut so it can't blow back in.

KELLEY *Aitken*

HATCHETFACE

HATCHETFACE. She was short, five two or something, and dark-skinned. She tanned easily to a nut brown. Dark hair, too. A hatchet-faced, raven-haired woman. I'm waxing poetic. At any rate, she didn't stand out, if you know what I mean. Not like a dove among crows or a lily among ... let's go for something short and dark. Pansies? And not exotic enough. There are flowers, since I'm on the subject, bromiliads and the like, spiky tropical blooms, ugly and captivating at the same time. You look at them and think, jeez, how does it work? Why did Nature make it? No answer forthcoming, but still, you can hardly stop staring.

Her feelings for me go back to when she found out about us, me and him. She said it hurt a lot because, "You're so blonde. So pretty." It's all relative. I mean, in Canada I'm not. But down there, a small village on the Ecuadorian coast, blonde was the red-hot ticket. Lots of variables according to culture and geography on "pretty." Nail it down in one corner of the world and lose sight of it somewhere else. An elusive concept. But Winona sure as hell found something pretty when she married him. Lord, was he gorgeous.

I'm justified in using the past tense. Age and drugs took care of his beauty. Took it away a cell at a time. Which adds up over all those weeks and months and years on that hot coast. And he's fat now, too. Looks go.

7

Beliefs get stale. Love takes a hike. You wake up one morning and the sense of adventure that beckoned you is long gone, hardly remembered except for nights when a visitor pulls it out of you and it rolls off your tongue like the rum you're drinking. The next morning, there's just your hangover, a too bright sun beating on the shrimp ponds, the sticky, stinking heat, and a sour taste in your mouth. It's the taste of nostalgia, of something that didn't deliver. The visitor goes back home and you're on your own again, melting into torpor. Endless tropical nights stretch out ahead, bug-filled wastelands to be endured. The kerosene lamps go *phht* and *ssss* and the cassettes are old and a lot of them just don't play anymore.

Winona's the only woman I ever had the pleasure of hating. I borrowed her husband for the briefest possible period. Long enough to have a leg up. Like a dog, pissing out a territory. Like a bitch in heat, consenting finally to the leader of the pack. Not even such a catch after all.

Winona talked about their sex life as if it were some raving roller coaster of positions and potency. "We did it down by the pump on the path. God, was it good," she said, into her cups one evening, just the girls, 'cause Gary was up in the capital. Sure you did, Winona, with the fire ants crawling all over your half-tanned ass. Sounds blissful to me.

"We made the house shake last night," she'd say in town, to anyone who'd listen. Like a cane house doesn't shake when you sneeze or just walk across the floor. Give it a rest, Winona. Everybody knows it's bull.

There's a phrase in Spanish, how does it go? The translation is something like "She put horns on him." Meaning, he was the cuckold; the husband of an adulteress. Winona fucked her way through the varied terrain of the country, up and down mountains and into the jungle, along the coast, up river and down river, putting horns on her husband with a certain geographical panache. Maybe it was a cry for help and maybe it's what a hatchet-faced woman does when her own husband no longer turns to her in the dark and maybe, maybe, maybe. Maybe I was part of some weird balancing act on the part of Fate: a ye-too-shall-be-screwed contract that floats around in the ether, one of the great karmic scoreboards in the sky. Fucking Gary was my way of evening the score. I was happy to fuck Gary 'cause his own wife screwed around on him. That was how I sold it to myself, at the time. I was happy to lean forward in the Boston whaler so that my round little butt showed underneath my short blue shorts, leaning over the bow like I was so interested in the colour of the water or were there fish in the channel or just how shallow is it here anyway. Pretty damned shallow.

Gary and I had one good night together. Sexy. Steamy. Sliding around in the sweat and musk of each other. The next day, he sent me home with a *racime* of bananas. If you've seen pictures of the plantations, you know these big bunches hang off the banana plant. Tiers of green fruit around a thick stem, like rows of fingers getting ready to catch something. And down there, in banana-land, they refer to the smaller bunches as hands, *manos*. Some of them were sure to rot before I'd get around to eating them. Maybe Gary wanted me to think of something sweet, to think of his *manos*, touching me everywhere. Maybe he wanted me to remember what was unlikely to be repeated, 'cause that was the last time Gary intended to stray. Guilt? Variety is not the spice of life? He just wasn't cut out for it, the life of sexual transgression.

Sometimes couples divide the roles and rules between them. Here's your outlet, honey; here's mine. Gary was happiest when he was taking apart a motor, grease up to his yingyang. He couldn't help being beautiful, being the kind of man women want, panting, parading their pert little buns and breasts around in his line of sight, hoping to get a rise out of him. I watched other women try after me; I knew he wasn't biting. One good night was all Gary could give me. But Hatchetface and I went many rounds. What's a man sometimes except a lever between two women, unconsciously throwing his weight and influence into one corner and then the next.

Y'see, I told her. I know, I'm a major league *idiota*, but we were drunk one night, me and Sandy and Winona. Sandy's the connection, right? She's my friend from back in Canada. She's why I'm here in this hot little back-water on the equator. She's Winona's friend, too, 'cause gringas stick together and sometimes you just wanna speak English. Sandy alternates between putting up with Winona and avoiding her. She's tired of fibbing to Winona, of having this secret on her.

"Okay, Sandy," I say, "I see your point." She's giving me this look: You better.

"Okaaay," I say. "All right, already. We can tell her the next time we're there."

"We?" Sandy's got her teacher voice. I let myself be shamed, be swayed. Why not, no sweat really 'cause I know that Winona in one of her guiltier moments had more or less offered Gary to Sandy. I figure the fling's been flung, the affair was pretty short-lived, she'll understand. What a dolt.

Within a few weeks, we're at the shrimp farm and Gary's away, up the coast buying larvae. I'm psyched. Tonight's the night. I'll make a clean breast of it.

"Listen, Winona, it was booze, okay?" Only I'm looking at her face and "okay" is not the word for that expression. "We just got a little, you know, carried away." Her hairline is moving strangely, like the hair is trying to separate from the scalp. Now she's looking over at Sandy, but Sandy's not looking at either of us.

"Just the one time, Winona." Ah yes, very reassuring. See that vein pulsing at her temple, the thin line of her lips pressing together, those two spots of colour high on her cheeks.

Hatchetface asks a few questions, mostly to do with when but the what is there, larger than life, a furry beast pressing up against all of us. Is it really hot in here or is it just me?

The miracle is that when I finally say good night and go upstairs, I fall asleep. Winona stays up all night with Sandy. By morning, I'm the *femme fatale* from hell and the golden princess all rolled into one. I'm hanging with metaphors, I'm reeking, stinking with symbolism. The other woman. Done her wrong. Her Gary does it once with someone else and she's the scorned wife, the heartbroken heroine; she's got story power in this one to outlast any and all of her infidelities. Sandy's acting all sanctimonious and pure, like you-get-what-you-ask-for. I'm sheepish, but at least less hungover than the two of them, and better rested.

"What did you expect?" Sandy asks when I mutter something about the morning mood. And then, as if I might have forgotten, "You slept with her husband." I can see the emphasis she places on that last word. It's in capitals, drawn and shaded to look 3-D, a big word in comic strip granite. It drops from the cartoon bubble beside her head and lands with a crash at our feet. I look down.

We're all acting out our parts.

Hatchetface gets a regular snit on about it, hates my guts. Sometimes, months after the fact, we'll have it out. Gary shakes his head at us, from a distance. He still sneaks a kiss or two when he can, but we both know it won't amount to a thing. I'm not drinking so much anymore. I never had the stomach for it. But Winona's always saying, "We create our own reality." She likes to alter the one she's in with whatever's handy. She and Gary go from the sweet, clear high of refined coke, down through the months and years into the gag-me stench of base, cooking on a wire screen. They can blow a whole weekend huddled around that screen.

At the end of that year, I leave. Four years later, I return. In the interim, my dad has died from pancreatic cancer.

Between finding out about my father's illness and his death, there was no time to fix decades of not saying what we felt, or even knowing what that was. I have remorse to last me the rest of my days.

I'm back in Ecuador 'cause something in me needs something here. I don't need trouble, so I don't go to the coast. I don't revisit the scene of the crime. The crime, as it were, visits me.

Gary and Winona have driven up from the coast with a cooler full of shrimp. Sandy has walked over the hills from the little house she lives in now. She got tired of the bugs and constant dirt of life, ocean-side. There we are, the four of us, in the living room of the place I'm house-sitting, thirty minutes southeast of Quito.

We've boiled, shelled, and eaten the shrimp, and scarfed down the cheese and bread. The wine they brought is all gone, and Sandy's up for it all of a sudden, in a real party mode. She says there's more wine at her house. She and Gary get in the Jeep to go and get it, which leaves me and Winona alone under the high wooden rafters of the adobe living room. I can't imagine how we're gonna get through the next twenty minutes.

She's still got wine in her glass though mine is empty. The room already looks hungover. There's a platter with four or five uneaten shrimp on the coffee table, the remains of a humungous pile; I swear, they brought half a pond. On the same dish are several squeezed and discarded limones, the small tropical fruit that's the colour of a lime but tastes like a lemon. I'm tapping my fingers at the side of my chair, staring into the fire, trying to remember a magic spell from my childhood that'll make me or Winona disappear, me to fantasy-land and her to some black hole, any black hole, in space.

A eucalyptus log is burning in the fireplace, but the smoke that surrounds us is from the cigarettes they've been smoking all evening: Camel plains. Shrimp juice, red wine, and the odd whiff from my own armpits—no, I'm not relaxed—add to the layered perfume of the room. Finally, as a distinctive top note, the tang of banana vinegar.

A jar of *aji*, hot sauce, stands open among the drained glasses and crumpled napkins. They brought it with them because every region in this country prepares it a different way and Gary likes the coastal stuff. It's intoxicating, that smell, and it's doing that olfactory trick of erasing years in a flash. It hooks me by the nose and drags me down the mountain to a cluster of small villages around the mouth of a river emptying slow brown waters into the Pacific.

Where the heat was like a second skin.

The sun on my head and the breeze on my shoulders and the mud sometimes up to my knees, all of it, was the land and sky holding on to me, a tropical embrace, an infiltration. When there was no breeze, the air itself was thick with heat and moisture so that it felt more solid than air but not yet like water. I loved it, invasive as it was. It made me into the kind of woman who could do that, sleep with another woman's man, because not only had the heat gone to my head, it had gone to my heart and hands and all the other parts of me. It wasn't right, but I knew why; I had slept with Gary because the tropics had melted a reserve at my core, and because he was there when that happened. I slept with him, but what Gary gave me had little to do with a hot night and his body.

Under a sun-blasted sky, we had often crossed the *boca*, the wide mouth of the river delivering itself into the ocean. Life is occasionally that simple. There is nothing like a fast ride in an open boat, with the light chop making a vibrato beneath my thighs and the wind in my sun-bleached hair and on my sun-toughened skin. And though it was, sometimes, someone else, it was often Gary behind me at the tiller. In my memory, he has become synonymous with that feeling of freedom.

Remembering that makes me feel naked here, in this high-ceilinged room with its smoke pall and the remains of our feast and a woman whose husband I borrowed.

"We create our own reality," Winona's saying.

Shit, I'm thinking, I'm not up for this.

"We design it; we alter it."

Too many *Omni* magazines, Winona, too many sci-fi paperbacks. I'm listening hard for the sound of the Jeep. She still has half a tumbler full of wine. She's tapping an unlit Camel on the coffee table.

"Airplanes fly ... "

" ... only because we believe they do," I finish her sentence 'cause it's a speech I've heard before. Her eyes narrow; she seems to be seeing me for the first time. Her gaze shifts to the drink in front of her. She reaches for the glass, almost slo-mo, raises it to her lips, takes a small sip, and then another. She puts the drink down, positioning it just so, as if she's illustrating a point.

"We create it. Our own reality."

Meaning you've created me, Winona, at least the role I've played in your life. Meaning your stupid theory works both ways. C'mon you guys, get back here. There's no sound from outside, no distant grumble of the Jeep's motor, of its chassis squeaking as it labours up the cobblestone road. Just the flick of her lighter and the sweet tobacco stink of the cigarette she points into the inch-high flame.

"What are they doing, picking the grapes?" I say. Even to my ears, this line sounds flat and pitiful, the way small-talk always does in a charged atmosphere.

"Sickness, injury, we bring it on ourselves."

Oh, Winona. Why did I ever underestimate you?

She knows how my father died, that his illness was sudden and merciless, but she doesn't know that he aged thirty years in less than two months. That, at the end, he looked like my grandfather, beaky and scrawny, a withered life, a wasted body.

"Like cancer, for example. It's something you do to yourself."

I'm screaming at her, "Fuck off, just fuck right off." She's getting back at me through the only man I've got and I don't even have him anymore. He's dead and it happened too fast and she's not just implying, she's saying he did it to himself, meaning he did it to us, meaning hurt is this thing we all carry around inside us and only get rid of by passing it on. Winona's gonna make me pay if it's the last thing she does.

Well, the weird thing is, by the time the other two come back, I don't even hate Hatchetface anymore. I'm screamed out, hated out, score's even, *punto.* That's the word for period or end. It's the severed tie; it's the whisper of an angel in the mountains lifting off a terra cotta roof and heading for the sky. It's like, Winona, maybe we create these shabby little lives, maybe we fuck around on each other trying to make up for the won't-get and can't-have. Go home. I'm sorry. Life sucks. Gary's turned out not to be such a hunk, after all. And wine is just the colour of this one night.

RANDALL *Maggs*

FER DE LANCE

I remember you, even here
where winter stops blood, nails water
to rock, where men who never go fifteen miles
from home except by sea or think to watch for
things like you in cracks or comfortable
sea-side grass, would turn from the
slit fish in disbelief confronted
with something like you,
your icy eyes, your
yellow ugly snout.

You're just another occupant of
dreams for them, not to be taken seriously,
like *quarks* or *escargots, ben-wa balls,*
something else from away too
foolish to talk about.

But I remember you. Trapped heat
in the orchard near *Tzin Tzun Tzan*, a wasp-sung
town. Ankle-high, the wasps as bright as sun
bore into fruit on the ground and overhead
the avocados droop like bulls' preposterous
scrotums taking me back to cooler fields, better-known
boys with dangerous, high-pitched voices and
hair-pin guns. Slit-eyed, we'd creep to the fence
and Simonette's grazing bulls, wanting the good
angle: something about those bulky
bags enraged us—

So, too late the warning, too
foreign: blown fuses in a
northern brain—not
rope I'd walked on, no slapstick
rake that leapt and whacked my shin.
I sank to the ground and glutted wasps, shouting
at a wobbly sky. What God would deal with
the likes of you? What Shepherd coil you
underfoot, deaf and so cleverly disguised?

Not that you hadn't gotten together
before. And those pickers like angels
in white—what were they grinning at?
One less gringo to eat the earth?
One more soul for a better land?
Or, being Mexicans, someone fierce or
foolish enough to rant at God Himself?
El hombre tiene cojones, I imagine they nudge
one another. *Si, muy grandes huevos.*
That's gold in the poke down here.

But they were pointing at
my boot and the rip an inch from
susceptible flesh.

O yes. I remember you.

My frequent visitor.

When snow slides over the cold
road or someone flips a hose across a lawn.
When I reach for clean socks in the back
of a drawer.

FIRST LESSON IN UNPOPULAR MECHANICS

KEN Babstock

As a boy, it was a scale-model Messerschmitt
pitched at the wall in a boy-scale rage—
Now? These grown-up middle-tones, wafflings, shit
flung deliberately wide of the fan. I remember the age
I began to ease off—thirteen, fourteen—
when busting one's stick meant a five-minute major,
and there, in the sin bin, thinking *what did I mean
by two-handing the crossbar?* Couldn't gauge or
properly reckon what point I had made (hoped
I had made) so kept my caged gaze on the raftered clock:
that massive, red-rashed, free-floating block
where the seconds of my sentence, my stasis, loped
toward zero, zero, and zero, in slo-mo.
The thing opposed, absolutely, my re-entering play; its rules,
                                        its flow.

KEN *Babstock*

TO A SISTER, WHEREVER

Why should I recall that brush you were beat
with for your fourth lie that week? Control
abandons the pious and scrubbed who eat
in thick silence, whose fists, tongues only unroll
when they're praying ... Christ, it's so easy now
to look back, analyze, judge, or deny
but I was there—watching—whispered "ow"
to myself as the welts boiled up on your thigh.
Bright-lit, bristling kitchen of angles, hair liquid coal
above stainless-steel chair legs, the linoleum lifting. How
to account for these visitations in daylight? Objects—
their imprints—stack up, grow like a subsurface reef.
Sister-ship, sister-swimmer, our estrangement connects
us. I hope you're well. I've found sleep a relief.

THE FAR SHORE

PAUL *Anderson*

(novel excerpt)

HE DRIVES WITH THE WINDOW DOWN as if to drive by ear. As if to clear his eyes. He is wearing a light tweed jacket, jeans, bedroom slippers. A T-shirt, faded blue. It is forty below zero. The point where centigrade and Fahrenheit collide.

Air shrouded in ice-fog ... Muscular cuts of ice rut roads burnished now to a high gloss, like sculpted meat. At these speeds, the ruts sometimes fling the car into slight fishtails. It is after midnight. He passes few vehicles. It feels as though he has been driving around for hours; it has been much less. Once, passing a phone booth, he thought to call her back, to tell her he isn't coming, he's never coming.

He finds himself following a tree-lined boulevard that winds along the river. It is not far from her house. He understands he has been heading here for some time.

Sodium lamps slip like orange flares up over the windshield and back through the darkness overhead. The river flows alongside, thickening with ice. It freezes where it pauses. Open water boils its cold into the arctic night.

The air is choked with ice, trees fog-rimed—crystalline, a fairyland petrified with hoar. The car slews wildly sideways. The gut-clench of dread he feels is familiar now. He has time to swing the wheel into the slide before the car explodes sidelong into the soft-banked snow. A dream—weightlessness—then impact, very real.

He opens his eyes to a lap heaped with snow. Into it, slow, beads a string of rubies from a cut on the bridge of his nose. His left temple throbs, an ache more frail than bone. The door is wedged shut against the snow. He struggles through the open window.

The black car's feathered track has missed the concrete pylon of a footbridge by less than a foot. He does not trust this hilarious urge to laugh bubbling up in his chest. He clambers up to the footbridge for a better view. The steps before him are heaped with snow like high-risen loaves.

He looks back, down, grateful for the tracks. The facts so clear. He is fascinated by the scene. He sits down in the soft snow blanketing the bridge. He slips his feet over the side and swings them lazily back and forth above the water, through the steam. One foot has lost its slipper. He rests his elbows on the retaining bar and looks out over the river of smoke, across to the far shore. Clouds of sodium orange, sky of India ink, a soft, prismed mist.

He rests his chin between his hands on the frosted bar. He shapes smoke signals with his breath.

Hahh ... Huhh ... Ahhhh ...

He feels a tender kinship for this small animal within, ally against the frigid night.

The arctic air claws at his nostrils, floods his eyes with tears. As a child would, he lets the cold weld his lashes shut. He feels the warmth of childhood memories he can never recall, smells cinnamon and toast.

Through a drowsy warmth comes the fabling croon that magpies make to bait a cat. A slow pulse blooms in his head. He understands he is about to freeze to death.

Eyelids balk, flutter—crack the weld of lashes. From beside his face on the bar, a shape flaps off, the feather rasp of its black and white motley still audible through the steam. He thinks the bird has taken out his eyes. He jerks his chin up, leaving the soft inside of his lower lip fused to the bar. White sear, trickling warmth, mouth filling with iron.

He can't open his *eyes*—panic in his eyelids, the delicate horror of moths. Both palms come away from the bar torn, flayed. *His eyes*—skinned fingertips scald as he wets them on his tongue to melt free the lashes of one eye.

He scrambles to his feet, stumbles back along the bridge, one eye shut, one blind to perceptions of depth. At the car, in the rear-view mirror, he glimpses nose and lips cased in ice the shiny red of candied apples.

Oozing fingertips freeze now to the key as he turns it in the ignition. But the car starts easily, pulls out of the snowbank easily. Everything will go easily now, if he can just get warm. Frost smokes the windshield glass as the heater fan blows powdery snow off the dash.

He pulls the car down a familiar side street, thrusts his head out the window to squint through the fog—on the glass, in the air—through the white flutter behind his eyes. To the freed lashes cling enamelled burrs, like tiny molars of ice. *If he could just see, just get warm ... Go to her.* The most natural thing in the world. He thinks she could have moved, changed apartments a dozen times since then. Snowy swingsets, slides, teeter-totters stilled and silent—like agricultural implements wintering, idled.

A harrow, a plow.

Bare branches, cracked trunks. Tiny tracks, wedged in snow. His own tracks up the walk. Each step forward leads him farther from what he's known.

Thumb jammed to the intercom buzzer, unanswered. His speech rising, slurred, a thread of chill tangled in the jaws. No answer.

He goes back around to the front of the building, hauls himself onto the low balcony though he has seen no lights inside. His raw palms again burn as they tear free of the railing. He is ready to break in if he has to, to smash the sliding door. He puts his face to the glass next to the handle. Through brushstrokes, he sees a faint light.

He understands that the windows are not dark. They are painted black.

It seems so obvious that the door will be unlatched. He slides it open, stubs the numbed, stockinged foot as he staggers in. His back to the warm, black wall, he slumps to sit on the carpet, cradles his right hand. The whiteness that flutters behind his eyes does not feel like rage, does not feel like anything he knows.

For a long moment, his surroundings do not register. Then another instant, as if through a negative, light made darkness, dark light. The dining room and what he can see of the kitchen are painted black beneath a film of condensation gleaming under candlelight. Black matted carpet, black walls daubed in crude, red glyphs.

He thinks he can hear the thrum of water boiling.

On the cheerful red-and-white checked tablecloth, three stub candles gutter in black wax pooling on the linen. It is humid. He has begun to sweat.

The table is set for three. Oblong wicker basket, white linen napkin, loaf of bread, heels cut off. Saliva floods his mouth. A pang of hunger. His lower lip throbs.

The plates are heaped with a red-brown mass like stew. Drawing nearer, he sees in the dim light that the pieces are not diced but halved or whole.

He stands, hungry, sweating, staring down at the plates. But he has not moved to feed himself. It is not until he has stared for a moment at these strange vegetables that he understands that this is a heart. Heart, liver, kidney.

The room reeks of meat.

NO VACANCY

IRENE Guilford

WE SPEND ALL SUMMER HERE, my mother, my grandmother, my grandfather, myself. We have eighteen cabins and one cottage, laid out in two horseshoes, not feet together as you might expect, but with the mouth of one open to the street and braced up against its back, the two feet of its partner. My father comes on weekends but not often. He has a job in Toronto as a foreman at Canada Packers.

Our house is to one side, on a raised island of lawn mowed by my grandfather and edged in turtle-sized stones whitewashed by my grandmother. There is a lawn table, umbrella, and chairs, where guests sometimes make the mistake of sitting, thinking them for their use. The first time I saw this, strangers sitting naturally, as if they had the right, I was jolted by the violation. I am used to it now, but my mother still sucks in her breath each time.

Can't they see it's private, belongs to the house? How stupid can you be? If they'd asked, not just sat down, maybe that would be different. She stalks out, telling them to leave so the chairs may be left empty.

My grandmother and I clean. I don't mind working in the cottage. It feels like a real place, with a living room, kitchen, two bedrooms, and a washroom. The air is cool and dark from the smooth plywood walls. It is the cabins I hate, with the burry, grey boards, the two double beds in one room, the green metal hot plate, and, in one corner, the triangular sink so small that you nick the bony tops of your hands on the underside of the taps when you reach inside the bowl to clean.

We dive our hands into dishes toppled into the sink, opaque crescents of bacon fat congealed along the rims. We change the beds. The sheets are always too short for the mattress. There's never enough to reach over the foot or to tuck under the sides, so that it will hold. I wonder how people don't mind, for the sheets must slither loose into a gather of wrinkles as soon as they pull back the blanket.

The blankets are rough, grey army-issue. A few have a red stripe at one end that my grandmother and I, in unspoken assent, place at the top of the bed so the stripe will be near people's faces, under their chins when they sleep. Some blankets have patches worn so thin they could not keep anyone warm. If we can, we camouflage this beneath a fold. But there are others that we can no longer get away with and that one of us must take to the house, where my mother, presented with a sheet or blanket we can no longer use, takes it, sucking in her breath and shaking her head, as if only she could understand the significance of this loss.

Sometimes we are cross and my grandmother snaps at me because she can't get me moving—and I do feel like I am moving through molasses, my limbs are so heavy, and I know she must think me lazy or sullen—but mostly our work is brisk and companionable. When we emerge at its end into bright afternoon sunshine, my grandmother strikes a pose in the middle of the yard. She wears her head scarf factory-style, knotted above the forehead. She plants her broom, crosses her forearms over the tip of its handle, and, cocking her hips, gives a whoop at this exaggeration, this making of her own merriment, and I laugh.

My grandfather mends the screens in the wooden doors and windows. With tiny nails, he tacks down the stiff curling mesh that lifts away from the frame, or patches a hole where someone has put an elbow through in a drunken loss of balance. He hefts up the big, red Adirondack chairs, lifting them from the neighbouring cabins to which they've been dragged, carrying them back where they belong. They sit, one on each side of the front door, their wooden planks splayed like fingers, waiting for customers to lean back.

Every few seasons, he paints the outside of all the cabins, working his way around each horseshoe, starting at cabin one, the darkest and smallest and nearest the house, until he gets to cabin eighteen, the one farthest away, the one requested most often by groups of young single men. He paints the cabins grey with red trim. Sometimes as he's painting, my mother pushes open the screen door from the kitchen at the back of the house and leans out calling, "Father, will you mow the lawn today?" Without looking away from his work, he gives a smooth wave that only reinforces his rhythm.

As he moves, for he is always moving, he is slow and steady, not so much carrying himself as letting his weight drop unattended, so that it falls comfortably within each step, finding its own rest in the sway. As he works, he whistles—quiet, content, and private, for himself, not the world, drawing the sound out like the thread from the centre of a ball of string.

But mostly it is my mother who does the work, though sometimes my father comes up on a weekend. She thinks at least he will help maintain order, she asks only that in her telling of weekday troubles, the stories of men getting drunk on cheap wine in the afternoon and climbing into the trees to swing like apes. As I hear her tell this story, I look up into the high rustle of the pine canopy, visualizing men's bodies draped along its branches, their legs dangling, and from the tips of their fingers loosely held bottles of wine that they raise to drink. I can't see how it's possible, for the lowest branches are too high to be reached from the ground.

But mostly, my father just stands in the yard, a broom in his hand, laughing at the comings and goings, so my mother makes friends with the police. It is the presence of their car—the cruiser, my mother calls it— gliding through our yard like a ghost, silent and low to the ground, that keeps the peace. She gives them a bottle of rye at the end of the season.

It is my mother who rents out the cabins and takes in the money, using as an office the long narrow sun room that runs across the front of the house. It is lime green, with windows around three sides. At the back of the house, in cabins already rented, there is dusk and collecting danger. At the sound of a crash, or a rise in revelry, she is out, slapping the screen door open, barking for them to be quiet. When she pulls herself back sharply, her smile wavering between surprise and satisfaction, I see how her life is split like the halves of a hard green apple, which she tries to keep stuck together.

When she rents a cabin, she puts an X in a square on the bristol board I rule up for her, a new sheet for each month, the days across the top and the numbers of the cabins down the left side. The board is white and stiff, its shine thinly spread over the surface like water, its gloss firm and smooth like icing. If you tap it lightly with a forefinger, you will hear hollowness beneath.

With the tip of her ballpoint, she gouges the channels of the X through the sheen, laying black rivulets of ink in the furrows. Sometimes, she jerks the tip of her ballpoint back and forth, her lips set, staring unseeing at the whiteness. With each X, I know we are getting closer to the squares being filled.

But sometimes, sometimes, there is that last customer. He is ordinary, round-bellied, and unsmiling, taking bills from his wallet to lay down flat with one palm while holding his folded wallet like a thick sandwich in the butt of the other. My mother stands and waits, gathered to herself. She waits until the thud of his boots recedes, until the floorboards cease to shake, until the window glass, set rattling by the slamming of the door, turns quiet.

It is then, only then, that she bends over the white bristol board. Taking her weight on her left palm, her right shoulder slightly drooping, she makes the last deep X. She puts down the pen. She lays both palms flat on the table, and taking her weight there, she lifts her face. With eyes shut, she holds the moment in her mouth like a taste.

Meanwhile, I am hopping like mad inside, waiting and waiting for her to say it, to say the words, hoping it's to me that she'll say them. Shivering herself free, swivelling away first to one side, then the other, she casts about for something else that needs doing, all the while delaying, delaying, deliberately delaying, as if this moment means nothing, as if this happens all the time. Finally, she says it.

"All right. I guess we can hang the NO VACANCY."

Before she can stop me, I am flying to the dark space under the back stairs, the shadow where we keep it.

We have two signs, not just one, not like those people who just drop a NO in front of an already present VACANCY, a small square left to hang crookedly, in a different colour. We have a separate board, long and narrow, with the two words together.

I take it to the strip of lawn at the edge of our property, where we have the sign marking our establishment: ESTELLE GARDENS. The sign is like a little house on two posts, with a roof overhead and a light we turn on at night. The curling letters, painted in red, proclaim underneath—ALL CONVENIENCES.

I stand the NO VACANCY in the grass, propping it against my left leg, loosely bracing to keep the balance. I reach overhead. As I lift off the old sign, its bottom edge comes so close to my face I have to lean back to avoid it. I stand the sign in the grass at my right leg. Then, picking up the NO VACANCY, I let it drop in front of my chest from the hand holding it into the one waiting. I lift it, hook it into place, and guide it slowly into position. It hangs on rusted hooks like kiss curls.

For a moment, it is sweet. We are shut. We are closed.

One day, when my mother and I are alone, I ask her for money for the work I do.

We are in the kitchen at the back of the house, a big room with a linoleum floor and a strip of fluorescent light over the sink. My mother is heavy-treaded as she sets out dishes on the table, thick white ones with a green stripe around the rim, or thin Melmac ones that settle with a hard rattle, their pink beige the colour of the flesh of store mannequins.

She stops, pulling herself up. Her face is haughty, disdainful, but I make my way through my asking. As she listens, her mouth twitches slightly.

"How much do you think you're worth?"

I have learned to proceed cautiously, for when she speaks, there is sometimes false reason in her voice.

"Twenty-five cents a cabin."

From the way she snorts and turns her back, I know she enjoys this toying.

But why not, I fume inside. It's not like I'm asking for an allowance, though I know other children get them. Allowance. Just the word alone is redolent of a life out of reach, a life of golden rooms and chandeliers and satin, a life I will not allow myself to imagine beyond this glimpse through a crack in the door.

Allowance. Something you give just because you can, something you get just for being. I'm not asking for that, for I know we are a family unlike others. We have no money. But this is money for labour. I make beds and clean cabins. I carry stacks of folded linen, their solid heaviness against my chest as I go cabin to cabin, dropping off sheets and pillow-cases. I pick up empty beer cases, their damp cardboard collapsing in my arms, the bottles rattling. It is pay for my labour I'm asking.

I stand, stunned and silent, waiting to see if she will turn back to me, waiting to see what she will give. But she remains facing the sink, giving only her silence.

At night, the face of our property is a vaporous light that falls like a thin yellowed curtain from the overhead string of bulbs to the thin strip of lawn below. There is a frizzy halo around each light, for these are not lanterns, just bulbs, green, blue, or white, picked up from boxes in the basement.

Beyond the strip of grass that is the demarcation of our property is the no-man's land of the road. Beyond that is the other side—not so far, it takes only a few strides to cross, but far enough.

At night, cars straddle our strip of lawn, parking in a relaxed off-hand manner, two wheels on the road, two wheels up on our grass, like a guest who has thrown a loose leg over the arm of a chair in which he's taken up friendly residence. Big cars, blue, green, or white, their generous curves gleaming, they stay pinned within the faint curtain of light, left behind by owners who, with a casual forgetting, gather up friends as they saunter across the road to the Allistonia Hotel.

My mother comes out of the glassed-in porch from where she has been watching. She stands on the strip of lawn, hands on hips, teeth tight, glaring at the parked cars blocking the entrance. Her anger bounces like a bright light off the curving hoods. She struggles, readying to launch herself across the road, then stopping, readying then stopping, until finally she is off. I follow her. She crosses to the beer parlour, ignoring the door marked LADIES WITH ESCORTS, slapping open GENTS instead.

"Who owns the Buick?" she barks into the rough jostle of laughing men, their fists pounding tabletops in making jokes. The noise drops as faces swivel in her direction. No one replies.

"Whoever owns it, get it moved," she pushes the words out, a sharp shove at their shoulders.

A man, a thickly muscled man, slowly rises from his seat, placing his hands on the table. He has a worker's tan, and his sleeves are rolled up, showing a swell of bicep. He leans forward, staring at her, his eyes mean and hard. The room falls silent.

My mother shudders into stiffness, her eyelids fluttering closed.

Then, smacking his stomach with both hands, he guffaws. He jerks a thumb in her direction. His open mouth is a cavern rimmed with white teeth. Nodding, he collects his audience. All around her laugh. My mother is swallowed up.

Later, I stand out on the lawn, by the fine grey sand lying in waves at the edge of the road, and by all that remains of her crossing, the dents of her footprints, and the puffs of dust hanging in the air above them.

It is humid and dark. When I move, the air is like moist silk at my face. Beneath my feet, the grass blades are wide and stiff, the type you search for to stretch between the long sides of your thumbs like a reed so you can shoot that sudden, high shrieking whistle. My hair is frizzing, lifting itself slowly like a ballet dancer from a pose on the floor, an unfurling, uncurling of limbs. I stand very quiet and still, feeling life creep along my hairline.

The summer day I turn seventeen, the age at which Canada Packers will take me, I go to work with my father in the city. On weekends, he comes up no longer. Now, I come back alone.

With my earnings, I have bought a second-hand car, a dark green Mustang that I park with its nose pointing into the side of the house, under the NO PARKING sign. This space belongs to the house, but I pretend it is held for me, waiting for my arrival, mine even when I'm not there.

I get out of the car and stretch. High overhead, leaves rustle. The sun glints through.

On the island of lawn surrounded by the whitewashed stones, my mother, grandmother, and grandfather are sitting at the umbrella table and chairs. They do not greet me, but wait and watch as I approach. I have been away, making money, and in all this, they know, forgetting them.

It is like stepping onto a flat stone. As I come near, I can see there are no empty chairs. They are all taken. I stoop to stand in the space held under the canopy, the tassels along its fringe catching in the top of my hair like dry, discarded blossoms. I try to laugh, but it is a forced city cheerfulness. It hangs on me like ill-fitting clothes. No one is fooled.

TANGENTS

HELEN Pereira

I FEEL AWFUL and want Tim to hug me right now, up here in my mother's attic, but he's changing our son Paul. I have that dead-weight feeling I always have when I'm leaving for home after visiting Mom. The disappointment.

I come back to her bringing the good early memories—her teaching me to read, singing to Andy and me at night after our baths when we were small and Dad was away. It's like a little parcel, that bundle of good memories. When I return at Christmas, I bring a kid's excitement, hoping to open the parcel, hoping that finally Mother's early love will spill out again. It never does.

"Let's not drag out the goodbyes today, Tim," I say, and watch his reaction, afraid he will think I'm just being mean. Maybe I am, because I get mean when I'm hurt. And I hurt a lot, now. "I'll go downstairs and bid my filial farewell," I say. "You guys follow. The confusion should help."

Tim turns to me. His face shows concern.

"What are you going to tell Annie, Margaret? *Are* you going to tell her? I thought that was the whole purpose of the weekend, this pre-Christmas trip."

"How could I, with Carlos around? And us going back and forth to Dad's?"

"But you told your dad, and it went okay." Tim swings Paul to his feet. Paul chortles happily, his bare pink feet running on the spot, tippy-toed. I look to see if Martha has seen this intimacy between father and son, to see if she is jealous. She is still busy printing NANA.

"Dad's different. Rational. He just said what he's said to me all my life: 'Well, well, Margaret. Now isn't that something?' Mother is the loose cannon."

"Give her a break. She's your *mother* for God's sake. She has a right to her feelings."

"There you go," I snap. Now I'm mad at Tim because it seems that people I care about always side with Mother.

"See you." I sling my overnight bag over my shoulder, heading down two flights of stairs. At least, she's done a good job on this *house*. It's nice. I smile in spite of myself. Only Mom could have her living-room walls painted slate green and apricot and pull it off. But why do she and Carlos need this house, all this space? I know what she'd say. "So you can visit, dear." Right. Yeah.

I drop my bag in the hall, take a deep breath, and stride from the dining room into the kitchen for the Big Speech. Mother is darting back and forth around the kitchen. Good. I'll just go ahead and tell her. While she's too preoccupied to interrupt.

But no, before I can even open my mouth, she beats me to it.

"Everyone's getting it," she says.

Which *it?* I've come home from Montreal to tell her I've accepted a contract to work in Kenya, and that we'll all be gone for two years. Tim, me, and her precious grandchildren. Her question throws me. Which *it?*

I watch her bustle around the kitchen, draining water from jars of foul-smelling soybeans, wheat, and chick pea sprouts, opening and closing the fridge doors. She is dressed like an athlete, wearing my brother's torn red sweats topped with an oversized Canadian Masters' Track Team T-shirt and thick wool socks, one blue, one green. She actually looks purposeful instead of erratic. She always did seem confident in the kitchen, even when she was married to Dad. A good cook. Baked special whole-wheat bread in little clay flower pots. I really loved them, Mom's crusty loaves.

When she *was* home. After we started school, she went back to social work "to keep in touch." Then began all the various classes in acting, yoga, and weaving, "as a relief from social work." I felt as though I hardly saw her. When she was home, though, she was always in the kitchen.

"John Travolta drinks wheatgrass juice," she announces, tilting a jar of sprouts toward the sun.

I want to scream. I haven't found out what the first *it* was. Now she's on to John Travolta. Listening to her is like watching a decathlon competitor on television, leaping from javelin-throwing to broad-jumping to sprinting.

Why do I keep coming home to this? Why should I have to prepare her for my next absence? Her non sequiturs drive me crazy. Maybe if she *had been* a decathlon competitor, she would have leapt from event to event instead of subject to subject. Maybe I could stand her for more than half an hour. At least in Kenya I won't be expected to return for visits.

She rinses her hands under the tap and can't find a tea towel, so she dries her hands on her T-shirt. Canadian Masters' Track Team? Where did she get that shirt? She doesn't even belong to the Canadian Masters' Track Team. God knows, she's old enough. Is there a grey-haired marathoner in her life? How does her new husband, Carlos, stand her? Dad couldn't.

Tim, Martha, and Paul arrive. Paul grabs my knee with one hand and waves a Lego toy in the air with the other.

"I have to make some sauerkraut," Mother says, throwing red cabbage into her food processor. I'm still wondering, which *it?*

"You should make your own sauerkraut, Margaret. Buy a food processor. You'll eat more salad and get fewer colds." I try to interrupt, but she darts to the Kleenex box, flips out a tissue, and wipes Paul's nose. She doesn't miss a beat. She washes her hands, dries them on her shirt, and is back zapping cabbage into the machine.

"As I was saying, dear, I have so much energy. It's all the enzymes, you know? They have special healing properties."

I'd love to crash her goddamn sprout jars through her precious greenhouse windows, tell her what I think of her crazy medical theories, remind her that I'm her daughter the doctor and that her inability to complete conversations is a symptom of thought disorder.

"Have a nice orange drink," she says, handing Paul a fizzing glass of Redoxan. "Nana's having one, too, so she won't catch your cold."

"Really, Mother, I think ... "

"Don't interrupt, dear. I know what I'm doing." She bends down to hold the glass for him while he gulps, his round blue eyes turned up to her face.

"You should take him off dairy products, Margaret."

"Who? John Travolta?"

"Don't be a smartass. You know very well I was referring to Paul. Your son."

"Mother ... "

"I wish you wouldn't keep interrupting. That's always been a bad habit of yours. Now listen to *me*. I read about it in the *New England Journal of Medicine*. One of your reliable sources."

I haven't found out what it-*A* was, that everyone has, and now she's on to it-*B*. Which *it* was in the *Journal?* Travolta and wheatgrass? Sauerkraut? Lethal dairy products? I've got to tune out. I'll focus on the kitchen. It's a nice kitchen. Nicer than the one we had when I was growing up. This one has pine walls covered with my daughter's paintings. Mother did that with ours, too—tacked them on the kitchen walls.

She pushes shredded red cabbage into a crock, covers it with leaves, and sets it on a radiator. "While we're discussing medicine, what do you think about our friend Sarah?"

"Who's discussing medicine? And what about Sarah?"

"I mean your professional opinion. You are a doctor."

"What are you talking about, Mother? I mean at this moment, about Sarah."

"You doctors. So smug. Well, you don't need to worry about revealing professional secrets. She already told me everything."

"Oh." I wait, watching Mom. She is beside the fridge but looks puzzled, as if she doesn't know why she went there. Maybe she's finally winding down.

"How will they treat it?" she asks. "What's the prognosis? Leukemia used to be so lethal. When she told me, she just sat here and cried. We both did. I didn't know what to say. What did you tell her? You're her best friend."

"She's *your* favourite. One of your young pets," I snap. Sarah. We started nursery school together. She was my bridesmaid. I walk into the dining room and turn up the thermostat.

"Leave that alone!" Mom yells. "If you got more exercise or dressed sensibly you wouldn't feel so cold. What's your opinion of megadoses of Vitamin C? For cancer. Do you agree with Linus Pauling?" She flips the thermostat down to sixty-five.

"Margaret!" she persists. "Really. You must have some opinions about these things."

"About what, Mom? Exercise? Active wear? Dairy products? Linus Pauling? Fuel costs?"

"You know very well I'm talking about. Sarah. One day she'll phone and talk about some new guy she's met, and how she plans to settle down and raise a family. Or sit around reminiscing about you two, when you were teenagers. Next thing I know, she'll break into tears because she thinks she's dying."

"She's confused. It's like that. She's sending mixed signals."

"I know. I picked that much up."

She shoots me the look. Her don't-patronize-me-doctor-I'm-your-mother look.

Now I'm furious. But with what? With *it?* With mother for being the way she is? Just letting me into her life between yoga classes and lovers, so that I could never get close when I needed her? Or because my best friend Sarah can love her just the way she is? Sarah never even told me. She told Mother. Am I jealous of Sarah for loving Mother? Or Mother for loving Sarah? I want to say something, but I don't know what the topic is, and my mouth is dry.

Tim carries our suitcases downstairs and out to the car, followed by Martha, our giant four-year-old. They are speaking French. I think, Please Tim, hurry for God's sake! I'll hit Mother if I have to stay here much longer.

Her face lights up. "It's just wonderful, Martha being in French immersion. That's the only way. One never truly learns a language, later."

My French is so-so. Tim went to university in Montreal. Will he and Martha grow even closer? No.

How can she say that about language? After all, she has lived in Brazil and carries on endless conversations in Portuguese with her neighbours and with Carlos.

How does he stand her? Or her, him? They seem to get along. Seem. Hugs, snappy dialogue. The way she is with Andy, her darling son. My brother. And how she used to be with Dad.

Now she's washing dishes. She looks tired. Should I help? If I do, she'll say, "No, dear, you work too hard." If I don't, she'll sigh with fatigue after I've left and complain to Carlos. Whatever happened to that enzyme-produced energy? I never win.

I will go back to Montreal feeling three years old. I will waffle, apologize to everyone at the hospital and let the kids walk all over me; I will get a migraine headache and Tim will say "Jee-sus! Never again!" I'm a doctor pushing thirty-five, but she still wipes me out. Kenya is my only escape.

It'll be okay for her. It sounds dramatic and she gets off on drama. She can brag about her daughter the doctor working for World Health in Africa.

I wait, but she is, for once, concentrating. On the dishes. I pick up a dish towel and start to dry the china in the rack. It's a mix of dishes—the dark brown pattern from my childhood, the good gold-coloured pattern she bought later on when she was working. The new dishes were just stoneware, but they were a matching set and she was proud of them. That bloody china sets off so many memories. When she was with Dad, long ago when they were still happy.

"I want to know all about leukemia so I can help Sarah. What to prepare her for. What I should do."

"There are different kinds, Mother. Different stages. Sarah should ask her own doctor. It's really not your ... " Mother turns around from the sink to face me, her hands wet and soapy.

"Margaret, please—what are her chances?"

"It depends. On how far it's progressed."

"Could she get better?" she asks, and returns to vicious, noisy dish-washing.

"Look, Mom. Let's drop Sarah, please. We only have a little more time here with you before we have to shove off."

She turns from the sink again. Her face is white. She looks scared. She's lost weight, quite a lot. And she's turning grey. Finally. I never noticed those wings of white at her temples before. She almost looks like a mother.

"It's just that Sarah's being so good. Dropping in ... "

Gawd. A crack at me, I suppose. Another guilt trip. It's a wonder I never went completely off my trolley and got locked up for life. Nearly, during the seventies. Getting high. Trying to rise above the Broken Home. She tracked me down from commune to commune; leaving notes, messages with Sarah; loaves of bread.

"Yeah, and I dropped out."

"No dear, I wasn't talking about ... that. About the past. I'm talking about now."

Martha comes in from helping Tim load the car and attacks Mother at the thighs.

"Nana, oh Nana!" Her grandmother's daughter. Same sense of theatre.

"Nana, please come and visit us."

Oh gawd, no. Anything but that. I fling the dish towel down on the counter and glare at Martha.

Mom crumples over the sink.

Now what? Tim and I exchange desperate looks. What's up? This performance could go on for another hour and we'll never make it to Montreal before dark. Tim walks over and kisses her cheek, sets two bottles of wine on the counter. Then he bends down to pick up Paul.

Her face softens under Tim's kiss.

"Goodbye, Annie," Tim says. "Have a great Christmas! Enjoy the *Beaujolais nouveau*. We've got to hit the road." Martha darts over and strangles Mom's legs.

"Let go, darling," she says, gently pulling Martha's arms away. "I've got some things I want to give to your mother." She goes to her antique hutch, and from the back, where she has hidden them from me all these years, she brings out a Crown Derby demi-tasse; a candy dish that belonged to my great-grandmother; a tiny Spode cup and saucer, gold-banded; and her mother's silver teapot. She sets them all on the dining-room table.

"Just a minute. I'll find a box." She has never found anything, for as long as I can remember, but she rushes to the greenhouse and returns with a carton.

She wraps the cups with ripped pieces from the morning *Globe and Mail*: stuffs crumpled paper between saucers, cups, dish, teapot. She pauses, closes the carton carefully, tucks the corners firmly under each other in the centre. She stops, bracing herself against the old oak table we've had ever since I can remember, the one from the suite my father and she bought when they moved to Toronto.

I tighten my lips. When I see her tears, I cry too, but don't know why. I walk over and grab her, and we cling together. I suddenly realize that I am taller than she is. I feel her trembling and hold her tighter, feeling strong, protective.

Why are we crying? Because we both know Martha will love her father most, the way I did? Or because my mother and I never risked showing how much we loved each other until just now? Has she guessed we're going away? *She was always good at that. Knowing what I was up to.* Or are we crying because of Sarah?

"There, there, Mom."

"Shut up, Margaret, shut up." We stand clinging, weeping, until Martha tugs at us, upset. Mother strokes Martha's hair, then says to me, "You'll be all right, dear. Really. Just take a couple of aspirins and call me in the morning."

I smile and follow Tim and Martha to the door, remembering, "Everyone's getting it." The *it* that Mother said everyone was getting? Which *it*?

I take Paul from Tim, hold him close, bury my face in his soft blond hair. Mom reaches over to kiss his snotty face. As we move toward the door, she slips into her Birkenstock sandals and follows us out to the car. Passing her garden, I see papery orange Chinese lantern plants sticking out of the snow, and the frosted skeletons of spring shrubs. Mother stands in the freezing cold, holding the carton, waiting while Tim buckles the kids into the car. Then he takes the package from her and sets it on my lap. I tighten my arms around it.

"Thanks for the cups, Mother. I'll take good care of everything— guard them with my life."

"Hide the cups from Martha," she whispers, "the way I did from you. You've finally got them. They're yours now."

Tim clears his throat and starts the motor. Martha strains from her seat belt and reaches toward the window, whimpering, "Come and see us, Nana."

"I will. I will, darling." She kisses Martha, shuts the car door quickly and runs toward the gate. As she leaps across snow piled against the curb, a sandal falls off.

I'll write and tell her, I think, as I double-check Martha's car seat with one hand and balance the parcel on my lap with the other. I'll explain about Kenya in a letter.

The bundle of heirlooms, my mother's lifetime treasures, is heavy.

As we drive away I feel like crying, but smile and wave.

I turn around. Mother is not looking back. My last sight is of her red-clad figure outlined against white snow, hopping on one foot as she bends over to retrieve her sandal, the other green foot bent in the air.

WHAT'LL
YOU HAVE?

SUE *Wheeler*

1.

It was always the same: Coke, 7-Up,
Dr. Pepper. As if the only odds
you got came locked in one of three
flavours. This was true, actually,
everywhere but country gas stations
and roller rinks—those birthday parties,
winding ourselves tight in one direction
till we sat in a row on the bench,
each set of four little wheels
still itching to spin.
A mother as glazed as the doughnuts
would pass the bakery box, plain or jelly,
plus your choice of Grape-Ade, Nehi,
R-C Cola. The bounds of the possible
could also blow to dust at any roadside—
low on gas, a kid needing to go.
Not much around but baked fields,
the farmers paid not to plant.

(Maybe it was April, and bluebonnets
breasted the distance like the bodice
of a flower-print housedress.) We'd stand
under the canopy, the only shade
for miles, and swig cream soda till
our heads were an ache of cold empties.
If the city-of-origin was one
we didn't have, we might get to walk away
from the nickel, running our fingertips
over Tucson, Peoria—those bottles
really got around. The car would pull back
onto the blacktop, the settlements
of the wide earth chinking softly
from the floor at every turn.

                    2.
The drinks keep rising from the brass tray
in the house across the road from Lazarus'
tomb. Our hosts are thirsty, we're thirsty,
all God's chillun got thirst. First
the jugged ice water, then Orange Crush,
hot tea in a glass with a mint leaf—
they ask before they sugar it, North
Americans don't always want four spoonfuls—
Arab coffee, back to the water
for the next round. Take more, take
some chicken, some baklava, you must
be hungry, and we are, we've come a long
way, the No. 10 bus down Suleiman Street,
the driver overcharging and still
the fare was only pennies. Out the door
the goat who's just had his throat cut
isn't about to pull any back-to-life
stunt. Not with that lightning gash
through his neck, not the way his arteries
fountain red heart-rhythms over

the courtyard. The children laugh
and scream, leaping to keep it off their feet.
Lickety-split the carcass is skinned
and gutted and hung from a tree branch.
Later, the grandmother in the embroidered
dress will read our coffee grounds.
She'll swish them round the insides
of our cups and set them upside down
to dry. *Journey,* she'll say. *A man.*
You may not get everything you want
right away.

SUE Wheeler

THEIR FUTURES DRIFT
LIKE ASH ACROSS THE CITY
(Triangle Shirtwaist Factory, New York, 1911)

Young women sturdy as pine trees
veins resinous with dreams
abandon needles mid-seam
in Egyptian cotton, leave
black bread radish and onion
in the chipped lunch pails, hearts
treadling terror hot as the knobs
and hinges on the locked fire escape
doors. The girl with the purple ribbon
smashes a stool through the cobwebbed
glass and they leap and leap, the sky
is a shudder of petticoats, skirts
are bells pleating the morning
air, their hair untwists and spills
above them, epiphanies of flame.
They are bridal bouquets tossed
and tossed from balconies, a Calvary
of reaching arms, fingers spread
like the ribs of the tightrope
walker's umbrella.

ASHA'S GIFT

RACHNA *Mara*

ASHA LAGGED ON THE WAY to Doctorsahib's. She stopped to exchange quips with Chuddi, who was scrubbing pots outside her hut, then she hurried to the bungalow without picking the brilliant hibiscus she usually gathered for her hair. She must not let the Angrezi Doctorsahib think she was afraid to face her. But Doctorsahib had already left for the clinic.

Asha fumbled with the key tied to the end of her sari, unlocked the door. Everything was just the way Doctorsahib always left it—a few dishes in the front room, the water gone from the bucket in the bathroom, bed unmade, dirty clothes in the basket in the corner of the bedroom. No indications of Doctorsahib's state of mind.

She gathered the dishes from the front room, stalked into the kitchen, and clunked them into the basin. She picked up the broom and started to sweep, glass bangles tinkling discordantly.

These Angrezi-log, what arrogance they had. Why hadn't Doctorsahib Parkinson said anything yesterday? She'd caught Asha red-handed and she'd said nothing except, "I do not have time now, I will talk to you tomorrow." She'd said it in Hindi, of course, her awful Hindi, with that *pah-pa-pah-pa-pah* voice, which Asha and all the villagers made so much fun of.

It was a mistake, agreeing to work for this Angrezi doctor. So many strange ways she had. The way she spoke. The clothes she wore, such dull colours. And her skin. Not nice and fair so much as boiled looking, with ugly, dark blotches. Her eyes were pale and watery and she had no eyelashes to speak of, just a few scrubby, straight hairs, like a cow.

At the Ungoli house, at least you knew where you were. Ungoli Memsahib may be a terror, but she didn't toy with you like a cat with a mouse. If Ungoli Memsahib caught you at anything, she gave you a quick, hard slap, and that was the end of it.

I will talk to you tomorrow. Asha spat onto the dishes in the basin. And again. She scooped up the dirt, half-considered dumping it in Doctorsahib's bed, then swept it vigorously outside.

She'd been working for the Ungolis when Doctorsahib Kamla told her about the new Angrezi doctor coming to the village, asked if she was interested in doing her housework. Asha'd had enough of working for the Ungolis.

Burra Memsahib always sat on the cot at the head of the courtyard, watching everybody with a serpent's eye. Mean, she was, grudging every bite the servants took. True, she handed down the odd bit of worn clothing, which came in handy for Asha and for her sister Sundri and Sundri's two children. But for the clothes, Asha would never have stayed.

Yes, she would have. She would have had to. Sundri's husband, Tilak, was always complaining, complaining about having an extra mouth to feed. He never noticed the cleaning, mending, cooking, fetching water from the well, even helping in the field. All he noticed was an extra mouth to feed. Particularly since the day behind the bushes. She'd shown him the knife, described what she'd do. He'd never bothered her that way again. But there were other ways.

"Why does that girl have to live with us all the time?" he'd shout at Sundri. "She's always eating, eating, eating. Why can't she get married? One woman's enough."

Sundri, hands fluttering, would say, "You knew when you married me that she was going to live with us. Where will she go, no mother and father? You promised Dr. Kamla Sahib when she gave you my dowry that my sister would also be welcome here."

"Yes, but that was years ago, and she's still here. I didn't think I'd have the girl forever. Look at her, nineteen and still not married."

"How can she get married with no dowry, you tell me that? All our extra money you drink away, so how can she get married?"

And Asha would shriek, "I will never get married, never."

"You see, you see," Tilak would yell. "There's your sister. Wanting to live off somebody else's hard work. There are boys willing enough to marry her and Dr. Kamla Sahib will provide a dowry, but ... "

"Dr. Kamla Sahib has done enough for our family. I will not ask her."

The arguments always ended with Tilak hitting Sundri and Sundri crying.

In the end, Asha had found work with the Ungolis. The servants hated it there, but with the uncertainty of the rains and the cost of borrowing money for seed and tools, most of the village families were glad of any steady income, however slight. So when old Rukhma died, Asha quickly applied for her job. Tilak had still complained, even though she handed over every rupee she earned.

Now she was grateful to Dr. Kamla Sahib for offering the opportunity to her first—there wasn't a lot in the village that Dr. Kamla Sahib didn't know about. She'd always kept an eye on Sundri and Asha; she'd looked after them in Najgulla, brought them to Barundabad. She'd watched out for them ever since that time, long ago now.

"Eat, you must eat," Dr. Kamla Sahib says to Sundri in Najgulla Hospital. Sundri is silent, creeping back to the bed their mother died in.

Asha eats everything she's given. The patients complain she even steals their food. The knife she carries makes them uneasy.

"You must stop doing that," Dr. Kamla Sahib says, bandaging the gashes on Asha's arms and legs. Asha says nothing. Later, does it again. She feels only a fierce exultation as the knife cuts her skin. How to explain to Dr. Kamla Sahib that this is a preparation for returning to the streets? Any day now, they'll really be on their own. No doll, no mother, or father. Toward the end, it was her mother's anguish for them that was the real burden.

It hadn't taken Asha long to sum up the new doctor. She said *aap* to Asha as though she were an equal, instead of the familiar *tum*. She requested, never ordered, and always said *shukria*, thank you. She never locked up food, the flour, sugar, rice, *dahls*, and she even gave Asha a key to the tiny bungalow.

The only thing Doctorsahib was fussy about was keeping the place clean. She examined corners, insisted everything be properly dusted, mopped. She hated dirt as much as the heat.

Such a small place, so easy to keep clean. Asha's body didn't ache the way it used to at the Ungolis' and she was paid a little more. And no one to watch her. At the Ungolis' with *Burra* Memsahib and all those people scurrying around, it had been impossible to search the bureau drawers and cupboards, let alone help herself to even a handful of rice.

But the best thing about working for Doctorsahib was her Hindi. It was so funny, her accent more than anything else.

It came in particularly handy over the food. Doctorsahib couldn't stand anything hot. As she ate, her eyes would stream, her face turn red. She would struggle to say, "*Khana tikha hai.*" *The food is hot.*

And it was easy to think she'd said, "*Khana theek hai.*" *The food is fine.*

Asha would smile, say, "*Theek hai,* Doctorsahib, *shukria.*"

Then another day, Doctorsahib would try again, "*Itna lal mirchi nahi dalo.*" *Don't put in so many red chilies.* She would say it slowly, carefully, having practised.

Asha would smile, nod. She'd stop using red chilies, double the green chilies and black pepper.

When Doctorsahib complained about the food, Asha would look crestfallen. "Doctorsahib, you don't like my cooking?"

"No, Asha. No, it is not that, but ... "

"So you like my cooking, Doctorsahib? I work hard for you."

"Yes, Asha, I like your cooking, but ... "

"*Shukria,* Doctorsahib."

When the food was hot, Doctorsahib didn't eat much. Sometimes there was even enough to take to Sundri's hut. On those days, Tilak didn't grumble so much.

She'd ease off the chilies until Doctorsahib grew relaxed, even compli-
mentary, then slowly increase them again. How it made Doctorsahib run to
the toilet! Asha would stand outside, listen to the firecrackers.

Chalak, she was, sly. You had to be in this world. Look at her, free to
come and go, and look at Sundri, already big with her third child. Sundri
had the same glazed eyes their mother used to have, worrying, worrying,
over children.

In Najgulla, begging, it is their mother's fear for them that is hardest to
bear.

Some days they fare well; other days they eat out of garbage bins. They
sleep where they can, doorways, alleys, the knife always handy. They sleep
outside a temple for a while until the *Sadhu* approaches their mother. They
need temple prostitutes, young ones, he says, eyeing Sundri and Asha. Her
mother, visibly with child, afraid to invite a curse from a *Sadhu*, says,
"Forgive us, but not now." They never go back to the temple.

There are so many partition refugees, people are afraid or impatient.
It's impossible to get work. The only offers they get are for the work of
women unaccompanied by men.

And yet, when the very thought is ludicrous, their mother still worries
about finding husbands for them, still hopes the baby will be a boy, miraculously curing their problems.

Occasionally, she talks about returning to Hyderabad, Sindh, now in
the new Muslim country, Pakistan, talks about embroidering wall hang-
ings to sell, about meeting their father there. Other times, she forgets the
happy years in Hyderabad, Sindh, slips back to the time when they'd left
their village because of the drought, the argument they'd had when they'd
left—should they go east, past Rajasthan, into Madhya Pradesh, maybe
south, to Bombay, or should they go west to Hyderabad, Sindh? Hyderabad,
Sindh, is closer, but how will the girls find good husbands there, with so
many Muslims?

It is worst for Asha when her mother remembers. Asha cannot bear
the look. It's there because of the unborn child and because of them,
Sundri and Asha.

Asha hadn't searched Doctorsahib's bureau right away. She suspected a trap. At first, she'd pull open the drawers and look. So strange, the Doctorsahib's clothes, so fine, the material, the stitching. Finer even than the stitching Asha's father used to do. And her underclothes. The *chuddi*, the underpants, had no string, just thread that snapped back when you pulled it. The material was silky, not the rough cotton the villagers wore, those who had underwear.

The village women were curious to hear about the new Doctorsahib. When Asha took Doctorsahib's clothes to the river, the women would cluster around, eager to touch. Meenu even smelled Doctorsahib's underpants once.

Asha laughed and shouted, "Hey, Meenu, an Englishwoman's bum smells the same as an Indian's. Want to sniff mine?" How the women roared. From then on, they called Meenu Chuddi.

The women were interested in all the Doctorsahib's Angrezi things. The stick with bristles that she used to clean her teeth, no *Neem* twig for her. The wonderful soap, smooth, that smelled better than flowers. The white liquid Doctorsahib used on her hands. One time, Doctorsahib gave Asha some. It made her skin as soft as a petal.

And all the bottles of medicine Doctorsahib had. There was a blue bottle that Doctorsahib always ran for after eating hot food. One time, Asha had hidden it. Doctorsahib had been frantic until Asha produced it, claiming to have moved it while tidying up.

Asha mimicked Doctorsahib's Hindi, described her habits. So dirty she was, she never washed properly when she went to the toilet, used paper not water. And she ate with her left hand. *Chee*, imagine not knowing the left hand was for cleaning the body, the right one for eating. The women wrinkled their noses, giggled.

Gradually, Asha became more daring. She examined the contents of the bureau drawers, the items underneath, always careful to replace everything exactly as before. That was the only trouble with Doctorsahib: she was too tidy. With a messy Memsahib, it was easier to poke around undetected.

Already her search had been profitable. She'd seen the box with white, rectangular objects in the bottom drawer. Bandages, Asha had thought, until she'd seen Doctorsahib carrying the box into the bath-room, later seen one wrapped in paper, soiled. Imagine using something like that, so smooth, soft.

Asha covered her face, went to Doctorsahib. "Excuse me, Doctorsahib. I don't like to mention it, but ... "

"Yes, what is it, Asha?"

Asha lowered her head, whispered, "Do you have any spare rags? It's my time of the month and I need some more."

Doctorsahib had given her some pads, and even a belt to hold them in place. The next time Doctorsahib had gone to Najgulla, she had bought a whole box for Asha, and from then on, every month, Asha was well supplied. She had told Doctorsahib how heavy her blood was. Asha did well selling two here, two there for a paisa.

"*Arre*, Asha, you're getting too bold," said Meenu, one day, by the river. "One of these times, she'll be on to you and then you'll get into trouble. Big trouble."

"What do you mean, trouble? You watch your mouth, Chuddi. If you say one word to any of the *Sahib-log*, I'll come after you, pull your hair out by the roots. D'you hear?"

"*Ai-yai-yai*. I'm not going to say anything. I'm just worried about you."

"I can take care of myself, Chuddi. You better watch yourself, I know how that Rohet watches you when you go behind the bushes. Careful you don't get it. Right between the legs."

The women laughed. Asha banged the clothes against the rock. Get into trouble! As if she was so stupid. She could take bits of food, even the odd piece of clothing—it floated down river during the wash, she was so sorry, Doctorsahib could stop the money from her wages. Of course, Doctorsahib never did.

But Asha never took money, except for a few paisas in change when she shopped for food. Doctorsahib kept her money in the top drawer, underneath her underwear. Asha couldn't decide whether the woman was extremely simple or extremely clever. Asha counted the money but never took so much as one rupee. She had no intention of being dismissed from a job that, on the whole, was satisfactory.

It was the morning after the interchange with Chuddi that Asha found the embroidery threads. She'd never noticed them before because they were folded in a long piece of cloth, inside a clear plastic bag. Asha had seen the cloth and ignored it. It looked like a piece of cheap coarse cotton.

That morning, she took out the plastic bag, unfolded the fabric. Out fell embroidery threads. Red, orange, pink, peach, every shade of green. On the cloth was printed a pattern of flowers.

Asha sat on the floor, the cloth in her hand. How fine the threads were. In her village, the threads had never been like this.

"Asha. Asha, come here now, right now."

Asha ignored her mother. She was happier playing outside or helping her father in the field.

"Asha, come now or I'll give you a beating."

Her father looked at her. "You'd better go, quick, or you'll get it."

Asha ran back to the hut of her parents, her grandparents, and her older uncles' families.

Her mother shook her head, clicked her tongue. "What a wild thing you are. Why can't you be like Sundri, now? See how nicely she's making that *choli?*"

Sundri sat in the shade, hands flying, covering the short blouse with vibrant threads in the geometric pattern distinctive to their family.

Her grandmother said, "Leave the girl alone, she is only five."

"Yes, but she must learn. Get going, Asha, work on your cloth."

Asha pushed her hair off her face, took a small drink of water from the pot in the hut—you had to be careful, it was always short. She pulled out her grimy piece of cloth. *Khhsss!* What a dull sound the thread made. *Khsss!* In, out, in out.

Her grandmother smiled. "Come. I've got a gift for you."

She opened the worn trunk in the corner of the hut and held out a rag doll, with coarse, dark threads for hair, brown embroidered eyes, and a wide, red mouth. "See, you can make clothes for her and embroider them. That will be more fun, yes?"

Asha sighed. How strange to think of Doctorsahib doing embroidery.

At the Ungoli house, Parvati Memsahib had sometimes done simple, flowery patterns, nothing like the bold work in Asha's home village. But Asha could hardly glance at Parvati Memsahib's work, let alone touch the threads.

It was only when they'd still lived in their Kutch village that Asha had disliked the work. It hadn't seemed special then. Every woman in the house did it, every wall hanging, every quilt, every garment they wore was covered with colourful embroidery. But after they left the village because of that drought, Asha missed the colours.

And it was their making in Hyderabad, Sindh. Nasser Aziz, a Muslim tailor, taught her father his trade in exchange for the embroidery Sundri, Asha, and her mother did. Soon, her mother had gold bangles.

Her mother said Asha had a real gift for adapting the village styles, combining them in fresh ways. She'd embroidered clothes for her doll, such beautiful clothes.

Asha's hands shook slightly as she carefully put away the embroidery threads, folded the cloth, and returned it to its plastic bag.

She gathered the dirty clothes and went down to the river.

The women were talking about Ungoli *Burra* Memsahib, how badly she treated her daughter-in-law, Parvati Memsahib, all the work she made her do, and her big with child.

Asha's voice was harsh. "What're you going on about, poor Parvati Memsahib, poor Parvati Memsahib. Poor, my arse! She's rich isn't she, with wealthy parents? She can go anywhere, do anything. Stupid fool, she's got no spine."

She spread Doctorsahib's towel on the flat rock, scrubbed it with hard soap.

Jaya, a wiry old woman who worked at the Ungoli house, shook her head and clicked her tongue. "Listen to you. You've got no pity for anyone."

Asha pounded the towel against the rock. "Why should I have pity for *sahib-log*? We're the ones working our guts out. Look at this Doctorsahib now, what I have to put up with, her dirty habits, eating with her left hand, her awful Hindi. She's been here for months and she still can't speak properly. And fussing, fussing, fussing about food, never satisfied. I don't know how much longer I can stand it."

"You'd better watch your tongue, Asha *rani*. You have it cushy at Doctorsahib's, and all you do is abuse her, trick her, cheat her."

Asha hawked and spat into the water. "All of a sudden so pure and lofty? I've heard you many a time abusing Ungoli Memsahib."

"Yes, but Ungoli Memsahib is a different sort. I've also been to the clinic. Doctorsahib treated me well."

There was a chorus of agreement from the other women.

"*Chumchas!* Sucking up to the Angrezi-log."

"What's Doctorsahib done to you? She feeds you, pays you well, and look how you treat her. She's all alone, a stranger. You have no heart, no pity."

"You're too old, Jaya. Your brain has dried, sitting out in the sun." Asha banged the towel so hard against the rock she grazed her knuckles.

She gathered the clean clothes and strode back to Doctorsahib's bungalow. In the kitchen, she noisily set about preparing Doctorsahib's lunch, chopping up an extra large green chili for the *dahl*.

After the meal, Doctorsahib called Asha, who instantly put on her smile.

Doctorsahib's face was still flushed, her eyes moist. "I will not be in for the evening meal today. I am going to Najgulla and I will be late, so I will eat there."

Asha lowered her head. "Doctorsahib, you don't like my cooking?"

"No, no, Asha." Doctorsahib blinked uncertainly. "It is just that I have to go to Najgulla. I have work to do. So I might as well eat there. That way, you also will have a free afternoon."

Asha smiled. "Very good, Doctorsahib."

When Doctorsahib left, Asha ate the leftovers, quickly cleared the dishes.

She walked into the front room, slowly looked around. No evening meal to prepare and she could iron the clothes tomorrow.

Almost involuntarily, she went into Doctorsahib's bedroom. She knelt in front of the bureau, opened the bottom drawer. She took out the threads.

She hesitated, then pulled a length of the brightest red. The red of the *khameez* of her *gudiya*, her doll.

In the frenzy, Asha grabs her doll.

"We don't have time for that now." Her mother slaps her. "Get something useful."

"Never mind," says her father. "Let the child have something to comfort her." He picks up the kitchen knife.

Asha stands frozen, clutching her doll. Her mother thrusts a bundle at her. She's snatching up clothes, food, pots, hissing orders to Sundri, who also rushes around, gathering things.

Why do they have to go? Why in the middle of the night?

Nasser Uncle is there, helping them load the bullock cart.

"Take the machine," he says, putting the new sewing machine from the shop on the cart. "And here, my wife sends this food. Hurry, you must hurry."

In the warm August night, her father swings her onto the cart, Sundri clambers up behind her. Her mother is crying, her mother who's always so strong?

Nasser Uncle reaches up, hugs Sundri and Asha. His mouth shakes, his face is wet. "Allah be with you."

Her mother takes off two of her gold bangles, holds them out to Nasser Uncle.

"No, you will need them. Allah guide you."

Her father embraces Nasser Uncle.

"Go now, my brother. And don't take any trains. There are terrible stories."

Her father climbs to the front of the cart, swings the whip, *kaa-thaaa*. They lurch forward. Asha doesn't know why she's so frightened. Maybe it's because everyone else is. She can smell it.

"Shh." Her mother's voice is low and fierce. "A big girl like you, there's no need to cry. You must stop. D'you want to get us all killed?"

"But why are we going, Ma? When will we come back?"

"Shh! I don't know, don't ask any more questions. Just be quiet." Asha presses her face into her doll. Her mother's hand strokes her head, but her movements are rough, jerky. They frighten Asha into silence.

Asha sprang to her feet, ran to the window. What if it was a trick, what if, right now, Doctorsahib was sneaking back?

No one in sight, no noise, just the steady pulsing of the afternoon sun.

She knelt again by the bureau, fingered the threads. You couldn't do much with one piece of red. She pulled out strands of crimson, fuchsia, emerald. What was a little thread to the Angrezi-log?

The Angrezi-log are leaving the country at last, but they're determined to make Muslims and Hindus fight each other; they have broken the country in two.

Asha doesn't understand. She's seen many Angrezis, but they don't seem so strong that they can break the land. Do they snap it like a biscuit?

Her mother is angry. Maybe it's just rumours. Half their belongings left behind, a new baby coming, a boy this time, pray God. They've seen no trouble. This is just Nasser Aziz's trick to get their goods.

"Stupid woman," cries her father. "He risked his life to warn us. We're all right so far because we left soon enough. And we're not there yet."

"There, there. Where is this new border, do you know? You're too trusting and here that Aziz, *sala gandoo*, is laughing with our things."

Asha, jolted, parched, clings to her doll. The world has gone mad.

It was that stupid Doctorsahib's fault. Typical of the Angrezi-log, they never trusted anyone. Hadn't she told Asha after the midday meal that she would not return until late that evening?

She'd done it on purpose, of course, to catch Asha. Asha had been kneeling by the bottom drawer, trying to decide which colours she could safely take more of, when there she was, Doctorsahib herself, at the door.

"What are you doing?"

Asha had been unable to speak, had felt her eyes filling with tears.

Doctorsahib, her mouth a thin line, had said, "Put it back. I do not have time now, I will talk to you tomorrow. I came back for something I had forgotten."

Asha hadn't had the wit to pretend she hadn't understood or even to invent some excuse, however implausible.

She tucked in the last stray end of the mosquito net under the bed. How could she have been so absorbed, that she hadn't heard?

Voices wailing, crying, whimpering, shouting. The long stream of carts, people walking, heading from the border area. Both ways. Hindus, Muslims. The terrible things they've seen, heard, the talk. Women weeping, dead bodies by the roadside, naked women, blood between the legs.

Her father keeps the knife handy. Her mother's nose is swollen; the slit where the nose ring was torn off, infected. Her eyes when she looks at Asha and Sundri. So many families have lost their children; some have sold their daughters.

Asha hugs her doll. When they get there, wherever that is, she'll wash her doll's clothes, and everything will be clean, bright.

Down. Her father jumps to the ground, overturns the cart. Her doll, the quilts they have pieced over the years, the ones they are to sell to start again, the sewing machine, bouncing, bursting. Asha screams, can't reach her doll. Her father thrusts them under the cart, pushes it down. It bangs against Asha's head. Cattle bawl.

Screams, her ears are soaked in screams. Her mother calls her father's name, pulls Asha and Sundri close against her, one hand on each of their mouths. Drowning in the thunder of her mother's heart, her familiar smell, her sweat and something else. Sundri must have soiled herself. No, it's her, mess in her pants, stench of fear, her mother wailing. Asha presses her hand against her mother's mouth, presses hard. Cries burst uncontrollably against her palm; snot runs over her hand.

There weren't many clothes to wash; if she is still here tomorrow, she'd do them then. Otherwise, someone else would inherit the Angrezi woman's stinking clothes. Besides, she didn't want to face the women at the river. Would they guess? They'd find out soon enough. They'd pretend to commiserate, but they'd be delighted. They'd even fight over who was to get her job.

Asha gave the chair in the small front room a last rub. The house was clean, and she'd already cooked the *bhaji*, the hottest ever, three large green chilies. It even made her eyes water. She hawked, spat into the *bhaji*. There, Doctorsahib, a goodbye present from Asha.

She didn't need this Angrezi Doctor. She'd go back to the Ungolis'. And if she couldn't get on there, she'd go to Najgulla, where plenty of families needed servants. She'd never be forced into marriage, have children. Look at Sundri now, so worn.

When her mother's water breaks, two months too soon, no one will take them to the hospital. Asha screams; people ignore her. Just another mad beggar.

Half pulling, half carrying, they drag their mother the mile to the hospital.

The gates are shut to keep marauders out. Once a Hindu crowd broke in, killed a Muslim patient and doctor.

Asha shouts to the *chowkidar*. "Hurry up, my mother is having a baby. Hurry."

The small, thin *chowkidar* looks at them and sniffs. He puts finger and thumb on either side of his nose, blows expertly. His snot, greenish-yellow, globular, lands in the dust by Asha's bare foot. Her mother moans, clings to the gate of the hospital, knuckles white.

"Open the gate, you *sala gandoo*," screams Asha. "Open it, you mother-fucker, or I'll cut your dick off."

"Who d'you think you are, you piece of garbage? Get out of here. This is a hospital for decent folk."

"My mother, she's having a baby."

The *chowkidar* swings his stick. "More likely drunk, by the looks of you. Out of the way, move, or I'll call the police."

He bangs his stick against her mother's fingers, and pokes it through the bars of the gate.

In the distance, Asha sees a white-clad figure.

"Doctorsahib," she yells. "Doctorsahib."

Sundri weeps, her nose overflowing, clinging to their mother.

Asha holds on to the gate, eyes closed, shouts, over and over, "Doctorsahib, Doctorsahib."

Her fingers are bloody from the *chowkidar*'s stick before a voice says, "What is this noise?"

Asha looks into the dark, pocked face of a woman in a white coat.

"What's the matter?" she says in a voice that is low yet annoyed.

The *chowkidar* licks his lips, talks fast in a whining tone, but the dark woman stops him.

Her mother's labour is not very long. The doctor with the pocked face delivers their dead baby brother, tries with a nurse and another doctor to stop their mother's bleeding.

Asha stares at her mother. Still. Her awful eyes closed at last. Sundri is at the foot of the bed, sobbing, a heaving bundle of brown rags.

Slowly, Asha picks up, from where it has fallen, the knife her mother had taken from their father's body.

Doctorsahib. Asha carried the food into the front room, put it on the table with a thud.

Doctorsahib sank into the chair, her face red. She fanned herself with the newspaper.

"It is a very hot day, is it not Asha?"

What was the woman playing at, speaking so politely? Still trying to torment her. Doctorsahib gulped down a glass of water, looked at her.

Asha's heart beat faster. Tilak would be furious. Would she be able to work for the Ungolis again? Her place had been filled. How would she get a job with no reference? She'd end up back in the streets, babies thrust inside her.

"What were you doing with my things?"

She'd prepared for this. From her waist, she pulled the rag on which she'd worked the embroidery.

Doctorsahib frowned.

"What is it?"

"A doll's *salwar*. We used to do this kind of embroidery in the village I come from." She hadn't meant to say so much.

"I do not like stealing," said Doctorsahib.

Asha stared back, her face expressionless. This ugly woman. *Burra Angrezi Sahib*, sitting there, wanting to extract penance, like a tooth.

"But since it was not anything ... " Doctorsahib hesitated, continued, "anything serious, I will overlook it this time."

What did she expect? Asha to touch her feet?

"The next time you want something, you ask me. Understand?"

Asha nodded, almost imperceptibly.

"I do not want you to go through my things again, understand? I want to trust you. And I want you to trust me."

Asha stared at the plate of steaming food.

"I also like to do embroidery, but here I do not have the time. My aunt taught me, my mother's sister, in the village I come from, in England." She paused. "If you like, the next time I go to Najgulla, I can get threads for you. As a gift."

What was the woman's game?

Doctorsahib pulled the plate toward her, bit into a piece of *chapati* wrapped around the *bhaji*. She sucked in her breath sharply, her ugly blotches drowning in the flood of colour.

"*Bahaut tikha hai*, so hot." Eyes watering, she said stumblingly, "But I like your cooking."

Asha curved her mouth into a smile. What a fool, this Doctorsahib. A slug with weeping eyes, pathetic.

Doctorsahib blinked rapidly, licked her lips, gathered another mound of food with her left hand.

Asha's smile widened. So many things she could do, worse than chilies in her food, worse than spit.

She couldn't help it, she started to laugh. She laughed and laughed, unable to stop.

Doctorsahib looked at her, puzzled. Then she too was smiling; then laughing, helplessly, foolishly.

Asha, bent over double, saw Doctorsahib through streaming eyes. Why was she laughing? Didn't she understand? Didn't she know what could happen? Stupid, stupid woman.

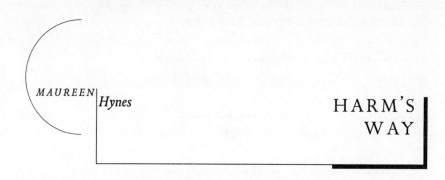

MAUREEN *Hynes*

HARM'S WAY

Some of us wear a piece of the road as an amulet
over our breastbones: may harm not wind its way back to us.

The first three times were scorching, I can feel
the small disk of heat on my chest. Risk insurance.

A man sits down in the ditch and whets his knife with a stone.
Traps and kills a weasel, siphons a jar of blood

and bricks it into his calcified wall. A woman draws
a yearly bucket of water from the well a child drowned in

to make a thin soup for her family. A girl
braids silk threads to tie around her wrist, while

the boy takes a small vial of water from the waterfall, stashes
it behind his mother's hatbox, lets it thicken to oil.

There's that noise again.

Some kind of a basement noise, but you're outdoors.
Your ears flinch, your eyes sharpen into the dusk.

Striding down the gravel shoulder in your too-new Reeboks
and far off, a Zamboni, a cyclone, a minotaur.

Alone but that's okay. Until now. Fragile suddenly
and thunderstruck. Peel your hands off your throat

and scream, why don't you scream? Jump into the field,
into the hay with the rest of the sneezes. Turn back, peel

the road back to your rumpled bed. No, stay still and listen
for the frogs or the stars falling out of the dusk.

This is Harm's Way and no escaping, no Tahiti or
Bora Bora for you, no flights to and from,

no slipping out or nodding off, no sitting around
singing sad songs, *Goodnight Irene, Swing Low Sweet Chariot.*

This is Harm's Way, the traffic ahead is bad. Bulldozers
heaping and curling a wave of hazards and the loudest trouble

is distilled into something tiny and deep, the first kiss
of breast milk ticks with odds, one in nine, one in three.

This map's no good, takes you right into the nuclear plant.
Good paved road, the forest's cleared, the atolls gone.

Melanoma or divorce or stroke or military coup
chugging its particular noise directly toward you, no

signature required. Oh, says your mother,
that's just Harm's Way telling you to get out of its road.

—It's all right, she says tenderly from aloft. She brushes
your hair and strengthens the terror. Perpetuates it.

Summoned or shunned doesn't matter, no pleading
a special case, no spreading laurels to rest beneath,

privileges peel off and crackle, a stained old pair
of evening gloves. The rosary mumbles its beads.

You search overhead, scope the sky for the baking sun.
Why is this road so empty when you know you're not alone,

why is it always night on this particular stretch?
Rip a poncho out of your pack, spread it on the dark wet weeds,

lean against the whitewashed oval of a roadside grotto,
and recite the alphabet of what's given and received.

Here's a thread of dawn. Tie your shoelaces, scramble on.

PRECAUTION

Three hours of hesitant driving
along guardrails in the cold coastal rain
and the houses staring with a certain closed
belligerence. This isolation, each from each.
Pull over. Step out of the car, stretch your
arms and legs against the salty details
of the rain, lean against the car door,
finish your cooling coffee.

Just inside the brown slat fence, two small girls
stand in a packing crate.
Their eyes and arms brim its edge.
"This is our spaceship," says the younger one,
maybe four years old.
You ask her, "And where are you taking it?"
"To New York, and the moon and the sun
and all the stars." Across the field,
from the doorway of his house
a man calls to them. You watch him stride
across the wet meadow in his black rubber boots,

the same orange band around their rims
as your brothers' boots when they were paperboys.
He summons them from the box, takes each
by a hand and hurries them back across the field
into the house.

A welter of words has died on your lips, mostly
yes and no. Wild irises, stunted by the cold
salt air, grow at the edge of the wet grass.
You get back in the car, drive
up the twisting ocean road to the lighthouse.

NINO'S WORK

JOSEPH *Maviglia*

Nino has sheared sheep
for thirty years: packed
and carried wool
to lower towns by mule.

This spring,
a fabrics factory from Reggio
plans new service,
offering synthetics at cut prices.

Nino says, "My customers—they know
wool is wool.
Besides, my mules know these roads."

Outside,
beyond the braying stables,
truck tires rattle past.

STEVEN *Heighton*

TO EVERYTHING
A SEASON
(novel excerpt)

4   THE FALL WIND

A CHINOOK WIND BLEW in over the passes and
the clean powder snow falling since Remembrance Day turned soft and
wet and began to vanish. The streets of Banff, full of skiers and sightseers
up from Calgary for the day, ran with meltwater smelling of spring, the
sun in the clear sky was summer-hot. Jessie and Stratis stood at the plate-
glass window of their busy café gazing up over the bright crowded streets
and dripping roofs of the facing shops to the peak of Mount Rundle, where
snow was being churned and spun by the westerlies like spume off the tip
of a wave. And Rundle did look like a wave, a huge tidal wave of blue-grey
water frozen solid in the second before breaking. So Jessie thought. She
was a painter, part-time—a too small part of the time—and she'd told
Stratis how the mountain looked to her, but he always said he just couldn't
see it, a mountain was a mountain, wasn't it?

She turned to him. The sunlight through the plate-glass window did
him good, brushed his greyed face with colour. For two weeks he'd been
in a state of unexpected remission and ten days ago he'd come home from
the hospital in Calgary. The doctors, Stratis warned her, were not optimistic.
She knew that. She knew not to expect miracles. But on a day like today

anything seemed possible, even likely, with Rundle holding its precarious poise against the blue sky, the sunlight, the chinook breathing sweetly through the open door of the café, winter deferred for a few more days, the café full of cheerful customers and the new help, Glen, working out just fine—much better than the last student she'd hired in June when Stratis first went into hospital.

"Jess?"

Glen needed help at the till. Jessie spun around and in a few strides crossed the tiny Olympos Café. She and Stratis had long fought over the décor—he wanted posters and framed, doctored tourist photos of Greece, she planned to cover the walls with the sketches and paintings of Bow Valley artists—but from the start of his illness she had acquiesced, so in his absence the café had come to look exactly as he had always hoped. A few of her paintings he could live with, he said, gladly he could, but all that other stuff? There were enough mountains out the window, who wanted air-brushed Alps when you had the real thing a few steps out the door? So while a few of her watercolour landscapes still hung behind the till, it had been months since she'd hung any new work by friends. A yellowing map of Greece instead, the Acropolis from five angles and through lenses aimed with wildly differing degrees of skill, Mount Olympus viewed from the sea, beaches with fresh-painted fishing boats drawn up, the Aegean an implausible postcard blue and the matching forgery of Grecian skies.

A tightness now in her throat and belly as she passed them, these aquamarine clichés, these touched-up dreams that would soon remind her of a fresh and unretouched sorrow. But no. Stratis looked so well these days; he was cheered by the café's increasing success, and the weather, and most of all by being back in Banff with his children. And Jessie. He had smiled weakly, then laughed out loud and hugged her on seeing how she'd put up all those extra images of Greece.

"But soon my dear you will take them down."

He said it softly, without malice.

Jessie had met him eight years before in Calgary, where, at twenty-six, she was trying to finish a fine arts degree part-time while waitressing wherever she could. Stratis managed the dining room where she worked weekends. He was the owner's son and he'd surprised her, over time, by erasing her stereotyped image of the Greek Boss. "My father, mind you, is the real thing," he would laugh, his long black feminine lashes meeting. "Me, I hate it here."

Stratis had no particular interest in art and that suited Jessie just fine. She'd had enough of dating art students. Stratis's consuming interest, she learned, was family—not the one he had, mind you, but the one he hoped to have. He wanted a small business of his own somewhere a long way from his father's city and he wanted his own big family as well. So his lean olive features lit up and furrowed in a broad smile whenever a family with small children came into his father's place—partly, Jessie teased, because he didn't have to serve them.

"Strange," he opened up to her one night after work, over his beer and cigarettes. "We were never happy as children. I think sometimes I want to do right what my father didn't."

Stratis was ready to settle down, it was clear, and Jessie had long been ready. So after getting her degree she moved with him to Banff, which she loved and he didn't think was really far enough from Calgary but did offer good prospects for the future. They both got work in another restaurant through one of Stratis's seemingly countless uncles. They lived frugally and began to save. They were made floor managers, Jessie days and Stratis nights, and the money was better. After a year they got married and a year later they had their first child—a girl, Calla. Then twins, Larissa and Paul. They made an offer on a closing crafts shop and did it over as a café.

With each passing year Jessie smuggled a few more of her friends' paintings into the café and deported a few more of her husband's Grecian atrocities. Stratis fought a stubborn rearguard action and sometimes resorted to guerrilla tactics, one night replacing three watery Alpscapes with chromatically similar Greek scenes, then pleading, "Jessie, *pethi*, we're a Greek-style café, think of the customers!" And she had to nod. But this was no more than a minor check. Eventually, she was sure, the Olympos Café would be a kind of local art gallery.

The impending realization of her dream could do little now but depress her. As if the dream itself were partly to blame for what had happened? Stratis looked so thin here, silhouetted in the window with the mountain above him; snow churning steadily off the crest.

She showed Glen how to unjam the drawer of the till, and when she looked up she saw Stratis weaving his way back through the tables. He riffled the hair of a small blonde girl who grinned up at him, her chin, lips and teeth flecked with nuts and sticky bits of *filo*. For a moment he seemed to flush, to glow with that contact, but as he neared the till, his face faded again from rich colour to shades of chalk and charcoal, black and white. The furrows in his cheeks and around his eyes sank deeper. Deeper still as he tried to smile.

"It's such a nice day, Jessie. Too busy to leave Glen here alone. Let's close at four and go for supper with the kids."

At home, after the children were in bed, Jessie asked Glen to come down from his upstairs apartment so she and Stratis could go out for a while. The chinook was still blowing and the streets still ran with meltwater and the Bow River, sluggish and half frozen just a day before, was flowing swiftly in the dark. But the air did seem colder and Jessie wondered if it was more than just the absence of the sun. A change in the weather? They walked arm in arm along the river, slowly. The path was deserted. Then, straight ahead, a black, massive shape bulked up out of the river onto the banks: a huge elk, his hide and antlers dripping, glistening in the faint lamplight, his body like a great barrel rocking back and forth as he shook off the cold water of his crossing.

Jessie and Stratis stood very still. The elk ignored them, his heavy snout upraised and snuffling the wind. After a few moments he ambled, with solemn dignity, into the pines.

They lagged back up Wolf Street toward the café. Stratis said he wanted to check the place seeing as they'd closed early—and since Stratis was the kind of man who would stop the car halfway to Calgary and turn around and drive back to Banff just to check if he'd turned off the coffee machine, Jessie was not surprised. She was not even exasperated, as she had been in the past by his worrying, his occasional laziness in the café, his stubborn matter-of-factness (*a mountain is a mountain!*)—and his refusal to quit smoking till it was too late. How strange, how very wasteful such exasperation now seemed! Even about the smoking, perhaps ...

Rundle brooded above them again, a tidal wave in silhouette. Jessie would never tire of its power, its tension, the sense of massive implacable movement, stopped. Yet always in motion; never complete. It was a masterpiece of tension and whoever could reflect it perfectly in paint—and not just its essence but its *shape*, which could never be improved on—would have a masterpiece on her hands. She had sketched and painted it many times, in charcoal, *conté*, watercolour, and oils, in as many versions as there were tourist views of the Acropolis. By the path near the bridge over the Bow River where she and Caleb had come walking years before, she would set up her easel in the sun. Mondays, for a few stolen hours. So that when she came home, Stratis—making the *baklava* that had added, with the children, twenty pounds to her frame—smiled at her freckles and said it looked as if someone had sprinkled her face with nutmeg.

And she would laugh. But the mountain escaped her.

They came back to the modest clapboard two-storey on Marten Street and thanked Glen. Jessie noticed how uneasy the boy looked on seeing Stratis's face. And when she and Stratis were alone and she got a good look at him under the hall light, she realized he did look worse. And she sensed he knew it.

He told her he felt fine.

The mountain and its halo of blue air still hung above them when they were in bed—a kind of abstract Greek Orthodox icon, framed above their heads, in encaustic. Jessie's. She frowned up at it as she got under the down quilt beside her husband, who was almost asleep but seemed to stir himself, rubbing his long-lashed eyes like a child resisting sleep. And with those white pyjamas he had started wearing in the hospital after years of sleeping nude, he looked even more like a child. So small and shrunken, even now, after a week of eating well.

His body again giving off the faint sour odour they had both noticed in June. For the last week it had been gone and his body had seemed, to Jessie, as fresh and pure as a wind off the snowfields.

"I smell again, Jess. I stink."

A kiss of denial. "Hush."

He puts his arms around her and pulls her naked body onto him. His clasp is so gentle, she thinks; and then she thinks, weak.

She helps him undress. Gently she holds him and rubs her body over his. He is so weak, not like two nights ago when he seemed almost as before, laughing, reminding her of when sex was something lively, raunchy, a terrific joke with endless variations and the same gut-wrenching punchline that seemed new every time. A warm fragrant gust of chinook rattles the blinds and passes over them and perhaps it stirs him, wakes him a little, breathes strength back into his lungs because his cock hardens in her hand and quickly she guides him inside her and moves over him, and over him.

They go on for a long time in near silence, Stratis with his eyes closed and a look on his face so peaceful, the long lashes twinned, parted lips like a sleeping child's; she with her mouth open near to his. Exhaling deep as if to revive him. Now his eyes open, widen, and he clutches her buttocks with hands so gentle she could weep, she arches harder and rubs against him and pulls back and feels a kind of fear as if the smooth motion of her cunt soon to clasp and suck the crisis from deep inside him with his seed will weaken him too much, bleed life from his core. He is coming, groaning weakly and she lets herself go, she pushes and as the storm breaks under her womb and pumps long sweet warming gusts to the tips of her arching toes and clenched fingers a breeze blows through the room and just to feel it caress her bare skin as she comes is too much, the sweetness is too much, the pain, goddamn it, the sorrow. A second climax wells from her belly but this time it is all pain, an orgasm of pain that racks her whole body dredging up all the things she has kept down as she sobs and collapses on top of this man, this good man, this fucking heartless bastard who is going to leave her.

So soon. So soon his cock softens, wilts, and slips out of her. She can't stop crying, her head pressed into the bony crook between his neck and shoulder. The sour reek of his poor body.

"It's all right, Jessie. Please. It's all right."

It's not goddamn it and you know it's not. It's not, you're going to leave me. What the hell am I going to do?

At four she wakes and his side of the bed is empty. For a moment she lies propped on an elbow staring at the imprint his body has etched into the sheet. That sour smell again, stronger.

She stumbles into the hall. A white form glides toward her out of the dark. "Stratis?"

"The children," he whispers, short of breath. "Just checking. You know how I am. To close their windows."

She guides him back into the bedroom, so cold now, icy, the weather has turned and by dawn the unmelted snow in the yard will have a crust a child can walk on without sinking. Ice knitting up in the melt-pools and forming along the banks of the Bow. Cold air bleeding in through the walls and settling into the drawer by the window where she keeps all her portraits.

She tucks Stratis in and closes the window for winter.

"In the morning," she says lightly—trying to sound casual, in control—"darling? In the morning we should probably go see the doctors. In Calgary."

His mouth is open as if to form a response, but he says nothing. Asleep, so soon. She lies beside him and studies the familiar yet subtly changed contours of his face, thinking of the weeks to come, and Rundle: the blue sky above it and the chinook blowing snow like foam off the grey rock crest of a shape she will always be painting. Down the sloping backside of the frozen wave to a small graveyard of crooked limestone slabs. She has painted there, too, but she won't be able to do that again.

She leans over and sets her palm, like a mirror, an inch above the open mouth and feels the warm soft breath of her husband moistening her skin.

TILT

JOHN *Donlan*

Dear body, snow fell many miles
as if to be with you today.
The river with its ruff of ice reminds you
to protect the warm column of blood
around your voice—the voice you sometimes feel
there is no use for.
Dear body, the birds have voices, don't they?
So let's not have any more nonsense of that sort.

You love surface geology: here—
take this slope anchored in pines and grasses,
this jacked-up slab of crumbling sea-floor we call Mountain;
wear the earth as if it was your skin.
Don't forget you have that wet red muscle
pushing heat to your limits, dear body,
beyond any extremity you know.

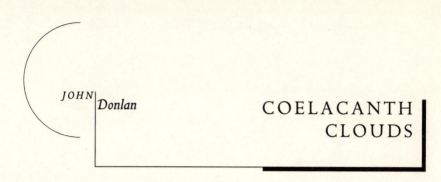

JOHN Donlan

COELACANTH CLOUDS

Mule deer moving across rough country:
cartilage slides smoothly in its socket.
The wind's voice, translated through the low
hiss of pine needles, says, "You belong."

Overhearing, you're unsure
of your inclusion: you're used to hearing the wind say "Die,"
chiselling away at concrete towers.

Here it scours grains of mountain ice
against the rock face, perfectly indifferent.
Two ravens play in its upward rush as if
celebrating gravity's overthrow:
fly up like bingo balls, drop like rags,
soar where prehistoric fish once swam
suspended above the ocean bed. They glance
sidelong at you, tumble and call. You laugh
to see such sport. Coelacanth clouds drift by.

STRING
QUARTET

MÉIRA Cook

PRIMA PARTE MODERATO

This is not about music this is about desire. The desire that rides
us, four horses on a carousel. When the music stops we are obliged
to change horses. How did I, the first violin, learn of desire this
temperate man this musician of controlled vibrato and perfectly
creased trousers? There was a spot on her hand, it preoccupied her
immensely. She rubbed at it, a cat with buttered paws.

So little it takes.

If I were of a poetic mind I would say she holds her viola
to her chin as if it were a head. A beloved mortal head aah the
degeneracy of that mouth composting kisses. She is rotten as
camembert I tell you.
Also she is holding her bow too high again and slicing.
Slicing. Tonight I will tell her of the moderate elbow that pivots
in its ballbearings. No more slicing I will whisper in the secret of her
ear. And I will slice her open like a letter yes. And she will be all
paper and flutter at my feet ... *moderato moderato.* ·

SECONDA PARTA ALLEGRO

Why always the long wet slant what am I *donnina allegra* a loose woman?
always with him the gaze brimming over eyes swimming little fishes in
brine surely she sees him her husband watches him watching me

watching her

she is so distant tonight the reflection of a woman caught in the
mirror who was it said beauty is measured in the distance between eyes
the length of the nose her neck is too long the sad nun's throat of a
modigliani nude a bowl of lemons in the foreground someone should kiss
her all over bite that hard red berry make her moan i would like to
hear her moan see those flat eyes fly open watch the palms for stigmata
I would like to make her moan does he make her does he there is blood
moving below the surface of her wrist sometimes in my sleep i see that
pale drowned face hanging over his shoulder like a scarf as he ramps
and plunges her eyes fathom green and salt sink to the bottom of sea
she takes me between her thighs plays me like a cello

RECAPITULAZIONE DELLA PRIMA PARTE MODERATO

Moderato *moderato* ... and she will be all paper and flutter at my feet.
And I will slice her open like a letter yes. No more slicing I will
whisper in the secret of her ear. Tonight I will tell her of the moderate
elbow that pivots in its ballbearings. Slicing. Also she is holding her
bow too high again and slicing. She is rotten as camembert I tell you.
A beloved mortal head aah the degeneracy of that mouth composting
kisses. If I were of a poetic mind I would say she holds her viola
to her chin as if it were a head.

So little it takes.

She rubbed at it a cat with buttered paws. There was a spot on her hand
it preoccupied her immensely. How did I, the second violin, learn
of desire this temperate man this musician of controlled vibrato and
perfectly creased trousers? When the music stops we are obliged to

change horses. The desire that rides us, four horses on a carousel. This is not about desire this is about music.

CODA LEGATO MOLTO

What the first violin loves the second violin tries to love. What the first violin desires the second violin is obliged to desire so it goes so it goes. What an excursion into the grotesque what a parody this is and I quite aloof from it all, angular and undismayed. Tonight as always he will blunder to her door I will hear the bedsprings and his sprung cries, a fugue of desire. Then I will smooth out his trousers lay them flat on the board and iron and iron the creases to darts.

What goes around goes around.

And of course he hears them too, the second violinist, their aleotoric grindings. And I wonder for whom he throbs at these times, for him or her, the object of his desire or the object of his desire's desire? As for me I have long ceased to throb I am all calloused fingers now suppleness of wrist is all.

Round and round.

Thing is, the music changes every night the horses dance up and down up and down who knows where I'll be next time round. Perhaps then, the next time this body this cello will be tuned *con molto affetto*

with love.

JOANNE *Page*

HOW YOU
MIGHT BE
LIKE ALBERTA

O_h
        look
the mountains are doing a star turn,
showing off—aren't we divine
and couldn't we be a row of Rouen cathedrals lined up
in the sun now taupe now
sand now rose now mauve
against a mackerel sky?
Worship here.

Never this, you,
Johnson Canyon's more your style,
casual signage and a turn off the road,

there being only the one way in,
easily missed, dictated by years of persistent backscarring
and previous attempts which have often failed for haste or
bullying, not a place to overwhelm
but be taken by, to come upon gradually,
tacking along the catwalks mostly up,

geological layers for the asking at eye level, switchbacks
for the elevation.

No need to strike up the band,
there is honky-tonk at the first winter waterfall
pouring behind frozen drapery
into the plunge pool, chunka-chunk and off,
a blue streak playing musical tag
with itself, hide and
seek downstream,
pooling where the cut is deepest,
oldest, then diving beneath the mute snow,
now you hear me, now you
don't.

Snow pillars brace canyon walls,
shadowy,
you seem to hold your breath at Upper Falls
and so do I, nothing moving but sunspots and vapour,
butter on ice, enough crystal daggers
to fend off trouble; the music smooths down to glass
and I would stay forever if I could
within this blue, this a cappella.

JOANNE *Page*

THE PURPOSE OF
JOHANNES VERMEER

W oman Reading a Letter

The woman with the letter
measures
two words:

drop of light
    in each
        scalepan

Outside the room
waterwheels stop.
Discovery and sails of ships
fail
for windlessness.
Every working of the hand holds
to itself.

Nuns keep vigil,
songs fall silent,
the room gives out the sound
of moonlight
        or flowers.

Clatter is defeated.

No surrender here,
only the ferocious
utility of the heart's salutation.

ROSEMARY *Blake*

DIVING OFF
THE WRECK

Everyone's swum out there at least once in summer.
The painted harbour. Stylized
white distances of sea and sky.

Light spirals over the dust jackets
on your shelves. *Analysis of Dreams, Dream Images.*
Day's unwavering. In these pages, the precise sails
drift over a poised horizon.

Someone asked her what difference
it had made her father dying then.
"Not much," she'd said.
"We were very young."

Now far from sea the asphalt's heat films
above the narrow side streets east off Bay.
These memories search into sheet-glass mornings.

AFTER THE
NIGHTMARE

ROSEMARY Blake

"It's all right.
There's nothing there."
The room washed bare and yellow
by the light. She smooths back
the damp sleep on his forehead.
"It's only the wind," her father
used to say.
Cliffs and hollows of her room.

The Norway maple on the neighbours' front lawn
reaches almost to their eaves.

He'd told her, once,
that in Ireland, in the south,
they picture death as a rider
in the high winds around the house.

Her son's asleep.
Nothing there.

Even when it's still,
the row of white pine,
newly planted by the fence,
shifts.

TIDAL
BELLS

BRUCE Hunter

Awash, rising from you
like a grouty sea lion,
my whiskers askew with kelp.
In my hair and yours, sea grit,
our fingers salt riffed and foamed.

Shells in the slow tumble
from the westward current.
The spill of liquid sand,
whiffs of us.

Like those bright glass bulbs
loosened from the Japanese fishing nets.
Those clapperless tidal bells
tinking in the upcurl of waves,
lapping, just lapping like our tongues.

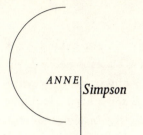

ANNE Simpson

WATERS OF IMMORTALITY

BECAUSE OF HIS FATHER, Allister ran away from home when he was ten years old. He wasn't going to listen to news of the war on the radio. He had what he needed. Water in a tin canteen, maybe the same kind the soldiers used at the Front. Sandwiches. Peppermints from the drawer in the front hall. Two undershirts, because his mother always said they were necessary. A pencil with the end bitten off. A black comb. A handkerchief. First he was going to Halifax, and then he was going to war.

When Allister left Verna, years later, he didn't know where to go. He stood on the front steps thinking he should go back inside and explain this, but the door was closed. It was dark and his children were in their beds. Finally, he drove to Truro and took a room for the night, in the place near the tidal bore. There was a mustard-coloured duvet on the bed and a Bible in the drawer. In the morning he saw the muddy waste below him, where the Fundy came in, taking everything with it when it ebbed, except the red mud. But in the middle of the night he couldn't see anything and he sat down on the bed with the Bible in his hands. Asunder.

Let no man. On the wall of the room was a mural of Cape Breton, with the dark hills sloping down to blue ocean. He lay down fully clothed on the bed and slept.

On his way to war, Allister came across blueberries just behind Aunt Dot's house. He picked a few, ate a few. It was hot as blazes so he lay down under the elm tree, thinking about what he knew of war. Willy Crowley had come back without legs or arms, just a torso and a head. He didn't come out of the house, except on nice days when they brought him out and put him on a blanket. They'd seen him, Frank and Allister, from behind the woodpile next door, wondering what he'd stepped on to rip off all his limbs. He looked like a bundle that his mother could pick up in her arms. Like a baby.

Allister's Uncle Lester was missing then. There was a photograph of him in the living room. Smiling. Once Allister picked it up and ran a couple of steps, zooming it over the sofa, like a plane. But Uncle Lester didn't fly planes. He was in the navy. Allister put the photograph back on the table and it fell over. He propped it up again, but it wouldn't stay, so he just put it down with Uncle Lester looking up at him, at anyone, who came into the room. It didn't come as a surprise when they told Allister his uncle had died. He thought of Uncle Lester looking up as they shovelled dirt over him. Over his black-and-white face, his mouth, his eyes. Over the glass and the frame. Maybe he knew it was coming.

Verna had told Allister she couldn't go on with it. Being married. He thought it had something to do with an old boyfriend of hers. Bart couldn't keep a job for longer than he could spit and turn around. In the afternoons. Maybe. In their own bed. He got up, turned on the light, and saw the scenic hills of the mural spread out in front of him. Vista. Her legs, her flesh, the mounds and hollows of skin. His legs, his flesh. Allister went over to the mural, pulled back his arm, and let fly with his fist. It didn't damage the hills any. But from the room next door a sleepy, angry voice called out, "Whaaaat?" He went back to bed and turned out the light. She'd said that there was no one, that nothing had happened, and he needn't worry on that score. But there was something she wasn't saying. Some little thing she was holding back. *What? What, Verna?* Nothing. So he left.

Allister's father drowned at Pomquet. He could have died another way. For years, Allister pictured it. Rope, fire, electrical shock. Trampling stallions, poisoning, falling, flying. He saw his father looping through the air in a biplane, scarf blown back, tracing figures in the air. G–O. Then another oval. O. A downward stroke, an arc. D. And the last few letters. B–Y–E. The plane suddenly askew and out of control, flames leaping from the fuselage as it plummeted to earth. His father's little joke. But it didn't happen like that. Maybe he didn't die at all. And it was some other body they'd found at Pomquet. Somewhere, his father was alive, because it was a different body they put in a coffin, earth settling on top of him, spadefuls of earth, while his mother wept. Soundlessly. Her red mouth making a shape. O.

This was what Ooch MacVicar told him about it. Allister's father was upset because they wouldn't let him go and fight in the war. His father's eyes weren't good enough, for one thing. But Allister knew his father didn't want to go to war. He could see it in his face when they went to the beach after church on Sundays. Once or twice his father sat in the car while the rest of them played in the sand, looking out to sea, as if there were something they couldn't see. Staring. After a while he fell asleep, the *Tartan* newspaper folded over his face until it slipped down to his chest, exposing his wide-open mouth, slack jaw, head to one side.

Allister remembered the plaid of the blanket that day at Arisaig. Yellow and blue. Clover at the edge of it. The flies on the sandwich bag that Verna had pushed out of the way. Her legs, the way her skin became softer, a little fleshier on her thighs. Her hand at the back of his neck, her mouth partly open. The pleasure of it. Rising, falling. Her quick breaths. *My. Oh my.*

These were the things, Allister's father lectured him, that they were losing. General knowledge. Informed knowledge. Take the horned toad. *Phrynosoma cornutum.* Family Iguanidae. Who knew that it could spray its enemies with blood from the corners of its eyes? Who knew the nesting habits of the bald eagle? The Code Napoléon. The basis for civil law in Quebec. His father sat at the kitchen table, staring into his tea cup. Empty. Who knew anything? He poured himself more tea and continued, measuring a little sugar into it. Or even, he went on, such things as hedgerows. Allister said he didn't know of any hedgerows in Canada. But Allister had missed the point. People didn't know how to grow hedgerows properly anymore. His father moved his hands in the air, showing Allister how they ought to grow, tangled together to form a natural fence. Home to thrushes, warblers, hedgehogs, voles. Hundreds of creatures. He dropped his hands. Or take cathedrals, he said, those great houses of the spirit. No one could build them now. There were maybe a handful of master masons in Europe who could do it. Soon they'd be dead.

He took up his cup again, though the tea was cold. They were in danger of losing everything. He drank and grimaced. To think of all that had been accumulated in knowledge. Then a gleam in his eyes. If they forgot these things, they would all be forgotten. Like Atlantis. Cities in ruin under the sea. Fish swimming through houses. His fingers floated through the air to show Allister.

The day would come.

Verna said it was a shame Allister's father had never been diagnosed. She thought he was manic-depressive. Ran in families. She knew someone in Goshen like that. Afflicted. But Allister's father didn't seem afflicted. Frank wasn't afflicted, or Bunny. Or Allister. He loved his father. His mother didn't play with them because there wasn't any time, but sometimes his father did. Once he let them tie him up to the chestnut tree, a kerchief over his eyes, so he couldn't see. He stayed there patiently until Allister's mother freed him. He made a tree house for them and one night they went up there and lay flat on the platform. His father and Frank and Allister. Squeezed together so they'd fit. Allister thought he was going to tell them about the stars, which were mostly obscured by the leaves. Something about Aquarius. Sumerian constellation. Pouring the waters of immortality upon the earth. Something like that. But he didn't. He told them he was born five years after the new century, which made him too young to go to war. The great war. Frank and Allister lay in the dark listening to him, thinking of him young. It was a century of discontent, he told them. Century of sadness. Frank told him they would win it, though, in the end. *What?* The war, Frank assured him, now that the Americans were in. His father made a little sound. *Whuuu.* Breathing out. Of course, he said, and if not this one, then another.

There was nothing to do in Truro. Allister couldn't sit on the bed reading the Bible anymore, so he drove back to Antigonish. Thinking of what to say when Verna opened the door. But she wasn't inside. She was around at the back, pulling weeds.

"Vern."

Not looking up.

"I don't know what I did, Vern."

"You didn't do anything," she said.

"Well, something's the matter."

"No."

"I can't do this," Allister said.

Her hand pulling out some dock, laying it on the heap.

"Vern."

She sat on her heels, looking across at Dyson's.

"Say something."

"I can't," she said. Nose red at the tip.

He put his arms around her, kneeling on the heap of weeds. She sobbed while he held her in his arms and rocked her, the way he had with the children. He wasn't going anywhere.

At his father's wake, people came to Allister and put their hands on his shoulder, on his back, on top of his head. They spoke to his mother. But they didn't know what to say to him or Frank. Bunny was sitting under the table eating a piece of frosted white cake. She was too young. Any other time his mother would have called her out of there, for heaven's sake; she was too big a girl for that nonsense. Allister wanted to curl up under the table beside her and eat the cake that was full of the rationed sugar he hadn't tasted for months.

"You poor things. You poor, poor things," said Mrs. Crowley.

Allister looked at her red lips and yellow front teeth, and then turned and ran, out the door, down Church Street, and under the hedge at his Aunt Dot's, flinging himself down in the field behind her house. He lay on his stomach, screaming like a stuck pig, kicking his legs, and pounding his fists into the grass.

His father found Allister under the elm tree when he ran away to war. His son's face was sunburned, pink as boiled ham. He lay down next to him, and when Allister woke, he found his father's arm around him. They lay there looking up through the greeny-light, greeny-dark leaves, way up high. They lay still and didn't say a word.

RICHARD Lemm

LOVE POEM ON POGEY CHEQUE NIGHT

The young men are breaking
bottles on the street, they grip
gear shifts, shove in tapes, leaving
their black marks on the pavement.
They have eaten something too long
dead, and now they sing outside
the dark windows in a choked language
white rhinos shot for their horns
understand. It is silence
I need to hear you. But they're crying
that the bars have all closed, even the bootleggers,
and no one wants them on the blood-swabbed decks
or bearing shields through German forests.
When you were here, moving as you love to
on top of me, everything could have fallen—
the banks, our last few heroes, the slow dots of
light that circle earth with our intelligence—
and we would have been safer
than I am alone, with my brothers howling
out there, hanging themselves
from nobody's moon.

SHED NO TEARS
(novel excerpt)

DOROTHY *Speak*

It was the first true autumn day. When I went outside to fetch William, he was putting the gardens to bed for winter, turning the soil with a spade, cutting back the perennials, pulling up the dying annuals, the soft-stemmed begonias. Ours is a pie-shaped property, for we are situated at a curve in the street. The backyard fans out to hedges planted by the neighbours, the McTavishes on our right, the Langs on our left—boxwood, hemlock, burning bush—grown now the height of a man.

I crossed the lawn under the shade of many trees, randomly planted over the years by William: an ash, heavy with its weight of orange berries; a clump of birch releasing today a golden rain; a horse chestnut blazing like Judgment Day. William grew up on the prairie, where the earth is flat or sometimes gently rolling, but everywhere bald and cruel, spare as bone, shelterless, and therefore all his life he's professed the purest of love for trees. But no sooner does he plant one than he brings out his pruning tools, believing he can improve upon nature. It makes me wonder if he's not in fact fonder of the noise and the raw power of his chainsaw than of the trees themselves.

"It's the hewer and hauler in me, Hortense," he will grin unrepentantly, pulling the starter cord as I press my hands over my ears. "It's the prairie boy!" he shouts above the engine's roar.

"But, William," I call back, "on the prairie there was no wood to hew!" Of course, he doesn't hear me.

In a corner of the yard stand the oldest of the species, two apple trees planted forty years ago. *The Man and Wife Trees*, William and I have always called them. Look at this pair, we'd say, these partners, these Man and Wife Trees, a married couple standing so close together, so united and loyal and enduring, their branches intertwined. The Man Tree is taller, more slender than the Wife Tree, which used to have a lovely round shape, as though she were with child. At one time, she lifted her arms so gently, so modestly into the sky, but today her branches are clipped and topped and pruned and painfully twisted. William tells me that because she will no longer bear fruit, she must be brought down. But I wonder if, after all these years of hacking at her limbs, he simply cannot rest until he sees her fall to the earth.

Though the trees have begun to shed their foliage, our yard, the grass still bright and green with a prolonged summer, is leafless. The Langs and the McTavishes swear that in the autumn William stands under the trees and catches the leaves as they spin down so that they will not lie and rot upon the earth. And indeed, since his retirement, he has been as devoted to the yard and gardens as a man smitten by a new lover. Solemnly, he sows his seed, his gestures tender, ardent, shaking with wonder. So many trees on such a small property have heaved the ground so that, as I crossed toward William, I feared turning my old ankles in the lumpy grass or tripping on exposed roots twisting like snakes across the lawn.

"Too many trees, William," I've told him. "Haven't you noticed how their roots have ruptured the basement walls? The foundations of the house are crumbling." But he only nods and fertilizes and prunes.

When I reached William, I noticed he was breathing heavily from his bending and digging. "You're retired, William," I reminded him. "Why don't you rest?"

"I've got a labourer's body, Hortense," he answered proudly. "I was born for physical work. It's in my blood. The prairie did that for me. All my life, the only thing I've wanted to do is work. There doesn't seem to be any other reason to live." I wondered if he was warm enough in his old coffee-coloured corduroy jacket, his felt hat with a small red feather blooming in the oily band.

"But what's the rush, William?" I asked, looking around at the yellowed hosta leaves he'd tossed onto the lawn, at the pruned rose, astilbe, bleeding heart, peony, hyacinth branches lying in heaps at our feet. "Should you be turning the whole garden today? Have you sat down at all? Dr. Pilgrim said you shouldn't work such long stretches. Let your heart calm down."

"I feel something, Hortense," he said earnestly. "There's urgency in the air. There's a smell of winter. You know, Hortense, I can't believe that through all the tedious, useless jobs I've done in my life and all the years I've wasted in this goddamned province, I allowed myself to get distracted. I forgot that the only important thing in life is soil. Look at this, Hortense," he said earnestly. Stooping, he pulled at a clump of impatiens, its frost-hit stems translucent and brittle. The roots came up thick with earth. "I've got the blackest soil on the street, Hortense. Probably in the city. Maybe the province, even," he said. He rubbed some soil into the hand that is missing three fingers, lopped off one day in this very yard when he was cutting back the Wife Tree with a chainsaw that slipped. Only the thumb and pinkie remain on this hand, sticking up like two antennae on an insect's blunt head.

"What will I do when the snow falls, Hortense?" asked William, his voice suddenly fearful, and I knew he'd spend another restless winter pacing the living room and lingering at the patio door, gazing out longingly at the frozen yard, the white gardens.

"Morris is here," I told him, my apron snatched up by the wind, flapping now like a flag.

"Morris?"

"Your son."

"*I* know who Morris is," he snapped. "Why's he here?"

"I don't know."

William sighed deeply. "Has he got his preacher face on?"

"I didn't notice. He's driven all this way. He hasn't even slept. The least you can do is come inside."

"I've still got a lot of digging to do."

"It's time you took a breather, anyway."

"Why can't he just come out *here*, if he wants to talk to me?"

"He's eating raisin toast. He was hungry after his shift. He came straight from the factory."

When William came in reluctantly, pulling off his jacket, Morris did indeed have in his hand the small leatherbound Bible he carries everywhere, even to work, where twice it has cost him his job.

"You can't feed those boys of yours on the New Testament," William told him at the time. "The gospel according to St. John won't put meat on their bones."

"God will provide," Morris answered.

Morris was never able to stand up to his father until he was a man of thirty-five carting the testaments around. They seem to give him authority, as the tablets did Moses. They've become his voice, which is a pity, I think, because they contain the wisdom only of men and none of women. The Bible is a very thick book for a slow reader like Morris, who was never strong at school work.

"Why was that boy nearly illiterate until he tripped over the scriptures?" William has often asked me.

"I don't know, William."

"I don't care if you want to waste your time reading the Bible," he's told Morris, "so long as you think and question as you go along." But Morris, like me, is not a thinker, and so he has swallowed the Good Book whole, chapter and verse.

In the kitchen, where two small windows facing the street have for so many years been my eyes on the world, I poured coffee. Carrying it out to the living room, I found William sitting in his recliner and Morris pacing the floor in front of him.

"Come to just one service, Dad," he begged, "that's all I ask. Please. Just come and see what our church is like."

"I converted once already. I don't need to do it again. There's little difference from one religion to the next, anyway. You get the same hogwash everywhere."

"But that's where you're wrong, Dad. All religions aren't created equal. Our god is a better god than your god."

"I didn't know they were running a competition."

Morris faced his father squarely. It's strange for me to see him looking so strong and unassailable these days, when he was such a lost and timid child. As a little boy, he had a fresh, smooth, trusting face, like a miniature

Cary Grant. But in his teen years, his skin erupted with plum-sized boils that had to be lanced and drained, and now his face is leathery and purple with scars. At fourteen, when he bore a hundred newspapers on his back after school because William said it would toughen him up, the children on his route used to call after him, "Hey, Scarface! How'd you get so handsome?"

I remember him as such a small, skinny boy and so am surprised now to see him stand nearly six feet tall, with broad shoulders and great spreading hands and a big square face. When he was young, I tried to strengthen him with carbohydrates, at every meal placing a stack of white bread at his elbow. Dutifully, he buttered the slices one by one on the flat of his hand and ate them. I was never able to put flesh on his bones, but I notice he's filled out in recent years and I'm not sure if it's Olive's cooking that's fattened him up or the way he now feeds so greedily on Jesus, who called himself the Bread of Life.

I have six daughters. I never wanted a boy. When I was growing up, there were enough men on the farm to last me a lifetime. William, on the other hand, like a farmer in need of cheap labour, dreamed of a house full of sons but got only Morris. The baby I miscarried at six months and the other one that died after three days were both male and now I wonder if, all his life, we have not somehow made Morris carry the burden of those two dead boys. William wanted Morris to be a leader, and I suppose he is one of sorts, if you can call being a factory foreman leading. He'd like to be a minister in his new faith, but he doesn't have the mental capacity and so has to be satisfied with teaching Sunday School. *Church of the Fire of God* is the name of Morris's religion.

"Makes God sound like a pyromaniac," William has said.

"If you joined our church, you'd be a changed man," Morris told William today.

"Why would I want to change myself?"

"If you'd let God be your guide all these years, you'd have lived differently. You'd have made better choices."

"I can make my own choices. I don't need any goddamned god to think for me!"

"He doesn't mean any harm," I told William after Morris left.

"He makes my blood boil. He can see that for himself."

William went to the patio door and looked out at the sunny gardens.

"For him to think he could tell me how I should have lived my life. I'm twice the man he'll ever be."

"What *is* a man, William?" I asked quietly.

"I've got ten times the brains, too. That boy was never bright, Hortense, but religion has only made him stupider."

"Why are you so hard on him, William, when you had such a harsh father yourself?"

"My father loved me," he argued.

"With the back of his hand."

Friday being my turn to host the weekly bridge game, I carried the card table into the living room after lunch, snapped open the folding legs, brought in four kitchen chairs. At one o'clock, the bridge ladies arrived. All three are widows. Goodie Hodnet's husband died of heart failure, Muriel Pelter's of lung failure, Anna McCarthy's of liver failure. They called it cancer of the liver, but everyone knew it must be cirrhosis. Declan McCarthy died of the drink. Anna is the freshest of these widows. The earth on Declan's summer grave is still loose and unseeded.

"I do think I miss him," she confided today, but we didn't believe her.

"How could you possibly miss him? I mean—he was never kind," said Muriel.

"Oh, the church taught me to accept his ways."

Twenty, thirty years ago, Anna went to the parish priest, Father O'Meara, asking permission to leave Declan.

"Leave him?" Father O'Meara exclaimed. "Wasn't he a drinker when you married him?"

"Yes, Father."

"You can't leave a man you've promised before God to honour and obey because he's exactly like you knew he was when you walked down the aisle. Now, can you? For better or for worse. Wasn't that the holy vow you took? For better or for worse? Everyone knows an Irishman is born with liquor running in his veins. He can't help but drink. It's in the blood. It's a point of pride, almost. Ask an Irishman not to drink and you might as well ask a bird not to fly. Go home now and beg for God's forgiveness. Pray for strength and you'll bear up. You'll find things won't bother you so much."

"I never loved Art. I admit that now," said Muriel Pelter, as though we'd ever thought she had. Because she is the longest-widowed of these women, she finds it the least necessary to lie about the past. "Art was a victim and I can't abide victims. I tried to picture his face the other day. I can't even remember what he looked like."

Muriel is what people call *a card*. Life is a joke to her. She can laugh at anything. And, indeed, she was rolling in the aisles at a matinee in the local movie theatre the day Art decided to swallow a bottle of sleeping pills. A Steve Martin comedy. With Goldie Hawn, she reminds us. Art had had emphysema for ten years. The last two, he was chained to an oxygen tank, which kept him at home.

"I can't stay there with him. It drives me crazy listening to that coughing. I have to get out," Muriel would tell people, and sail off in her Pontiac. She lives alone now in the spacious cliff-side bungalow with the deck overlooking the blue waters of the reservoir. This is where Art died, but now that she's had every inch of the house washed down, floors, walls, ceilings even, she can no longer smell his illness.

Today she arrived in a winter-white suit, of which she has six; six suits in this one colour, I've counted them. Since Art's death, she has bought a suit a month, twenty-four so far, driving to a nearby city to find them. Pension money. Disability money. Art has come in handy, in the end. She is a mover, a go-getter, looking for lunches, shopping trips, birthday parties, funerals to which she might wear her thirty-five pairs of dress shoes.

Once these women trooped in, the living room, its tables and chairs filling every inch of wall space, seemed very small. For, though they say that losing a partner is like shedding a winter coat—ah! the lightening, the disburdenment—and though they are happy to be released from cooking three square meals a day, from sleeping beside a man, from *Hockey Night in Canada*, they are now bloated with widowhood. They eat and eat, expanding to fill the void left by their dead husbands. This is their sin of the flesh.

I linger at the edge of this group, an initiate. I will not truly enter their ranks until William dies. I must prove myself by becoming a widow. But I do wonder if, once William is gone, I will ever have enough substance to join this society of powdered and lipsticked, church-attending, money-spending, dessert-baking, 200-pound women. For I am a tiny specimen, shrinking, it seems, by the day, at present less than five feet tall and wearing a girl's shoes. So narrow have my shoulders become, so flat my chest, that I now fit a size zero, something I never knew existed. Am I disappearing, bit by bit? I have found I require less and less food to keep me alive. What does this mean? Perhaps I'm not living at all.

Of all these women, I find Goodie Hodnet the most intimidating. I fear her fearlessness. Into my living room today, she'd brought a back cushion, which she must carry everywhere because of muscle strain earned from a lifetime of hoisting milk cans onto a pickup truck. She is a big solid woman, shaped something like a milk pail herself, today wearing an olive skirt and tunic. She dresses always in browns, greens, russets, gold, the colours of the farm, of the earth, as though she hasn't yet relinquished her ties with the soil. Since moving into town, she visits the public library weekly, signing out books on history, politics, famous people, borrowing them by the dozen, the thicker and heavier, it seems, the better.

"On the farm I never had a minute to read," she's told us, and I can't help but think she must have been very glad the day she went out to the barn looking for Noah and found him dead on his milking stool, slumped against a stall while a cow waited patiently for him to grab her dugs and pull. "The world of ideas, Hortense!" she has said. "I'd starve in any other world. I nearly died on the farm. Noah was a simple man. He wasn't a reader." I've seen her marching to the library with her pounds of books, her head down, leaning into the wind with the same joyless, intrepid stride with which she must once have crossed the barnyard, weighed down in either hand with pails of chicken feed, rather like a beast of burden, her legs grown thick to support the encumbrance of her broad hips and her steep farmwife's bosom, her jaw thrust forward to meet adversity.

"Never look back," she's told me. "Never look back. Take the lot you've been given in life, move on, and don't let anyone or anything stand in the way of what you want."

Goodie will go to heaven, for she is now a great taxier of the elderly, a champion feeder of the bereaved, an organizer of bake sales, church bazaars, clothing drives. She records every charitable deed in a small black notebook, which she carries always on her person so that it will be handy when she reaches the Pearly Gates.

In the summer, Goodie drives a hundred miles to see *Hamlet*. She drives to Toronto to visit her daughter, with whom she attends the theatre, the opera, musicals. She has seen *Cats*, *Les Miserables*, *The Phantom of the Opera*. After she went to Mexico, she came over to describe it to William, because at bridge we'd cried "Stop! Stop!" when she tried to tell us about the rain god, the Yucatan, *Chichen Itza*.

For forty years, I've attended Sunday Mass with these three women. Together we've sung "Lord who throughout these forty days," and "When I behold the wondrous cross," and "Love divine all loves exceeding." We've knelt side by side at the communion rail with our tongues out to receive the crisp dry wafer. *Body of Christ. Amen.* We've followed one another into the confessional to spill our sins to a black curtain, emerged to whisper our penance to the same twenty-foot Christ, shamelessly naked on his cross, save for a flimsy loincloth the size of a hanky, his bronze thighs gleaming. But perhaps this history only makes us more dangerous to one another. You can't choose your family, to be sure, but isn't the same true of your fellow parishioners?

Today, Goodie and I were partnered. Picking up the deck to deal the first hand, I felt, as always, more alive than at any other time, enjoying the smooth, lacquered finish of the cards, the *slap slap slap* as they fell upon the table, soft as autumn leaves, the dizzying spin of the powerful symbols: hearts, diamonds, clubs, spades. The royal family in their heavy, embroidered robes—the troubled king, the stoic queen, the angry, self-absorbed prince with his golden rolled wig—seemed more mysterious than ever. I am lucky at cards, far luckier than in life. But I am also clever at them. "It's like you get a brain transplant when you pick up cards, Hortense," William has said. Cards are the currency of the elderly, and I know that I'll need this capital after William dies. A widow is only as valuable as the hand she's been dealt.

At three o'clock, William appeared, dressed in the first white shirt I'd seen on him in a month. He'd polished his Sunday shoes, carved the earth from beneath his fingernails, smoothed his thinning brown hair with a wet comb. The powerful smell of Old Spice filled the room.

"Good Lord, you're still around!" exclaimed Muriel with mock surprise. "I keep forgetting there are still a few of the endangered species left!"

Though they are content to be widows, happily stunned by their belated freedom, my friends are still pleased by the presence of a man, and when William sat down to replace me while I made tea, I noticed among them a sexual flutter, a shiver of excitement, like hens in a chicken coop when the rooster struts in. They shifted with enjoyment in their chairs, sending up yeasty winds, the whispering of stockings as their great thighs rubbed together.

"This is the only reason I can think of to have a man around the house," said Muriel. "A spare bridge player in the closet if someone comes down with the flu."

In the kitchen, I plugged in the kettle.

"Oh, William!" I heard from the living room. "You can't get away with that!"

"Try and stop me," he said calmly.

"You're being outrageous! Watch out, girls! He's up to his old tricks again! He's overbidding!"

"I have some decent cards," Goodie Hodnet warned him. "Don't waste them."

"Just wait," he reassured her, bringing out his charm. "Just bear with me, now. Let's see what happens."

In the kitchen, I sighed with frustration, hoping that William, to whom I'd entrusted a strong hand, would not destroy my winning streak.

"They'll be cutting the wheat out west about now, William," Goodie said, just to get under my skin. I tested the knife blade on the ball of my thumb, imagined cutting out her tongue.

"That Goodie," William has said to me. "Now there's a real woman. She would have made a great partner on a farm."

"Women were never partners on farms, William," I answered. "They were chattel."

"She's got gumption and brains, too, and substance. I like a hefty woman."

"William, you'll ruin us!" Goodie cried now with delight. He's allowed to be as unorthodox at cards as he wants, yet if I try to be the least bit creative, Goodie is onto me like a burr on a blanket.

"There's not enough risk in this game to suit me," William told her. "Not enough excitement. I'd sooner have a good round of poker."

"The game picks up when you sit down, William," Goodie said, then dropped her voice. "Hortense is getting blind as a bat."

My heart skipped a beat. A teacup rattled nervously as I set it on its saucer.

"She still has the one good eye," said William.

"You'd never know it. The time it takes her to play a card. Sometimes I think I'll die of boredom."

"She used to be a crackerjack player," William said.

"*Used* to be," said Goodie.

"She does her best," said Anna reasonably.

"When Hortense had that stroke five years ago," Goodie continued in a stage whisper, "did the doctors ever say anything about—brain damage? She *forgets!*"

"Shhhh!"

Toward suppertime, I saw an orange cast fall across the back lawn and gardens.

"It's truly autumn, William," I said from the living room, "when you see that light."

· No reply from William, but I heard him rise briefly from the kitchen table and open a cupboard under the kitchen sink, forgetting he wouldn't find there the whisky bottle that for so many years had helped him in the evenings to forget. For now his heart and his arteries are seizing up like an old clogged and stuttering machine and the doctor has forbidden drink. He sat again with a sigh.

From the kitchen doorway, I watched him sorting his flower bulbs, as though he were deploying model armies. Tulips. Narcissi. Daffodils. Hyacinths. Some large as a baby's fist, others tiny as pearl onions. On a piece of paper, he was making a diagram, trying to devise an arrangement in which to plant the bulbs for the best effect, considering the length of the stems, the colour, size, and shape of the blossoms, the moment of blooming: early, mid-, or late spring. On the table, the bulbs stood about in fleshy clusters, dense and meaty as organs, as colonies of miniature upturned hearts. So fertile, so pregnant with life did they seem, that, in passing the table, I reached out in a mad moment to pluck one up, intending to bite into its succulent fruit, its plump and glossy flesh.

"Keep your hands off those!" William barked. "They're delicate. You'll knock the skins off 'em."

And indeed their brittle, papery, toast-coloured skins were shedding everywhere, lifting, transparent and friable, floating away on the slightest breath, leaving the swelling curves of the tubers naked and gleaming. How could he tell me they're fragile, when he was about to bury them in the damp, acid, ruthless ground and these vulnerable skins would be letting go of the flesh even before he pressed the earth down upon them?

Looking over his shoulder, I saw that he'd made no progress with his drawings, but was tracing the same lines over and over, the velvety lead now so heavy that it lifted, smeared like oil across the heel of his hand. He moved the bulbs about like chess pieces, making small adjustments within each group.

"Stop fussing with them, why don't you?" I said impatiently. "Just put them in the earth. It can't be that complicated. We've been living with these for a week."

"Three days," he corrected me, but he rubbed his head in confusion. "I don't know what's wrong with me, Hortense. I can't seem to come up with a plan. I can't form a decision."

"Well, I wish you'd get on with it. Soon we'll be eating supper. Where will we put down our plates? I'm sick to death of the sight of these bulbs. I'd sooner sweep them into the trash than look at them another hour."

"That goes to show what your values are!" he thundered, his face suddenly red as a stoplight. "That tells me what you're worth. You never made a decent garden in your life. You know nothing about creativity and the time it takes."

"I believe I've been creative in my life," I said, my voice trembling, betraying me. "I gave you seven children, didn't I? And another two that died? Carried all but one of them nine months. I call that *time*."

"That's all you've been good for," he said, "and you can't even take credit for that. You were made to bear children. It's how the female body works and it's got nothing to do with thought."

In the basement, looking for something to give William for supper, I reached for a dusty Mason jar on a shelf. I recalled how, when the children were young and William forever out of work and the house empty of groceries, I used to go down there and proudly count my jars, thinking: this is our only wealth, these canned raspberries of mine floating like rubies in clear liquid, these peach halves golden as seashells drifting in thick syrup, these constellations of plump blueberries suspended like amethysts in their juices.

There are still jars and jars of these preserves down there, for out of habit I continued to put them up long after the children left home, foolishly expecting them to return on visits. But the visits became less and less frequent and gradually the grandchildren stopped coming and when they did come, they'd never heard of spiced pears or corn relish or peach butter or pickled crabapples, lovely bloated pale orbs. These things seem to have become old-fashioned.

I tipped a Mason jar in my hand, noticing for the first time that its old juices had grown thick and murky, the fruits soft and disintegrating. Returning the jar to the shelf, I reflected how much these preserves looked like rows of dark, meaty, jarred placentas. Then I thought of all my babies, those lost to me near birth and those relinquished to foreign landscapes, leaving me with nothing but these beefy afterbirths.

"What the hell are you doing down there, Hortense?" William called from the top of the stairs.

"Coming, William."

Merilee called long distance after supper, asking to speak to William. Curious, I kept the living-room phone pressed quietly to my ear, rather than hang up, while he took the call in the kitchen.

"Hugh and I are splitting up, Dad," Merilee told him, her voice cautious but firm.

"Who is Hugh?" William asked with mock confusion.

"My husband, Dad. You know who he is."

"Which one is this? I can't keep them straight," he baited her. "Is he the one who sweeps roads?"

"Dad—" I heard her sigh tiredly.

"Why are you telling *me?* Why didn't you tell your mother?"

"It doesn't matter what I do, Dad. She wouldn't approve."

"What do you want me to say?"

"I was just hoping you'd understand."

"I can't stop you from making mistakes."

"It's not so much a mistake, Dad. It's just—life."

"We never had lives like that, your mother and me. We stuck together. Through good and bad."

"Well, that's another approach altogether."

"Why get married at all? Why not just shack up? You must be supporting the legal profession down there single-handed. You're keeping the divorce courts in business, all right. How long did this one last?"

"Nearly a year."

"This is the fourth one, isn't it?"

"The third."

"Are you trying to set some kind of record?"

"Dad, this isn't so unusual. I don't know anyone who isn't divorced."

"You should come back to Canada," William told her, "where things are solid."

Merilee has gone to live in a part of the States where there is never any snow. She's quit nursing now and is a salesperson for a big corporation. She has an expense account and a company car, a small white convertible. I pictured her driving this convertible through the hot yellow palm-lined streets of a southern city, wearing dark glasses and a miniskirt. These days, she bleaches her hair and wears it in a cumbersome antebellum style. She diets until she has the waistline of a little girl. She's had breast implants, a facelift, liposuction, an abortion. She's sick enough to be in the hospital. She has nervous rashes, a stomach ulcer. She's like a gypsy, moving from husband to husband, apartment to apartment. She can't sit still or be alone for more than five minutes. William used to say to her, "You're running away from yourself," but she just laughed, her face, caked with heavy orange makeup, breaking into deep cracks. "Dad, you sound more Canadian every day," she told him. "I'll never come back to Canada. Nothing there is worth what you pay for it."

At nine o'clock, William turned the television to a profile of Adolf Hitler, sepia footage of German soldiers jerking like windup dolls across the screen. I said goodnight and went up the stairs. For five years, I've been sleeping in one of the girls' rooms, ever since William sent me creeping upstairs with my pillow under my arm because, he said, my snoring had begun to shake the walls of our bedroom. It doesn't trouble me. In fact, it's a comfort to sleep in the bedroom of my daughters. Sometimes, I lie awake at night and think of the sultry summer evenings when, to escape the hot sheets, the girls crept out of their beds in thin cotton nightgowns and lay like happy martyrs on the floor, imagining they could feel a refreshing draft sweeping along the bare boards. Reminded of this, I sense the cool of the wood along my own calves and feel in my old hip bones, my shoulder blades, the tough comfort of the hard planks.

I put on my flannel gown, crawled into bed, dreamt immediately of Katherine sitting on a train, her auburn hair shining like mahogany beneath the warm cabin lights. In the dream, the train was pulling out of the station and I was running alongside it, growing more and more tired and breathless. But there seemed to be no end to the station platform. It stretched on and on for miles. I heard my own footsteps striking the boards, growing heavier and slower until I began to stumble. When she saw this, Katherine raised the cabin window and shouted back to me, "There's space beside me here on the seat, Mother. Why don't you come with me?" "I can't come," I told her. "Your father's expecting his supper." Behind me, I heard a voice calling "Hortense! Hortense!" and then I awoke and heard William's real voice, which was not in the dream after all.

"Hortense!" he called from the foot of the stairs. "Hortense! Come down here!"

The radio clock read eleven. I got up quickly and hurried downstairs, wondering, as I always did, how the documentary had stirred William's penis in his trousers, if it was the action of all those ejaculating and recoiling war cannons, or perhaps the sight of so many German soldiers performing their *Heil Hitler!* salutes, their stiff and rising arms inspiring William's penis to ascend in sympathy. In the doorway of his room, I paused. He has the double bed still, which leaves only a narrow passage between mattress and dresser.

"What are you waiting for?" he asked impatiently.

"I can't see, William. It's dark."

"Just get in."

With his wounded hand, he lifted the hem of my nightie. I felt his desire against me, hard as a tree branch, then the thrusts of his thin pelvis against my buttocks. I heard his shallow breathing, imagined his poor weak heart beating tiredly against his ribs as our frail spent bodies moved together in an old luckless rhythm, like two elderly dogs. Closing my eyes, I thought of our young girls on summer nights, so fresh and untouchable in their cotton nightgowns, their bare legs downy, glistening with the heat, and I wished I were lying upstairs with them now on the naked boards, enjoying the cool, clean punishment of the hardwood, safe from William's mating call.

Later, coming out of the bathroom, I noticed the kitchen light on, and there I found William sitting at the table in his striped pyjamas with his hand pressed to his forehead.

"What's wrong, William?"

"I suddenly have a terrible pain behind my right eye."

"Is it a headache?"

"I don't know. I've never felt anything quite like it."

I went, then, to the linen cupboard and brought out a facecloth, rough and stiff with age, as all our terry cloth has become, just as our tea towels are full of holes from decades of fingers against porcelain, and our bed-sheets grown so ancient that their floral patterns have been erased where our bodies have scoured them, moving in the act of love-making or in the refuge of sleep, so that we have destroyed in our industry or in our unconscious journeys the splendid gardens that William so passionately desires to replace.

I softened the facecloth under the cold tap and brought it to William. He pressed it to his eye.

"Is it helping?" I asked, but he only moaned and shuddered. I stood there for a moment looking down at his ears grown large as cabbage leaves, at his nose, transformed by drink so that it now resembles a blunt and homely root vegetable. And I thought: How ugly we become in our old age.

I hadn't turned away but a moment when William cried "Jesus Christ!" The next instant, he was lying on the linoleum floor, the chair toppled over with him and his legs tangled up in its chrome ones. I rushed to him and went down on shaky knees, taking his face in my hands. A lamp on the kitchen table had also gone over in the fall, its shade askew, its bright light flooding William's face, which is pitted like the surface of the moon. Half a century before, he'd gone overseas, a new groom, with a complexion smooth as a pudding, came home three years later looking like this.

"William," I remembered weeping, when he got off the train with the other soldiers. "What has happened to your face?"

"Those sons o' bitches, Hortense," he said. "We all came back like this. Anyone exposed to the explosive mixture in the bombs. The crates were full of it. A fine dust. The wind blew it up in our faces, into our eyes. It's a wonder I'm not blind, too. The abrasion. The chemicals. But did they do anything about it? Even after we told them? Showed them our skin? Of course not. What did they care? Those sons o' bitches."

"William!" I called out to him now, as he lay sprawled on the floor. "William!" But his eyes remained closed and I could see a side of his face drooping as though with a great and sudden disappointment in life. I said to myself: You must do something. *Think*, Hortense, *think*. But then I recalled William saying I was not very good at thought and I wondered: What should I do? How will I get us out of this without William to think for me?

"You are no good, Hortense," he used to say, "in a crisis."

Then I thought: Morris. Rushing to the phone, I dialled his number, heard his sleepy voice come over the wire.

"Morris, I need you!" I said.

"It's late, Mom. What's wrong?"

"Your father has fallen. He's unconscious on the kitchen floor."

"You've got to call an ambulance, Mom," he said excitedly. "Hang up and dial 911."

And I thought: Of course. That is what I must do.

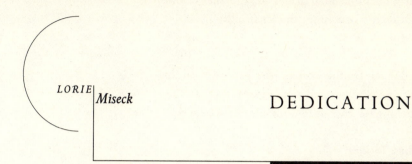

LORIE *Miseck*

DEDICATION

This is for the woman who will not read this poem.
The one whose lidded eyes were once question marks.
The older sister, now younger.

This is for her
and the others like her
who've stood on the edge
of landscape mapping a way in
and out.

For the woman in the alley bent over trash
whose address is her bones.
The woman in the park whose child stretches
her heart thin as toffee. The one under lamplight
packing small boxes so her husband won't notice
she's leaving.

This is for them
and the one so full of spring her bare hands
pull back soil to let the garden out.
The woman washing dishes and the one
plaiting her daughter's thick hair into
gold streams.

And this is for the woman who will not read this.
The one who hooked wool into landscapes,
reaching for rust, green, and bleached blue sky.

This is for her
and the one whose eyes have turned to lemon seed
and must look away.
And for the one who doesn't.

This is for all of them.

For the woman baking bread, rising before sunlight,
letting the dog, scarred by time's impatience,
out and in and out again.
The one who won't trap the pregnant skunk,
even though her night lawn is a ribbon
of black-and-white scent.

The woman whose hole in her breast is a moon,
not a wound pressing near her heart.
For the old woman whose clothesline
once full of shirts and sheets
now holds only hers.

The grandmother whose hips are rusted hinges,
yet moves across a room to take her daughter's hand.
For the mother who tells her daughter
she's a good mother.
For the mother who can't.
For the mother who won't.

This is for them, all of them,
and for the woman who will not read this poem.
The one trapped in a photograph with sisters,
eyes breathing similar light, each reaching for
something beyond the lens, something unnamed
outside the frame.

THE VOICE SAYS IN SUCH A WAY

LESLEY-ANNE *Bourne*

When we hear the swim-search siren
we run, undoing our clothes
as fast as we can
to the swimming area
where the siren keeps shouting

We may be at arts & crafts or
out canoeing—some of us
are sleeping in our cabins
when the alarm goes
that Sarah is missing—
still tagged into the pool,
the square marked off by docks,
suddenly a larger square
now that she's missing

A few of us line the docks,
wait for instructions
and the siren to stop
Others search the island—
check paths and cabins
—maybe she's simply forgotten

the tag with her name
still on the swimming board
after everyone left the water
this afternoon

We break the water feet-first
the way we were taught
when they told us
—you'll likely never need this—
underwater, three strokes forward—
eyes always open
hands out
ready
for something
in the dark

hoping it won't be Sarah

one kick back
and again—fingers open
for the thing coming into them

the girl we hadn't really known
or even tried to—
the one we talked about
at night, flashlights
whispering enough
for her to notice

never wondering if she did

until now

from the deep end
the voice says in such a way

No

LESLEY-
ANNE | *Bourne*

TEACHING
MY HUSBAND
TO SWIM

Wind gathers the lake
like a rug, then shakes it
up to his neck. Water
rises and I reassure him
it's not deep
and he can't drown.
He coughs
as a speedboat shoots

waves dangerously
near his head.
It's okay
I say again swimming out
for the middle, a mistake
I realize too late.
Grown up in this body
of water, I've left

him too deep
into the past
where his mother stands
on a bridge
holding him
over the railing
ready to drop.
Two years old, he

must look at the water
and kick. You'd wonder,
what the hell
was she thinking?
Cars slow. Someone
gets out. Stop her,
he is saying by the time
I swim to him.

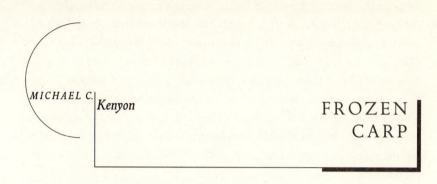

MICHAEL C. *Kenyon*

FROZEN
CARP

I AM A FREQUENT COMMUTER on the Japanese rail system, and today, as often on other days, I found myself charmed by the pretty women getting on, getting off, and by the buzz of wheels rolling on rails as one rides away from the city into the gentle and pure winter countryside. When the train passed my house in the suburbs—my usual stop—I settled comfortably back to plan the days ahead, my well-earned annual period of relaxation. I was fascinated by a poster advertising something I didn't understand: a group of peculiar symbols with attached prices. A strange dream took me into an encounter with my wife's friend. We were about to kiss. "Did you feel," she said, "I mean, were you going to do what I was going to do?" My wife was watching; she would leave, she told us; she would not say where. She took her anger and jealousy and—I can still see the door closing. The grain of the wood, so sensual. Now I was all energy, pursuing my beloved wife (I'm not being funny using *beloved!*) and at the same time kissing in a very Western manner her friend whom I loved very much.

Almost at orgasm, I believed I could hear the train staff urging me. "Hurry up, sir, we're nearly at your station." Gasping out loud at the images of these women, I guessed the trick. I was not to blame; it had nothing to do with me; this was some new gimmick by the rail company, another weapon in the long war for customers between the long distance bus company and the train people. They might have thought my earlier behaviour suggested desire, might have mistaken my fatigue and longing to be in the country for vague lust, a nostalgia for youthful passion. Still, they could not expect me to take this loss of self-control calmly. I felt like an anxious teenager. Would they really want me to feel guilty? That was it. They would assume guilt to be an integral part of this pleasure. Surely, yes. A moment before the long-anticipated fall, away from myself, I had a glance at another projection, as if shown another room. A traditional room, with tatamis, the one behind the door my wife had walked through. Inside was a murder, a violent death, bodies jerking in an awful sinking room filling with water, stains creeping up the paper walls. But as I said, just a quick look, then I came.

Rushed through the swaying train to take my ordinary daily position again, to look at the racing country, the boxed food changing hands as the caterers at the stop before mine sped through, women boarding (of less interest now; I was wet), the poster list of prices that I now understood. My erotic vision would cost me 450 yen; I would be billed later. The violent dream was more expensive. Obviously, it had been aimed at someone else, not at me. At any rate, if I'm charged for it, I will protest. Of course, I didn't think that then. It occurs to me only now, after I've had a chance to bathe, to put on a fresh kimono, to telephone my wife to tell her of my safe arrival. And thinking of the absurdity of being charged for a dream makes me smile. Standing at the open door, looking over this valley filled with night and moon and orchards of snow, alone in my favourite house, I feel calm and clear-headed. The house nestles in a grove of plum trees on the west slope of a hill a few hours east of Sapporo. Highest in price was a holocaust dream. I had no time to figure out the others—about three there were—the train was arriving at my stop ... My dream—which I decided was worth the insignificant charge—was called *Topic Fantasy*. Things moving more slowly ... I felt sticky, uncomfortable, as though everyone were watching ... The cold air of recent and undisturbed snow swept in to meet me as the door opened with a whir, and I shivered as I stepped out; the train quickly pulled away; in the blessed silence, I noticed the landscape beyond the small rural station as a detail, but a detail that in a moment swallowed me.

This morning my wife, my daughter, and my sister surprised me.

I had organized my five-day rest into units of work divided by simple meals, walks around the village at the foot of the hill; I'd had warm thoughts of solitude, of the project I had set myself: to make a list of birds resident in the area at this season. Still, I was not displeased to see them. My equivocal sister I had not seen for two years; and my daughter, after spending last winter at university in Tokyo, had been travelling in Canada and had returned only three days ago. My wife's placid, down-to-earth face is always satisfying to see. We laughed a great deal at our reunion.

Today has been a precious day, one I feel I will always remember. A completely shadowless day of indoor fires, familial love, easy talk. I showed my usual impatience to see the gifts they'd brought me. A soapstone seal from my daughter, my favourite tea from my sister, a new book of poems from my wife. How they giggled when I recounted yesterday's journey; though my wife, after we made love in the afternoon—the others had taken the Ski-Doo to town to buy cakes—asked me if there was truth in the dream. Did I feel attracted to her friend? I told her, of course it was true, but that there was equal truth in the anxiety I'd felt at her uncharacteristically abrupt behaviour, the violence associated with her retreat from the scene. And together we held our breaths and looked past the open door, at the blue sky beyond the breakfast room, the top branches of stark trees.

"How peaceful it is here," she sighed.

And I agreed.

It is night again, and late, but I am no longer a commuter on the Japanese rail system, nor a successful businessman, nor even a respected amateur ornithologist. I'm deeply content. A father, brother, husband. Tomorrow, I will watch for birds, but tonight, as the others sleep, I will try to capture this most perfect day. My desk and room are flooded with light reflected from the snow—the moon not yet above the trees. The house sighs with life, with the shifting bodies of three women, so full of the real gift they brought. For a while this afternoon as the sun set, we were spellbound; my sister had remembered for us one spring, one blossom-time years ago, when we all had been together here. We now lacked my mother and father, my wife's mother, my son, but they felt very close.

"Look!" said my wife. "The field of colza flowers!"

We gazed into the valley. We saw the field, I swear. And swallows diving. So many flowers; the children playing under the *matsushima* tree in the corner.

"*Matsushima!*" said my daughter.

Ah!

We knew exactly what she was seeing. These moments that pass, I ache to think. Here we are, my family. And though my sister is coming from nowhere and going nowhere, even she swayed with the magic. All day long, my daughter, excited with travel, proud of her new knowledge, could hardly cease talking. They joked, she and her aunt, as they dressed for the ride to the village. Threw gloves and scarves at each other. Outside, the sun bounced off their goggles; they were like devoted sisters released from their parents' authority. Deer tracks led into the trees. Our love-making was slow, my wife smiling back at me, telling me this is not a dream, this is not a fantasy. When the two returned, I drank a little saki, they drank beer, and we created the colza field. The women cooked miso, rice, and boiled tofu. I looked at the books in my room, touching each title to bring its tiny package of memories. We ate, then my daughter and my wife took turns reading passages from *Snow Country*. We decided to spread our kimonos on the thick snow in front of the house tomorrow if the sun continued to shine.

"We could dress warmly and open the doors and windows," said my daughter.

"Mmm," said my wife and sister.

"We could build a huge fire," said my daughter.

"Mmm!"

Before bed, we listened to Miles Davis's "In a Silent Way." I made them aware of the bird songs Miles Davis imitates in his solos. Black windows. Soft female bodies under goose down. Love. My face there, a weak reflection across the table, these hands clasped on the paper. The moon comes. A train in the distance. I'm a little worried for my sister. Tired in my bones.

When I finally slept, I took a journey of nightmares, each stop a violent wakening. I had chest pains, and this morning I feel feverish, but I won't mention it to the women; they have held on to yesterday's mood and are gay, poking fun at me for sleeping so late. They were out early, I heard their voices as I tried to rest; they sounded like geese. By the time I rose, they had already laid out the kimonos on the snow, four weird shapes like crashed festive planes. I will be careful not to show my own depression. How inattentive and self-concerned they are! The whole house seems populated with adolescents; my daughter sets the tone with her mindless babblings. I'm embarrassed when I think of my performance yesterday. We spent a good day, emotional and silly, but I find I acted in an undignified manner, telling my 450-yen fantasy, and now must suffer the unbridled giddiness I should never have encouraged. I can only try to overcome my low spirits by getting to work. I ask my daughter to carry my folding chair and blankets up to the old shrine in the woods; after eating, I will spend the afternoon in the silence I have looked forward to all winter. They must not interrupt. I forbid them to use the Ski-Doo or to play music. If they want distraction, they can go down to the village. My wife, it seems, thinks my words harsh, but as I explained to her, I have a project to complete. We had our festival yesterday. After all, I did not invite them, and because of them I have lost one day.

Nobody has been up here since the summer. Sometimes, years ago, the family came to celebrate the new year. We would visit the shrine and pray; in the cold, I'm reminded of those times. I want to stop thinking of the past because it hurts; it gets between my eyes and the beauty of the place. A fox trotted by a moment ago. Smoke rises from the village, from individual fires no doubt, though it hangs in a dull cloud under the sky. I should have let my daughter make a fire in the brazier beside my chair; she wanted to. So at last I'm alone. The bird names come unbidden; write themselves on the paper in my lap. The binoculars nudge at my eyes: the trees slip by. A branch loses its snow. There are my tracks up; my daughter's up and down. I can't see the house from here. Sun in a clear sky. The blanket wrapped round my shoulders. She said I looked like an American Indian. I sip from the Thermos of saki. Warm belly, cold toes, white hills.

The shrine, in sad need of repair, has been forgotten. The neighbouring family who owns the shrine moved it from the village a long time ago, an enormous and expensive task. This present generation must not be interested in its significance, religious or historical. It's not my position to pass judgment. They only visit a few days each summer; they have been successful in the computer industry. My sister, married, divorced, moves from city to city, job to job, writing letters that tear my heart they are so simple, so rigorous in sounding happy. I can't help her. She will no longer confide in me. Our eyes do not meet. She stays with family members all over Japan. I only stand and smile, like yesterday, looking at her, and bow, and bow. Return to my catalogue. I can do this: return to my birds that keep me from thinking of my work in the city and from wondering what it is like to be her, try not to feel afraid. I can't stop the sadness that seems to attend her desperate love of family, desire to escape. I don't know if she's fragile or strong. She has nowhere to go; she won't have children; it's too late for that. I remember things from our childhood. The surprise game. Her eyes so good then, so clear. She loved her nephew from his birth till he was eight and dead and in his little container. She loves my wife. Like a chicken, I bow and bow, and don't know what it means or what I'm doing.

My pen in falling has made a deep slash in the snow. Water drips from branches, polishing the decaying ice edges till they gleam, almost transparent beside the brown earth under the surrounding trees. Enough twigs for a fire; I could use paper from my pad but have no matches. Where are the pheasants this year? It requires too much effort to unzip my camera bag, fit the long lens. This in the past has brought birds, even flocks. Curious magic.

My wife approaches the shrine from the south along one of the overgrown paths. This traditional approach is foolish; it has meant she has had to cross diagonally in front of me from the house to the trees, then double back. The hem of her kimono is furred with white; her feet must be wet. She scoops snow from the *chozuya*, touches it to her mouth, rubs her hands. I'm happy to see her but will not show it. She claps her hands and, ignoring me for a moment, gazes at the shrine.

"Tonight," she tells me, "you must invoke *baku* to devour your nightmares."

"Um." So she is aware I slept poorly.

"I am sorry to disturb you. I will wait until you finish." She stands patiently while I pretend to make a note, while I scan the valley with my binoculars. A rhythmic *tock*, like wood blocks, has started below in the village.

I put down my pad. Motion her to come under the roof overhang. "I am concerned about my sister," I say, as if I have summoned my wife here to speak of this. "Do you know what she intends to do?"

"Ah. No. She washed yesterday when we arrived. She has not washed since. Do you want me to ask her?"

This requires no answer. We will let enough silence pass, then she will tell me what she has come for.

I shut my eyes against the bright sun. The wood-block sound echoes around the valley. Otherwise, nothing. I remember the bridge over the stream on the village road. The face of my son before he died. The one-armed monk at the funeral. My face mirrored in the window last night.

"Our visit is not without a purpose. Your daughter has asked me to tell you that she has an opportunity to study in Canada."

"Does she want to live in Canada?"

"There is a young man she mentions a great deal."

"You think she has fallen in love?"

"The young man will not come to Japan. He's an engineer. His father is an engineer with a company in Vancouver. She is too young to marry."

"Did she ask you to tell me this?"

"She speaks only of the necessity of learning in an English environment. She has slept with this young man."

"How do you know?"

A cold wind rushes up the hill. Branches freed of their burdens spring into the air. A thrush lands in the *sakaki* tree. I'm on a boat with my daughter in summer, drifting under the humpback bridge. My neck is stiff.

"You are shivering," I tell my wife. "Go back. Our daughter cannot return to Canada now. She must finish her education in Tokyo. In two years, I may consider the matter again. Do you agree?"

"Yes."

"You will say to her that this is what we have decided."

My wife shakes her head. "I think she will not listen to me. She knows how much I disapprove of her living away from Japan."

"Give me your hands." Under my blanket, her hands are frozen carp, dug from the ice one very cold winter when I was a child. I thought they would come back to life next to my skin. I slept with them all night, a bowl of water on the floor of my room for when they began to wriggle. In the morning, the stink was everywhere, in every corner of the house. "Send her to me, then."

I smile. So she comes straight up from the house, my daughter. I'm certain her mother would have advised her to take the southern access if she wanted to have a propitious dialogue with me. I give my attention to the thrush who has flown several times to other trees but always returned to the green *sakaki*. The bird has not uttered a note. I do not lower the binoculars when I hear my daughter move past me to stand at my back.

"I'm waiting for the thrush to sing," I say.

She is breathing hard from the climb. I expect her immediately to start talking. She doesn't.

"I can tell you are angry. But look around. Listen to this peaceful place. You have every possibility of a good life. You must not go away; you must remain. I have given it thought. I assume you will not have a child. You must take responsibility for your life, show your gratitude, and choose a path in keeping with the design I have created for you. Afterward, in a few years, you may listen to your heart. Do not be like your unfortunate aunt, my unwashed sister, who does not know how to listen, who will never learn, for whom it is too late."

I have stared so long toward the sun that when I turn she is a silhouette, and only slowly do I recognize my sister, standing just where my wife has stood.

"I'm sorry," she says. "I'm sorry. I could not speak. I wanted to give this to you alone." Into my lap she presses a box, which I hold out in one hand as she runs quickly away, slips and slides down the hill. I'm still gripping the box when she turns from the house and disappears behind the camellias lining the road to the village. A *megatama*, an exquisite specimen, curved jewel symbolizing love. I shake myself from the blanket and stamp about the shrine. How could I not have known? The open box sits on the railing. An indictment. I wash my hands at the *chozuya*, eat snow to rinse my mouth. I spoke nothing but the truth. Soon I have trampled the snow on two sides of the shrine. When I sit again, I'm warmed. It looks as though a ceremony has taken place, a winter ceremony involving many people. I feel nervous, can't concentrate. Again, I begin to pace the sacred area. Ever since my experience on the train two days ago, things have been troublesome. The passage of birds from one side of the valley to the other seems as pointless as symbolic love. What have I given? What have I received? It could not be a revelation to my sister that she is lost. She could have stayed with her husband. But what would she feel on hearing such words from me?

"My unwashed sister."

The pain comes fast. Knocks me to the slush. I pull the chair close, manage to heave myself into it. What about my life? Does no one care what happens to me? Must I decide for everyone? The smell of the carp, violence of separation, eroticism of the bleached wood of the shrine. The snow itself is defiled. I know my daughter will be next, up from the house, and I will try to guess which way she'll come. What she will bring. What I will send her away with. Ah, I do not want us to cut at one another; I want my daughter to take me in her arms and carry me down, I want my wife to bathe me, my sister to dress me in the cold kimono, and the three to build that great fire so that all the village will see our family and know that we persist in love.

I sit upright in the sun. It has moved barely an hour in the sky since I arrived. As white as a single knuckle. Water drips from my cuffs. Will no one understand I can't let go of what I love? If I'm to die now, I must prepare. *Matsushima.* "In a Silent Way." But the dream of violence, for which I will not pay, is as close and bright as the jewel on the railing. "O *baku!*" Wind rolls the smoke across the valley, the wood-block sound stops and the thrush begins to sing.

ORANGES

BARBARA *Scott*

IN MY GRANDMOTHER'S KITCHEN, there are no Ukrainian Easter eggs, their geometric lines poking fun at perfect ovarian curves; no orthodox icons in a sensuous riot of colour that always strikes me as poking fun at any attempts at strict asceticism. There are no traces of Ukrainian costume; those glorious colours and streamers are never seen, not even on special days. It was all my grandmother could do to trade in her pilled-over brown rayon pants and green acrylic sweater for a sagging green wool skirt and a navy cotton shell before heading to bingo on Wednesday nights.

On the sideboard in my grandmother's kitchen, children and grand-children are framed in cardboard, grey, navy, and black. There are no shiny appliances on the counters: no spots on the speckled linoleum. No wooden plaques with rhyming kitchen prayers on the walls; no coiled throw rugs on the floor. It is a kitchen marked by absence, bare of decoration, bare of colour, bare of all that could be called bohunk.

The strongest surviving presence in my grandmother's kitchen, now that my grandmother is no longer there herself, is the smell of food—the holubtsi, perogy, kielbasa, sauerkraut soup, and borscht that we heated up yesterday. She had enough food in the fridge, freezer, and pantry to take care of her own wake. She would have been proud.

The wake was yesterday. Today, my mother and I inhale the fading aromas and finish washing up the dishes. The chrome sink gleams; the dish towel, folded neatly in thirds, not in half, hangs with edges trim under the sink. The last time the three of us were here together, I watched with open mouth as my grandmother elbowed my mother aside, "Out of the way, Karolka. I can do it better myself." The source of tradition, a piece of the puzzle locking into place, the same words ringing down long years of my childhood, but from my mother to me. This kitchen is also where I learned the source of another tradition: my habit of slicing potato peels so thin you can see through them. It is a custom born in the Depression and useless to cling to now, but I remember my pride on the day I first held a slender shaving to my own kitchen window in Vancouver, first saw that murky glimmer. My grandmother's smile.

My mother sits at the kitchen table, peeling an orange, breathing from the clear green plastic tube that coils from her nostrils and hooks her up to a black box twenty feet away that chortles and chugs and keeps her oxygen levels high enough to sustain life. We have been looking at photos; the cheap plastic cases are spread over the table. "When I was young ..." she says. And I lean my elbows on the table while my mother talks past the phlegm in her lungs and mouth, past the tubes in her nose. "When I was young," she says, "I loved oranges even better than candy. You couldn't get them more than a couple of times a year in Kelvington during the Depression, and even then my family could never afford them. I didn't taste one until I was seven, and I thought it was the most wonderful flavour in the world. Later on, though, I discovered tomato sandwiches."

When he read the first ten pages of the family history my mother wrote for the Kelvington town history book, my husband, Leon, who is at the funeral parlour settling the last few details, said, "I don't know. It's just a bunch of detail with nothing *behind* it. I don't get a sense of where you come from, what your background is, who your people were."

My people. Sounds like Bostonians with several generations of gracious living behind them, not like the Ukrainian immigrants who scratched out a living in the dust bowl of Saskatchewan. This is the kind of cliché my mind slides into whenever I think back to the rare and infrequent stories my mother has told me. The stories scroll before me in black and white or sepia, not like those art movies that load every shadow with meaning, but like the photos on the table—flat, with a scratchy finish. My grandfather is Henry Fonda, with jutting chin and stoic bearing; my whole family stiff with peasant dignity—the Joads, but with Ukrainian accents. They stare into colourless sunsets and angle park by the drug store in clouds of grey dust. In my mind, the drug store always has faded wooden boards curled by the dust and dry heat, and inside, my mother is always thirteen, wearing a scratchy flour-sack dress. She is also in black and white. But the tomato sandwich frozen halfway to her mouth drips red juice and one yellow seed onto the Arborite counter.

When Leon says "your people," so pat, so easy, I see a family history whole and entire, custom wrapped, and handed down like an heirloom, something rare, to be handled reverently, with love. When Leon says "your people," I see *his* people, and I think "Easy for you," coming from that long line of born storytellers. My family hands down nothing whole and entire. Like the photographs, they offer to the world and to me only the smooth face of an eternally trapped present. But, occasionally, the flat surface buckles and tears; occasionally, it lets things slip. My history is something I have had to put together piece by piece, segment by segment.

Spirals of orange peel wind over my mother's knuckles, drop over her wrist to the Arborite table. She has lovely hands, fine-boned with delicate nails, and her skin, loosened by age, sits so lightly on those bones you could almost believe yourself capable, if you dared, of peeling it away in pliant sheets, of tracing the bright red pumping of arteries, the blue tangle of nerves. "The first time I ever tasted an orange," she says, "was in the late part of the Depression. When your grandparents were running the store on Main Street with your great-uncle Mike and his wife, my auntie Daisy. Your grandma's sister, she was. I wouldn't have been more than seven. They kept a canning jar on the top shelf for spare coins. No one ever took money out of that jar without all four adults agreeing to it. It was a communal jar; all decisions made concerning it had to be communal. This was mostly your grandfather's influence of course, coming out of his commitment to Marxism. Anyway, there I was in the grey wool bathrobe that was all I had for a winter jacket, and the rubber boots that were all I had for shoes. The boots were so big I had to wear three layers of your grandfather's grey work socks to keep them from falling off. Of course, there were care parcels from the Red Cross, but somehow the stuff inside never made it past the English families, who all knew the railway worker Mr. Thomas, to the bohunks across the tracks.

"December first, a box of oranges arrived at the store. A kind of miracle, especially at that time of year. They cost ten cents each. More than a loaf of bread. Mrs. Thomas came in with her daughter Jennifer in their fur collars and button-up boots and ordered a dozen. Your grandmother watched them leave with the oranges, and then she looked at me. All week, all we had eaten was baked potatoes with the skins on and some homemade cottage cheese. She did what she could to give the meal extra flavour by sprinkling it with the dill that she kept layered with salt and frozen in a jar by the back door. All the same, I was staring so hard at those oranges my stomach hurt. And she gave me one. Paid for it, too, by stealing a dime right out of the jar."

And I can see it all, pint-sized canning jar, with a red rubber sealing ring and glass lid and the raised letters in bubbles of glass on the sides. The pile of coins, their slow and painful pilgrimage toward the rim. Pennies mostly, from bright coppers to greenish-black lumps, but sometimes a nickel or even a dime flashing a defiant silver from beneath layers of grimy tarnish. I see the oranges, each in its wrapping of tissue paper, the smell a wild and sweet possession. Her mother packs them, one by one, into a brown paper bag and the other woman scoops the bag under her arm, handing an orange, carelessly perhaps, to her daughter. The door opens and slams; a wedge of light and a cold blast of air cut across the worn floorboards and are gone. My mother's rubber boots scuff the bare wood floor; her eyes, wet with longing, are fixed on the fruit's warm glow. She is the little match girl staring through a frosted pane; Lillian Gish locked out in the snow.

Her mother's face like ice when it has frozen too fast and cracked. The lines waver, shift, harden. She reaches one hand for the jar, the other at her lips to keep her daughter quiet. The ring of the till, the rustle of sweet-scented paper. And then an orange is smooth and heavy in a fine-boned hand and tangy and sweet on an urgent tongue. And for a moment, quick, before it vanishes—I am there, too, awkward in the grey wool bathrobe that is two sizes too small for me, reaching for the peel drying in the sagging pocket. Never quite touching.

"For the longest time whenever I tasted an orange, I could see her hand reaching for the jar." My mother's eyes are fixed on the orange; her fingers toy with the scraps of peel before her. "Your grandfather was very angry when he found out, her going behind his back like that." She pauses. "They never really were suited to one another. He was an intellectual. She loved to garden and can and had no time to talk. She and I would spend all day in the kitchen, making perogies." There they are, cutting perfect rounds of soft perogy dough with a glass, pressing a mound of warm potato mashed with cottage cheese into the centre, then crimping the edges to form warm, soft pillows. "Your grandpa's friends would come over at night and eat them with melted butter and onion. I remember sitting at the table with your grandfather and his friends, listening to them talk politics, government, revolution." Feel the fists banging the table, see the golden butter drizzling down their chins. "Sometimes, they let me eat with them. Back then, I could eat twenty perogies at a sitting, for all I was only five feet tall and just out of the San with one lung lost to TB."

My mother adored her father. You can see it even now in the slight tremble of lip, glisten of eye. There she sits at the table laden with food, sits not with the men but slightly off to one side, so that she can stare undisturbed at his animated face. They are freedom fighters, firm of chin, and stern of eye. And she glows with their reflected glory like Ingrid Bergman, all misty with emotion and soft light. And my grandmother? Perhaps that is her at the stove, with her back turned. Or maybe that is her in shadow, watching from the door frame.

My mother lifts the pale green hose from her nostrils briefly, wipes at them with a Kleenex, returns the hose. "Your grandmother never really wanted to marry your grandfather. She wanted to go to high school; she was only fifteen. But her family was living in a two-room house. A shack really. I've seen pictures of it. There simply was no money for food and clothing, let alone for school. She was the oldest of four children. It was just easier for her parents if she got married. And so she did. Of course, your grandmother didn't tell me any of this. Auntie Daisy told me. She thought I should know."

The last time I saw my grandfather, he pulled me on his knee, where I perched awkwardly, afraid to let him bear my full weight. I was fifteen. He was crying. He had not seen me for three years. Over and over he said, "Honest to God I cry, Blane. Honest to God." Sometimes, I can still feel the scratch of his beard against my neck. But then I only wanted to get away from the crush of his embrace.

The only time I saw my mother cry was on the long drive home from Kelvington to Calgary after my grandfather's funeral. We stopped to see my grandmother on our way out of town, and as my mother told her about the service, my grandmother's face was all bone. Nothing pliant to shift or waver; nothing to see behind. Two hours out of Kelvington, my mother pulled over and stopped the car, crying into the steering wheel with the hoarse sobs of someone unused to crying. "God, doesn't she feel anything? I'm so afraid I'll end up like her. Dead. Just dead." But when I put my hand on her arm, she snatched it away and started the engine, scrubbing roughly at her face.

"He wasn't a bad man," my mother says, more to herself than to me. "But times were so hard then. My aunt once told me that when they first got married your grandma used to paint the Ukrainian Easter eggs, that she had a whole basket of them, all in beautiful intricate designs. And one night

Auntie Daisy brought Mike over to introduce him to her sister. They had just started going out. Well, Mike had brought a bottle of vodka with him and one thing led to another and pretty soon your grandpa got into one of his tirades, ranting about the revolution and how it would smash these old customs and religious rituals once and for all. The opiate of the people and all that. He got Mike going pretty good, too. Daisy tried to get your grandmother to go with her into the other room; let them get on with their drinking and raving. But your grandmother shook her off and stood there looking at your grandpa, arms tight across her body and lips carved shut. He yelled at her to get out and still she stood there, completely expressionless. Staring. And then he stopped yelling and picked up an egg and held her eyes while he hefted the egg in his hand. And still fixing her with his eyes, he threw the egg against the wall. Your grandma didn't even flinch, not once, as one after another he smashed them. Every one.

"Some of them exploded into fragments, but some of them hadn't been blown, so green and brown slime ran down the wall. And still she stared at him. Auntie Daisy said she didn't even make a sound for all of her work; just mopped up the slime and bits of egg shell with an old rag. But the stench of rotten eggs hung in the house for days. And she never made another pysanka."

I clear my throat. "Why didn't she go home to her parents?"

My mother hesitates. Swallows. "It's so hard for you to understand. The way things are today. The things we had to do back then, just to stay alive. Dramatic as that sounds, I know." She smiles briefly. "I think she did try to go back. I think that's why we didn't see much of my grandparents when I was growing up. But what could they do? They had other children."

The photos at my elbow are of my great-grandparents, whom I never knew. They are dressed in traditional Ukrainian costume, which I have never seen on any of my other relatives. The photos, which we found at the back of the bottom drawer of the sideboard, are in sepia, the colour drained, the intricate patterns of the costumes barely discernible beneath the yellowing and cracking. There is something preternatural about the grimness of their expression. Their stoic bearing. Their impenetrable silence. No wonder my grandmother locked them away.

What I want to say is "What else did he smash?" The night he counted the money and found one dime missing and the smell of orange on his daughter's breath. Is there a point in this story when the crack of egg shell shifts to the crack of bone on bone? When bits of coloured shell cower beneath splashes of bright red? And you, mother. Are you there, somewhere in this story, somewhere I cannot follow, hiding, with your hands over your ears? There is no frame large enough for this story, no filter that will help me see what, in the end, I do not really want to see. And for this, I want to say, I am sorry.

Some traditions are too strong. I say nothing.

My mother rubs weakly at the smudges under her eyes. I think she would like me to touch her, to hold her even, but her body looks too brittle. I can't brave the attempt. And then I think, perhaps I am the one too brittle. Too well-versed in lessons from a tomato seed, a scrap of warm dough, a bit of rind in a bathrobe pocket. As my mother has said, and probably her mother before her, we do what we must. But I will dare what I can. I reach toward her, take the orange from her hand, and section it carefully. I offer one segment to her, place another in my mouth. Then we wait for the flavour to burst upon our tongues.

PANTRY

BARBARA *Turner-Vesselago*

BABAYO KEEPS THE FLOOR in here so shiny. Big green tiles about three feet across. The rest of the tiles in this house are grey, for some reason, and much smaller. They never look anything like as good when he's finished with them. But he always does such a wonderful job in here.

Will I ever have a pantry like this again, I wonder? A cool, walk-in closet lined with shelves for all my little hoarded purchases. Cans of bully beef and tuna, flat tins of smoked oysters from Onigbindi's, round drums of shrimp crackers for cocktail party dips. White, pink, and green I had last time, when Daddy was out here. Onion, pink caviar, and avocado. Babayo and Megan's Esau trying to hold the trays above everyone's bare shoulders. People were so jammed in, and all over the balcony—it's just too small a place for a big party, really. Felix Evans was out there holding on to the pipe rail, sweating in his pressed white shirt. I said, Why don't you go back in and talk to Mavis Cooper? And he said, Coals to Newcastle, my dear, coals to Newcastle. Did he mean he was always meeting older ladies? Did he mean he knows he's like one, himself? I should have asked him what he meant, but I didn't want to sound that stupid.

I hate canned peas, so why do I have five of them? Le Sieur Petits Pois, just because you never know when they might run out and Jean Robertson was buying a bunch. She told me one time in the Kingsway that you shouldn't buy chicken if the liquid in the packages has gone yellow. That means it's been frozen and thawed too many times. I thanked her—I mean, she was saving my life—but I felt awful. How does she *know* these things? It's as if I don't know anything when I'm talking to her, and all I can do is hope to God I find out before it's too late.

I should throw out that jar of Niger Café. It tasted horrible, even after all the time it took to get the lid off. Maybe I can give it to Babayo. How do they do these labels anyway? It's like a painting, but they didn't get a single one of them on without wrinkling it. That's something I never think of: How amazing it is that the labels on most cans aren't wrinkled.

I wonder if Babayo ever drinks any of this alcohol? He always makes a point of asking before he takes one of the sardine tins for lunch, but he might be afraid I'd say no about the liquor. B & B, Benedictine, rye, scotch— nobody ever seems to drink rye out here. I guess buying it was a waste of money, but it feels good to have one of everything. Gin, vodka, Pimm's Number 5 Cup. I suppose he'd drink scotch, but I don't know. Surely, I'd see it if he was drunk. He'd be laughing and falling around the way he does at parties. But maybe I wouldn't.

Maybe I should put a mark on all the bottles like everybody else says they do. But do they really? Dwight Smith's wife, Natalie, said in the staff lounge the other day that she'd come home early to find her new housemaid stealing the sugar. What does that mean, stealing the sugar? Americans can be so pretentious. It sounds like something she'd heard back home on tele- vision. Then she said, Well, she was eating a spoonful of sugar, right there in the kitchen, and she guessed she'd have to lock up the sugar drawer from now on, and maybe all the other ones, too. I said, How would you ever carry all those keys? And started reading a magazine to make my point. But she'll probably get one of those big steel darning rings to wear at her waist, like a Victorian matron. How could any single human being eat enough sugar at a sitting to make any difference to anyone? And it's so cheap out here. I don't like either of those two scrawny little Smiths one bit. I hope Megan doesn't start having them over all the time. They probably never had a servant in their lives—I mean, who did, really?—and now all they ever heard on *Upstairs Downstairs* is coming home to roost for them. Stealing the sugar!

But if I did put a mark on the edge of the label? Maybe just on the scotch—I don't think he'd be interested in the others. Then I'd know, anyway. Cyril Kandapper went out to his boy's quarters one night for some reason, Felix Evans told me, and he found half his stuff out there—I mean his shirts, stacks of his records, all kinds of camera stuff, and furniture. Do you mean he'd never even noticed that any of it was missing? I asked him. It sounds like he had a lot more than he could use; he might as well be relieved of some of it. I said, Maybe the guy was just borrowing it and he would have given it back if he'd ever moved out of there. It's not as if he took it away and sold it—it was right there on the back of the property. Felix said, Well, that's not the way Cyril saw it. He took him straight to the police. And then dined out on it for weeks at the Polo Club, I thought. But I'd already said enough, and it is a good story. Imagine seeing a whole world of the things you'd forgotten about, all assembled in one place, with somebody else sitting right smack in the middle of them.

There now, I wonder if he'll see that. Surely not, when he can't even read what's on the label in the first place. Maybe someone he worked for before did this, and he knows about it. No, that seems so unlikely. I'll check it in a couple of days. But what if the level does go down? I'll say, Babayo, why have you been drinking this without my permission? And he'll say, Madame? Why have you drunk this scotch without my permission? Ni? Yes, you. I put a mark on this label two days ago and now look, it's gone down two inches and I haven't had any. Kai, Madame. Now don't give me that pitying look. There's no one else it could have been. You drank it! Haba! Madame!

And then what do I do? Just keep repeating myself and finally order him out of the house the way Mavis Cooper did with Dandu and Usmann when they typed Dandu, Dandu, Dandu all over her good stationery, and then said they hadn't gone into her bedroom and certainly wouldn't have used her typewriter if they had. She sat alone in that house and ached for them for months and then she told them all was forgiven so they'd come back inside and play again.

So what's the point? Let him take it if he wants to. It can't be affecting his work if you can't tell whether he's been drinking. And you don't even know if he's doing it, so relax. He's part of the family, and that's all there is to it.

Didn't I have another jar of cranberry sauce, though? I could swear I brought three back from Canada.

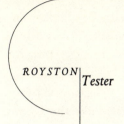

ROYSTON | *Tester*

CROOKED HOLLOW

QUARRY: any place from which stones may be obtained.

"SHE'S MAD AS A HATTER, SON," said Beryl, his mother. "You stay away from that Mary Bienenstock. I know her type. There're other ladies on Quarry Falls Road who give summer work, Scott. Leave that one alone. She's got plenty of men-friends who can help out. *And*, my lad, she's into the sauce. I've seen the blue box."

WELCOME TO MANTRAP, THE ALL-MALE CONNECTOR: FOR ONE-ON-ONE LIVE CONNECTIONS, *press one*. ON-YOUR-KNEES CONFESSIONAL, *press two*. UNCENSORED TALES, *press three*. THE BACK-ROOM, *press four*. PERSONAL COLUMN, *press five*. MAKE YOUR HOT SELECTION NOW.

"I'm only cutting the grass, Ma. What about tuition and books for RMC? You said you can't pay it all," said Scott.

"British like you, dear, isn't she?" said her husband.

"The worst, Doug," replied Beryl, handing Scott the *Crooked Hollow Star*. "Here, son. You get hunting for work. I'm off. I'll miss the bus if I'm not sharp."

To: Zachary Hollinger@freewebnet.kingston.on.ca
July 4. Crooked Hollow.

Hi Zack! Landed that summer wage-slave job—labouring for a Mrs. Bienenstock. What a nose on her! She talks like the Queen, too—doesn't move her lips—she kind of moans into the air. Whenever she raises that crooked schnozzle of hers to ... PRONOUNCE ... on something, it's as though she's snotting some fanfare with it, like they do at Stratford.

When I got to her place, first day, to build the fish pond she wants, she'd already dug a huge fucking pit herself. She was standing next to it all sweaty and panting. What a sight! Then she pointed to a pile of stones and pieces of marble, and introduced them to me, and to each other, as though they were people. Titled aristocrats: "El Roco de Alicante, Marfil del Coto de Pinoso, Marron de Albacete, Blanco Macel y Traventina de Almeria." And then she presented me, "Mr. Scott Haring." "Hi," I said ... to everyone. "Cerveza?" she said. "Beer, my boy?" It was eight-thirty on a Monday morning. Very, *very* weird. So I think we'll get on fine. Everyone calls her JACKY for some reason.

How's it with you, buddy? I know you're not there and all. But I think I've got a zinger of a plan for my "pretend graduation." Jacky's going to help me out. I'll keep you posted.

Miss you. Scott.

THE CONFESSION BOX:
TO RECORD YOUR OWN STEAMY, UNCENSORED TALE OR TO LISTEN IN ON OTHERS', *press one.* TO LISTEN IN ON MILITARY AND OTHER UNIFORM FANTASIES, *press two.* LEATHER, DEGRADATION AND VERBAL ABUSE, *press*

three. PARKS AND OTHER OUTDOOR EXHIBITIONISM, *press four*. LOCKER-ROOM JOCKS AND WATER-SPORTS, *press five*. TRANSVESTITE AND TRANSSEXUAL FANTASIES, *press six*. MAKE YOUR HOT SELECTION NOW.

"Ignore your mum, son," said Doug, after his wife had gone. "It's one of those British 'class' things. Mrs. Bienenstock's posher, that's all. And she's loaded and alone. You go gardening for her. She loves young men like you. Just keep away from the booze and her gentlemen friends."

"What do you mean, Dad?" said Scott.

"Fruits," he said, looking for the TV wand.

"You mean they're gay, Dad?"

Doug nodded gravely, waving the wand in the air.

"She's just begun having what she calls an 'at home' on Sunday afternoons," he said. "We met some. Very at home."

To: Zachary Hollinger@freewebnet.kingston.on.ca
July 25. Crooked Hollow.

Hi Zack! Guy, is this Mrs. Bienenstock—Jack—up your street! It's a real shame you two haven't met. She's really broadminded—and she's crazy about ... ADORES ... guys like you. Far East, Pacific, Africa, she's travelled all over. And these men she knows are really cool, too. She's always asking them to run errands, do her laundry, drive her places—like servants—even answer her phone while they're visiting. She tries to feed them occasionally, but they usually end up doing the cooking themselves because she gets into the gin.

Anyhow, *I'm* not getting much of her gardening done. She's already inviting me to her villa in Spain (where all that marble stuff came from). I've been to two of her Sunday parties. (Does she like to toke away with those "boys" of hers!)

Later. Scott.

"She a dyke, Dad?"

"Mrs. Bienenstock? I don't know, Scott. I doubt it," said Doug. "British women often end up like her. Look at your mum. People in their sixties aren't *anything*, son. She's probably their dotty old 'mummy.' You know how fairies are. Now, I wanna get the damn ball game. Is it on eleven, I wonder?"

"On Quarry Falls Road. Who'd have thought ... " said Scott.

"Go make money, boy. It's June already. You've got two months. We can't support you forever. I was out working full-time at sixteen."

GET REAL, GUYS. BE CLEAR AND SPECIFIC ABOUT WHAT YOU WANT. IF YOU'RE LOOKING FOR FRIENDSHIP; SAY SO. DON'T GO TALKING TO THE GUY WHO WANTS A THREE-WAY ORGY WITH POPPERS AND VIDEOS. BE HONEST ABOUT YOUR APPEARANCE AND AGE. FORGET IDEAL WEIGHTS AND SIZES: AVERAGE DICK LENGTH IS 4–7 INCHES. IF ALL YOU HEAR FROM THE GREETINGS IS THIRTY MEN WITH 8-INCH COCKS, DRAW YOUR OWN CONCLUSIONS. YOU KNOW WHAT THEY SAY ABOUT MEN WHO DRIVE BIG CARS.

To: Zachary Hollinger@freewebnet.kingston.on.ca
August 5. Crooked Hollow.

Hi Zack! Whenever I ask Jacky Bienenstock's age, she always says, "Late twenties, darling. You never ask a lady." She's at least sixty. "I just love young people," she says. All Oscar Wilde-theatrical. It's entertaining, I guess, but sad, too. I've told her all about RMC. We've talked about everything, including the Chatline. (SHE WANTS SHARES IN IT!!) She's really something, this babe. What a summer it's turning out to be!
Salutations, amigo! Scott.

Scott had three months before his parents would be travelling to Kingston for his fall graduation. The difficulty was that he had dropped out a year before, just after his best friend, Zachary, became very ill. Cutting lawns on Quarry Falls Road, like studying at Royal Military College, was a front.

He had already made more than the mint his father dreamed about. Scott-the-"Sysop" was managing his own communications company. It ran from a computer in his apartment in Kingston. The entire operation—"Mantrap"—was a brown electronic file—the size of a fishbowl—into which, for ten dollars an hour, thousands of men chatted day and night.

TO BLOW THE QUARRY: To sound a horn to call the hounds to the quarry.

Scott, in a rented dress uniform, stood at the entrance to Royal Military College. Barely visible from the road or driveway, he was leaning against a limestone wall, reading a newspaper. A car honked. Cautiously, he raised his head. The folks were right on schedule: four hours late. Jacky Bienenstock was at the wheel. Scott peered in. His mother, in the back, seemed too upset to speak.

"Darling," said Jacky, "it's all my fault. This wretched Rover just gave out in Oshawa. The middle of nowhere. I'm so terribly, terribly sorry." She was wearing one of her men's shirts.

"No sweat, guys," said Scott. "You know I hate ceremonies."

"The car seized up, son. No oil. Must've leaked," said Doug. "Your mother ... Well ... "

Scott climbed in and patted Beryl's arm.

"Look, Ma, here's the program. Look. My name. So I've graduated and you can be proud. Now, let's go eat."

TO STOP A CALLER FROM CONTACTING YOU, AND TO AVOID HEARING HIS GREETING, *press eight*. REMEMBER: THERE'S ALWAYS THE POWER OF PRESSING EIGHT.

"Well, the war was good to me, Doug," said Jacky sipping a fifth glass of champagne. "For a while, I was posted to a bomber station in southern England. Full of Canadians. Oh, those dashing young men from Saskatchewan farms, Alberta, all over. So young."

A weir ran noisily outside the open window of the Old Kingston Café.

AW, COME ON, YOU CAN DO BETTER THAN THAT.
YOU HAVE THIRTY SECONDS TO RECORD YOUR GREETING. DON'T LEAVE
IT BLANK. TELL OTHER CALLERS SOMETHING ABOUT YOU. A LINE FULL
OF BLANKS MAY APPEAR INTERESTING TO SOME, BUT IT'S FAR LESS
FUN. COME ON. WE KNOW THERE'S MORE TO YOU THAN A SILENCE.
PLEASE RECORD YOUR GREETING NOW, *then press star.*

"Well, those Canadian boys. Bomber crews. So far from home. My job was to
take the calls from Whitehall about the night's mission. All in code, of
course. The route, altitudes, targets. Top secret. Very important. Then off
they'd go. One night I'd be drinking and dancing with them in the mess.
Naturally, I had my favourites. And then, next time, a few faces missing. Then
more and more disappeared. Sometimes, I wished I'd get the routings
muddled and they'd be saved. In the end, I dreaded those calls. I felt I was
sending the boys to their deaths. Silly of me. I like to think they all para-
chuted to safety, missed the bullets and the trees, floated away from harm.
But, oh, I did travel, yes. They discovered I was good at diplomatic stuff. So off
I went chatting to the brass in all the European capitals. Getting people to see
eye to eye. Bloody exhausting, I might say. More bubbly, Beryl? Allow *me.*"

> *beep.*
> RAUNCHY FUCK-PIG MASTER. TOP. LOOKING FOR A BOTTOM.
> ANYTHING GOES. MY PLACE. DOWNTOWN. NO BULLSHIT. WANT IT
> ROUGH? CALL RIGHT NOW.
> *beep.*
> CUM-HUNGRY COLLEGE JOCK. BUBBLE-BUTT. SWIMMER'S BUILD.
> FIVE-ELEVEN, A HUNDRED AND SIXTY POUNDS. BLUE EYES. CLEAN-
> SHAVEN. BRUSH-CUT. EIGHT INCHES THICK AND CUT, SHAVED BALLS.
> YOUR PLACE. HOT SUCK AND FUCK ACTION. LIKE TO SERVICE.
> *beep.*
> YOU HAVE REACHED THE END OF THE GREETINGS. TO RETURN TO THE
> MAIN MENU, *press three.* TO RE-RECORD YOUR GREETING, *press one.*

"And what about Zachary, Scott?" said Jacky, sailing into another topic. "He must have graduated with you? I expect he's off with his family somewhere, too."

Scott looked across at his parents.

"Um, no," he said, smoothing the graduation program that lay open on the table.

"Perhaps Scotty didn't tell you, Jacky," said Beryl. The name "Jacky" seemed to stick to the roof of her mouth. "But ... Zachary passed away a year ago. Very tragically."

"Dead?" said Jacky, almost sternly. "Oh."

beep.

HI GUYS, JUST CRUISING THE LINE FROM OAKVILLE. SEEING WHO'S THERE.

beep.

IN MY CAR. DON VALLEY PARKWAY. LOOKING FOR A BLOW-JOB IN THE EAST END. SHOOT ME A MESSAGE.

beep.

HI. MY NAME'S STEPHEN. I'M NINETEEN YEARS OF AGE AND I'M NOT INTO BATHS OR BARS. I'M LOOKING TO TALK AND MAKE FRIENDS WITH SOMEONE MY OWN AGE DOWNTOWN. LONG TERM.

beep.

HOT GUY. SKINHEAD-TYPE. TATTOOS. GOATEE. TWENTY-NINE. EIGHT-INCH ROCK-HARD COCK. PURPLE MUSHROOM HEAD. SCOUTING OUT FOR A BOY OVER TWENTY. COPS IN UNIFORM A PLUS. WANNA PLOW A CREAMY TIGHT HOLE. NO FEMS. OR FATS. BUZZ ME.

beep.

ANOTHER GUY HAS SENT YOU A MESSAGE. HERE IT IS:

To: Zachary Hollinger@freewebnet.kingston.on.ca
September 14. Crooked Hollow.

Now that grad's done, Zack, I'm just going to keep the Chatline
running. I'm booked for Spain next June for a week—Jacky's invita-
tion. She's leaving next Friday.

By the way, I finished her fish pond. It's all crazy-shaped and
weird, like that whale's eye we saw on Grand Manaan. Remember
that? But I think the fucker leaks, too. All my fault. Thinking of you.

Scott.

"Oh, I'm so terribly sorry," said Jacky, turning to Scott who was looking
out at the water. "But Scott sends Zachary all those messages. I thought ... "

Two swallows dived below the open window.

"Fine lad," said Doug. "Part Native. Mohawk. Scotty's roommate at
RMC. Troubled boy. Very troubled. Pity really."

"I see," said Jacky, refilling her glass, clearly discomposed.

She glanced at Scott.

"Very sad," said Doug.

"May I see the graduation program again, Scott?" said Beryl.

"Aren't we all!" declared Jacky, draining the champagne.

"Oh, good heavens!" said Beryl. "I thought so. Look. Isn't this Zachary's
name here?"

Scott teased the program from her hand.

"It must be a mistake," he said. "Different Zachary Hollinger."

"Do you think it's to honour him?" said Beryl.

"They wouldn't do it like that, honey," said Doug.

"Well, whatever it is, your names are listed together: Haring, Hollinger.
Just like they must have been in class," said Jacky almost cheerily, noticing
the bottle was now empty.

"Imagine how his family must feel," said Doug.

"Oh, the family probably doesn't know, Doug," said Jacky, looking
around for the waitress. "If Zachary's dead, they wouldn't have come, would

they? I'd let it go. Don't ruffle any feathers—especially Native ones. Messy, messy. Miss!"

Doug glared across the table at Jacky, at Scott, then at Jacky again. "Let's be going," he said, gruffly. "I'll drive this time."

To: Zachary Hollinger@freewebnet.kingston.on.ca
September 16. Crooked Hollow.

Hi Zack. Still at Quarry Falls Road. But house-sitting for Jacky. She's Spain-side. Mantrap's running fine from my remote here. I've thought more about the grad. Jacky screwed up the program, of course—she wanted my name AND YOURS!! to be on it. Without telling me! Sometimes she's a giddy old biddy, you know—it's all that time she spends on her deck, pissed on gin, wearing her men's shirts, and staring at the tops of those fir trees. But I think we'll get away with it—my folks didn't quite clue in. Ma didn't anyway. So, congrats on YOUR grad.

Everyone thinks I'm nuts e-mailing you—but, hey, the World Wide Web goes everywhere, right? Who knows who's running it? Some god-gopher. But if it goes everywhere, it goes where you are. That's why I mail ya. On these humid nights I grab the cell phone and sit out back under the trees (Jacky-style by her sinking fish pond!!) listening to my own Chatline—it's crazy—I wait just for the blanks—the silent guys—like the fireflies, you know. Little shirts floating down, but with all your news. Blanks. That's how I see them, Zack. Shirts in the dark. Between all the beeps. And then you must be some place near. God, I miss you, buddy.
Later. Scott.

QUARRY: Certain parts of a deer placed on the hide and given to the hounds as a reward.

EATING WATERMELON

LISA Moore

I RUSH TOWARD CHARLOTTE, my fingertips burning on the paper coffee cups.

I say, Quick.

She takes the cups. The security guard with the dent down the centre of his forehead strolls between the tables.

Charlotte is late. I sat for a long time looking at a ship moored in the St. John's harbour. A giant wall of steel, dark red, curving against the sky. The mast strung with Christmas lights, dim in the grey daylight. A pile of sun-faded buoys sluffing off a snowdrift. A man ran across Water Street hunched against the sleet. After that, the street was empty.

When Charlotte sits down opposite me, her black angora tam sparkling with water droplets, I say, Are you married yet?

Married? she smiles. There's so much I'd have to give up.

She folds her hands over her tam and sighs. Her cheeks full of colour.

I can't believe how happy I am, she says.

For a moment, we have nothing to say.

I can't believe it, she says again. She shrugs.

After a while, I leave her to phone Philip. I watch her from the pay phone. She gets up to chat with Mel White.

Philip says, Come home. I'm in bed waiting for you.

I can tell by Charlotte's stiffening posture, she folds her arms, that Mel is talking about his wife, Charlotte's cousin. The receiver smells of cigarettes. There are initials scratched in the tinted Plexiglas shelf under the phone, a pointy heart.

Mel is probably saying, It happened just like that. We had plans, too. We were going to buy a piece of land in Cupids.

The guard walks by them, his forehead like two loaves of bread, rising side by side.

Well, get out of bed. You're supposed to be cleaning the bathroom.

I'd seen Mel's wife at a movie a month after she left him, in a seat a few rows ahead of me. The movie had started and Mel strode down the aisle, leaving a trail of popcorn. I could see his wife hesitate, a chocolate held before her lips, the green light of the movie pulsing on her temple, her cheek. Her face was turned just slightly, watching him step over a few people, and sink into the dark. She put the chocolate in her mouth and I could see her jaw move. Then her head turned, minutely, toward the movie, and she became absorbed by it. There was a lush English landscape, and the sound of galloping horses. I could feel the pounding of their hooves in the metal arm of my chair.

I tug Charlotte's sleeve.

I say, We have to go.

Mel says, You girls are looking good. I was just saying to Charlotte, keep up the aerobics.

It's not easy, Mel, I say. Happy New Year.

Mel had been on a pay phone at the Midnight Café the first time I heard about his wife. He was sitting on a stack of chairs, his eiderdown coat squashed awkwardly under his arms. He was making some arrangements about a car.

I had mouthed, Hello.

He covered the mouthpiece and grabbed my hand.

He said, Jenny left me just like that. She came back from Winnipeg. I met her at the airport. She told me as soon as she walked through the doors. I had candles, a bottle of wine. Sometimes it goes that way.

He slapped one palm off the other, like a plane leaving the runway.

Gone, he said, losing the receiver in the folds of his jacket. He grabbed it and said, Frank, how much for the timing belt?

Then he covered the mouthpiece and said, You're not doing anything tonight, are you? Are you still married? Don't count on it lasting.

Charlotte and I stand outside Atlantic Place on the sidewalk and look up at the sky. Snowflakes in her eyelashes. In a few days, she'll be in Greece with Harry, a honeymoon without the wedding. I had been at her house the day they decided to go. A whim. She prodded a torn egg carton with the poker until the flame touched it and the separate cups glowed orange, holding their shape. She said, I've been telling Harry my fires are impeccable.

Where are we going? she asks me. And then, Has Mel told you the story of him and my cousin?

Are you serious about Harry?

Yes, but what if I end up like Mel?

Charlotte's talking while she eats: prosciutto, anchovies, jalapeno peppers, ricotta. October sun still full of heat. We're on College Street in Toronto, an outdoor café.

She bites some bread and spits it into her hand.

Pah, it's mouldy, she says.

Is it mouldy? I look at a piece.

She flings the basketful on the sidewalk for the pigeons.

She says, He says I have to make up my mind. Can you believe it?

Sunlight falls through the leaves of a sapling growing in the concrete planter beside her. She holds out her hand and straightens a ring: That was it, that was the only thing he said.

The ring is from an antique shop in Shrinagar.

The sunlight rubs her shoulder like a delicate cloth, chamois. She turns her face toward it and closes her eyes. I used to sleep at her house. We slept in the attic and early Sunday morning her father would call, Rise and shine, girls, rise and shine.

Charlotte would say, without opening her eyes, Don't answer. Pretend you're asleep. But I had to answer; trout frying in the cast-iron pan, a pitcher of pulpy orange juice. Her father and I would get her out of bed just after sunrise.

I want her to come home to Newfoundland. To write a screenplay in her house on Prescott Street. To settle down with Harry. Charlotte thinks in terms of action.

I visit her in Montreal for two weeks. We are nineteen, and every morning in the middle of some story, she sneaks through the subway gate without paying. She does it by fishing frantically in her purse for her subway pass. Holding up her fingers as if holding the pass, flying through the turnstile, telling a story about Jennifer Snow.

And all the while Jennifer's hiding in the back of the van rolled up in this old Persian carpet, the windows all steamed, her husband and this woman practically naked, and Jennifer unrolls herself, shouting, You bastard, I got you, I got you! Below this Charlotte is whispering, digging in her purse for the non-existent subway pass, catching a pen that falls, You do it too, Marsha. Come on, do it, do it. Yes, Marsha, come on.

I wanted to do it. She's sailing through ahead of me, the tails of her raglan flapping. But my face burns, and I drop a token in the slot. On the ninth day, without looking up from his novel, the attendant jams the turnstile so the bar catches her stomach, knocking the wind out of her. He turns a page, eyebrows rising, but still not looking up, he taps the coin receptacle.

We tell each other everything.

She sops up the parmesan and olive oil with the last lettuce leaf. Speaks with her mouth full, Haven't you ever just been attracted to someone sexually, someone who has nothing else going for him?

No, Charlotte. I haven't.

We look into each other's eyes for a long time. Part of the leaf is still hanging from her lip.

Well, for me the sex thing is just ... Excuse me, she catches the waitress. The bread was mouldy.

What? I say.

Free floating.

Jesus, Charlotte.

Let's walk, she says, standing, stretching, working a kink in her neck.

She takes the bill and I let her. The luxury of depending on her.

Free floating?

Yes, chemical. Nothing to do with what he does for a living, where he comes from, just a tingling on the skin, lust.

There is a small scar between her eyes from when I hypnotized her. We are sixteen. She kneels before me. I swing rosary beads, the silver cross close to her nose.

I say, There's ink pouring through your veins, capillaries ... it's thicker than blood, darker, it pools in your toes, so thick you can't move them. Can you feel your toes get very heavy? Yes, you can. Now, your calves. When I get to Charlotte's waist filling with cement, only the whites of her eyes are showing and she topples over and catches the corner of the coffee table in the centre of her forehead. She rushes to the bathroom, pulling back her upper lip. My teeth, are my teeth all right?

Blood gushes from her forehead, over the bridge of her nose to the corner of her mouth.

We stop outside a junk shop; a silver compact/lipstick set catches the sun.

This place costs a fortune, she says, flicking the catch on the compact.

Blue eye, sky, clouds, jerky in the disk of mirror. Her mouth. She purses it, pouts. Then the lips whisper—I won't commit to Harry yet.

She snaps the compact shut.

This way, she says, linking arms, dragging me down a back alley.

Charlotte gets hay fever. When she's on a film shoot, she can go for three days with only a few hours' sleep. She can sleep standing up, her arms folded across her chest, chin tucked into her shoulder, frowning with the effort.

She drinks cognac, Pernod, beer, champagne. New Year's Eve, we are at the same party and I am standing very near her at midnight. I watch a tear slip down the side of her nose as she sings "Auld Lang Syne." I fill my cheeks to bulging and spray a mouthful of champagne over her face.

She drags me home, her arms under my armpits, her red mitts locked across my chest. Snowflakes land on her bare wrist. We can hear the muffled fireworks at the harbour, a long way away.

Charlotte wears a blood-dark green velvet gown to my wedding, a heavy cluster of rhinestones hangs in the dip of her throat. She's the Maid of Honour. When my daughter is born, she sends a box of chocolates so they arrive the same day, the white wrapping paper covered in her lipstick kisses.

Now Philip and I are at Atlantic Place and the same guard strolls past. An axe? A lobotomy? Blood gushing over his face, his blue uniform. Was he a child when it happened?

Philip stares out the window.

Is that ship moving? he says.

He's thinking about his thesis. Heidegger. Last night we were driving through Portugal Cove and he said, We impose our understanding of space on time. Space is the relation between one object and another, that church.

A white clapboard church loomed in the headlights and fell away. Then there was the ocean, mottled and quivering like seal skin.

But time doesn't come in chunks. We just think of it that way.

I had been thinking of the review of my stories that arrived in the mail a few days ago from a friend, a news clipping.

In these stories, meaning is always elusive.

There's no such thing as meaning, I say to Philip. I thought they decided that. Didn't they decide that?

Philip says, No, they didn't.

Yes, about twenty years ago.

Well, yes, they said there was no such thing, but they weren't convinced.

I think of Charlotte putting the candles down, in the centre of the table. They were Christmas carollers modelled in wax, their red caps melting over their eyes.

She said, It's such an artsy thing, to look for omens. If a fortune teller had told me that in the next month I'd fall in love and cross a great body of water, I'd never have believed it. So much can happen.

Harry said, Better watch the phyllo pastry.

I thought, staring at the candles, maybe there's meaning in objects. Russian novels, a sleigh might come galloping through a wood in darkest winter. Someone delivering a note, slush flying up under the wheels, vast acres of trees with no leaves, and 400 pages of elaborate construction, small print, musty yellowed pages, hinging on that note. The heroine tears open the wax seal with her lover's ring print pressed into it and the whole sway of the novel shifts like a ship moving away from the dock.

Each object on the table, the carollers melting lugubriously, their caps slipping over their brows, has to be tapped open like tapping a mountain with a ball-peen hammer to find a vein of gold, or tapping the shell of a boiled egg with the edge of a spoon.

Charlotte flips through cookbooks for a white glaze. She's making mille feuilles. She's wearing a grey skirt that hugs her waist and a waffle-weave T-shirt printed with tiny pink flowers. When she reaches for the vanilla in the top cupboard, her ribs show.

I phoned Harry late one evening and I said, Well, what do you love about her?

I was looking out the window at a snowstorm. There was a car backing out of the church parking lot across the street. A truck skidded down the hill and swiped the tail end of the car; they both swung like partners in a polka, the truck kicking skirts of snow to each side. My breath caught.

He said, For one thing, I can't remember the last time I took so much pleasure in just looking at someone.

The drivers got out and shook hands.

Harry says, Take it out, quickly.

She rushes to the stove with oven mitts. The first layer of pastry is dark brown and brittle, like parchment.

Their courting is an elaborate etiquette of cooking hints.

Take off the first layer, Harry says.

Do you think it will be okay underneath?

It'll be fine.

Are you sure?

Oh, look at that, he says. Perfect.

A breath of heat, the screech of the oven hinges.

But when I taste it, there's too much egg. It's like an omelette.

We each have taken a bite and we pause. She rests the tines of her fork against the pie plate, her wrist bent, her forehead resting on her wrist.

Not what I expected, she says.

It's lovely, he says.

I say, I'm so jealous of you, Harry, for taking Charlotte away.

India: in Shrinagar Charlotte and I get a shakara ride around Dahl Lake. We are twenty-one. We lie back on floral-covered cushions and idly write postcards. I fell in love with Philip just before we left St. John's. It takes a very long time to write one line. There's a silver teapot with mint and cardamom tea at our feet. We are being rowed to the hanging Mogul gardens, one of the seven wonders of the world.

The owner of the boat brings us to an antique shop at the end of our ride. There's a lightning storm, and the power goes out. The proprietor lights four white candles. The silhouettes of Thai shadow puppets strung from the wooden rafters leap and shrink, the fragile shoulders flickering with mute laughter. The dark sockets of Nepalese masks watch from the ceiling. A cockroach with an iridescent shell creeps over a yellowed scrap of lace.

Charlotte's cheeks are rosy in the flame, lips glistening, showing the pink inside her mouth when she laughs. She tries on a tall crown. Hundreds of tiny jewels and small bits of gold jiggle with each tilt of her head.

There is a tremor. Enough to make the wooden legs of the stools beside us dance. Charlotte and I grip the edge of the counter. The jewels on her crown bounce like a hard rain hitting pavement.

Is nothing, the proprietor says.

We're in a Bergman film, I say to Charlotte.

We look at cookie tin after cookie tin of rings and necklaces.

Philip and I stay in Charlotte's apartment in Toronto. Philip calls me into Charlotte's bedroom. He's ironing his shirt. He holds out a cardboard box. Inside, lying on a crush of white tissue paper, is a mahogany penis.

He says, It was just sitting on the ironing board.

But you opened the box, Philip. You took off the lid.

This room has a hardwood floor and vines lock around the window like arthritic knuckles caught in prayer. The cock is black and polished. Smooth. It hits my palm with a cool slap. The iron makes us jump. It hisses by itself, a thin vapour.

Driving on Bloor. Charlotte is taking me to a play, pay what you can. We're stopped at a red light and she leans over the steering wheel and looks into the rear-view mirror. She touches the tiny scar on her forehead.

Do you think I should get plastic surgery?

No way.

Me neither. I kind of like it.

Someone honks a horn. The light has changed.

She's acting in a film shot in the back alley. They are shooting night for day. I wake at three in the morning, shielding my eyes. I crawl over to the window. She stands below in the alley, in a concentrated white light, far brighter than daylight. Just down the alley, I can see how dark it is. The men behind the cameras are silhouettes. She's alone in the tunnel of light. I think of those descriptions of people who are brought back from the dead. She stands absolutely still, as if terrified, then she begins to do Tai Chi.

When she gets up the next morning, she wears a red satin kimono. A dragon embroidered on the back, breathing fire. Her roommate says, I want to dress like Charlotte. You know, the way Charlotte puts clothes together. Colours, textures. She has style, Charlotte does.

We walk for a long time on Ajuna beach, Goa, before we come upon the naked volleyball players. Grass huts. A child with gold ringlets and a necklace of beads, alone under the bushes. On the ridge, we can see slices of chrome through the palm leaves: several motorcycles. We keep walking without looking at the players. The next day, Charlotte suntans on a towel in an orange bikini. She has a migraine. Our skin turning pink. Two Indian men want to take my photograph. One of them keeps putting his arm around me.

American girl, he says, dreamily.

I'm from Newfoundland, I say. Please don't put your arm around me.

His hand down my back, his fingers under the elastic of my bikini pants. When I push his arms away, the other man slips his hands around my waist.

Charlotte runs toward us screaming, Get the fuck out of here. Leave her alone. Can't you see you're frightening her? Leave her alone.

Flailing her arms.

They pick up their towels and the camera case, and walk away. They look over their shoulders. When they have already gone a distance down the beach, she screams, Get the fuck out of here.

She shouts at me, Do you want to get us both raped? Her spit lands on my cheek.

Her hands come up and cover her face. The beach is huge and the waves pound.

Sshhh, she says.

I'm sorry, Charlotte.

She goes back to the room we've rented. The room stands separate from any building, made of cinder blocks painted blue on the inside. A clean cement floor. The sheets on the cots crisp and grey. She lies down on her stomach. I go to the beach-side restaurant to buy her a Limca. The icy bottle. For much of our trip, we've seen pop advertised on painted billboards, bottles beaded with condensation, frost curling from the mouth, the paint crackling. But the pop would be warming in the window, cobwebbed.

A baby goat has found its way into the room. When I creak the wooden door, the kid leaps onto Charlotte's back. Its four cloven hooves gather for a second in the small of her back, like four teacups piled on a saucer. The kid is pure white in a brilliant slat of sun. Charlotte jumps up terrified and the kid clatters and baas across the cement, scrabbling for balance and out the door. Its fleece brushing my knees, silky.

The surprise of a goat on the small of Charlotte's back, as if her soul has leapt out of a nub of her spinal cord, bone-white, graceful, shocking. We stand for a moment. A breeze sucks the door shut. She is trembling and I put my arms around her.

We pass a hotdog vendor and the smoke cuts across the sidewalk, the air above ripples in the heat. We have been striding down the sidewalk not minding where we're going. Four men, each one of them handsome, muscles bulging in their bare arms, block the sidewalk. They're saying softly, but so we can hear it, like a round of "Row, Row, Row Your Boat," Beautiful legs, those legs are beautiful.

Charlotte says, The Brophy sisters, all of them beauticians, all of them—

I interrupt, Champagne-blonde—

She says, They all live in the same apartment with Eugene. Poor Eugene has never been able to—

One of the men grabs her wrist. Her hair flies off her shoulders like the blades of a fan. She says, Pardon me?

She says it softly, her fist raised in his grasp, and the man parts his lips in an easy smile. All the men chuckle and say, Pardon me, mocking. I can see him in her sunglasses. We're all just politely waiting to see if he will let go of her wrist—he lets go.

We walk fast. She says, after a block, Exactly, champagne-blonde and these squeaky little Marilyn Monroe voices.

I'm afraid of Charlotte stepping into alleys filled with blinding tunnels of light. I buy the biggest watermelon on the stand at the fruit store on her street. It's almost too heavy to carry. Then we eat it on the deck of her apartment. I'm thirsty. The blade pink, gleaming with juice, catches the sky. A star of light skids down the serrated edge. The fibres of watermelon pressed against the roof of my mouth. A pink drip from the corner of her mouth. Her chin shiny, she is still talking.

I say, Look, what about Harry?

The afternoon that Harry and Charlotte leave, Philip and I come to terms with the fact that we're broke. I decide to take Charlotte's advice: If you don't have any money, you must behave as if you do.

I go out and buy us a truffle each. We lie in bed and eat truffles at three-thirty in the afternoon. Philip holds one to my mouth, then he bites it himself. We each nibble, until it's gone. Then we eat the other one.

I say, Imagine, we are lying in bed eating truffles.

As I'm drifting to sleep, I feel a wave of fright about not having any money, and then I remember the truffles.

I say, This is the only moment that exists. I'm thinking it will be a long time before I see Charlotte.

Philip says, That's not true. Heidegger says all present moments were made in the future and come hurtling toward us from there.

He would like to go on, explain it, and waits for me to say something. I wait to see if he will say it without my speaking. We are both waiting, but I fall asleep instead, deciding to swallow it whole.

Then I get up to cook supper and Philip works in the study. I've got potatoes boiling on the stove; the windows are steamed. I'm listening to a new Johnny Cash that Charlotte taped for me before she left.

Then, booming, something Charlotte has put on the tail end of the tape. The Rustavi Choir—hundreds of male voices blasting, powerful, deep, and just men, monks, making the glasses in the cupboards over the speakers hum against my fingers when I take them down to set the table.

I clear away the condensation from the window and it's dusk. The tree outside the window is covered in ice, and it's a pink gold, the last bit of sunlight firing down the branches like electricity or voices on phone wires, long distance.

THE LADY OF THE BEAN POLES

SHELDON Oberman

ALBERT BARRY WAS DIGGING a clumsy trench of a garden in his small backyard, his garden fork thrusting through mouldy leaves, probing deeply into earth, almost to the bed of Red River clay. Separating. Turning. Mixing.

Yet he knew he wouldn't get the vine-splendid beans and stout carrots of his neighbour, Mrs. Slawik. Her prosperous tomatoes weighed so heavily in the hand, they were something he could swear by.

Last year, she had let him have the pick of all her seeds. He had grown them the same way she did, in the same milk cartons with the same water, soil, and sun, but they hadn't favoured him as they did her. He'd caught her disappointment when he'd brought them out. She'd sniffed the way she did at Danny Stein as he was ruining his sneakers in the spring runoff. "That back-lane boy," she'd said. "He's growing every which way, but he's not growing up."

Composting didn't help much, either. Albert Barry's mouldy V8 juice had better enzymes than her spoiled pickles. His eggshells and grapefruit rinds mulched just as well as her Old Country borscht and cabbage rolls, which were, according to his books, a violation of all rules on proper rot. Yet Mrs. Slawik's garden smacked dark lips for more while Albert Barry's turned a cold, clay shoulder.

"Mrs. Slawik!" He called to her, not awkward or shy as long as he could speak from behind his fence. "Say, Mrs. Slawik, I've been gardening next to you for two lean years. How about telling me your secrets?"

She was patting her seeds into short tight rows, never bothering with markers. "No more than I needed tags for my five kids," she always said. Broad hips and sturdy legs. Grey eyes and silver hair. A smile, thin and pale as the newest moon. "Secrets? When I'm young like you, Mr. Barry, then I got secrets. Now I'm too old. All I got is habits."

"Then how do your habits grow such big tomatoes?"

She waved him off with a laugh and a promise that she'd fill his grocery bags if his crop was poor again and she shuffled off to her tool shed. He knew that she was flattered, for her garden meant more to her than her well-scrubbed rooming house, her mothballed Easter bonnets, and all her faded photographs. She may have shared her back lane with the shops of Winnipeg's Main Street, but Mrs. Slawik's garden was as close as she could get to the peasant farm of Ukraine where she'd been born—a world of fifty generations framed here by sixty feet of fence.

Albert Barry came from a straight and narrow line of bankers and ministers who never saw a piece of land as anything but a site for mortgages or burials.

He carried on their dedication to clean hands by teaching school recorder and conducting Boys and Girls Mixed Choir at Luxton Elementary, a few blocks away. Then his wife found what Albert Barry described as "another tune to beat her drum to" and left him for a jazz musician heading east. Barry, still conscientious to a fault, missed neither a beat of music nor a day of teaching. However, he did shorten after-school band practices and gave away his collection of Gilbert and Sullivan operettas. He began attending a church basement coffee house, where college boys in tab collars were singing the new-fashioned folk songs of the day. It was then that Albert Barry accepted, on faith alone, their testaments to the dignity of sweat and the sanctity of dirt. He bought himself a garden fork, a pair of denim overalls, and a stack of books on backyard farming.

Yet he hardly raised anything besides his own expectations and the eyebrows of his neighbours. It wasn't as if he'd even eat the vegetables he tried to grow; he took most meals at the Popularity Grill, where canned peas and parsley were strictly for colour on the plate and the special of the day was always hamburger.

The more he dug, the deeper he reconsidered. His fingernails were filthy. His underarms were soaked. His father's aversion to mould and pollen was burning in his nostrils, swelling up his eyes. He could hear his father preaching in his head, "There's no percentage in a garden, Albert. Cut your losses, son. You should not try to turn a profit with a garden fork." It was one of his father's many "should nots" that kept the muscles knotted in Albert Barry's neck.

He rubbed at his stiffness and felt a blister on his forefinger just where it would play the F on the recorder. Old Dad was right as always, Barry thought, but he kept on digging. I was meant to hold a tuning fork not a garden fork. If I had a penny's worth of practicality, I'd convert this misery of a garden into parking stalls for Ray Horobec.

Ray worked out of his garage down the lane. He was always looking for more space to botch another customer's transmission or to patch some rusted Chevrolet so it would shine like virtue till it was sold.

Just when Barry began to plot the cost of asphalt in his mind, he was jarred by his garden fork scraping something hard below. It shivered up his spine and grated on the edge of his front teeth.

What's down there? he wondered, testing with the fork. A brick? A stone? Maybe one of those ruptured pipes the city workers love to hunt all summer with their backhoes.

He pried at it, muttering at himself, "You damn fool. You're harvesting a crop of rocks just to break your father's heart." He worked at it with the fork until he felt it loosen. He knelt, probing, and reached something smooth and firm, though too slippery to grip. Wiping away the muck, he spotted the gleam of gold.

And he thought of Lydia's wedding ring as he had spun it again and again for hours at the kitchen table, watching it glitter like a hollow golden seed. The ring he'd found stuck in the soap dish after Lydia had left him.

He thought, Why am I digging this damn thing up? It's probably some pipe. I could break a line if I disturbed it. Still, his fingers played on the shining metal in the earth until the muck caved over it, burying his hand, clotting his flannel shirt sleeve, to leave only the stump of an arm.

He removed his muddy shirt, folded it carefully, kneeled, and scooped away the earth until he saw a streak of gold.

A cloud-shaped ornament

Albert Barry had been a boy who once went wild for gold, who'd charged through the tangle and decay of vines in the gap between two garages. Flinching at rough leaves. Crashing over a huge Scotch thistle. Just so he could grab what three girls in party dresses shrieked that he should never touch, though they had lured him on, after games of spin-the-bottle and pin-the-tail, and had gotten him even dizzier with a maypole romp around a laundry pole as they teased him saying, "If you touch it, you'll be sorry."

"Don't you even dare to look."

—To look inside a steamer trunk they'd said was rich with bounty; goblets and golden crowns seeded with pearls and diamonds; a horrible fate would get him if he tried to open it—a witch had guarded it with bloodsucking things that would pull him in with a thousand suction cups and ripping teeth, first tearing off his clothes, and then—

"Lies! Lies! You girls are all such liars!" he'd yelled, trying to shout them down.

"And then your skin's ripped off and—"

"Nuts!" he'd shouted. "You're just nuts and crazy!"

"And then the witch will make a zombie to look like you, so your parents won't ever know you're locked inside the trunk and screaming through her poison slime."

"There's no such thing," he'd sneered, "because nobody can live without a skin."

"Albert Barry, puff and blow," they'd chanted at him. "Albert Barry, you don't know!"

"You're just stupid girls trying to scare me from your hiding place!"

"Smarty pants! Full of ants! You just go and see." They'd flounced their skirts as he rushed for the trunk.

His heart had drummed a wild tattoo, as he swept past a burst of nettles and thistles slashing at his face, while his ears were shrilling with the wail of girls—

"She'll get you! She'll get you!"

Then he swept away the rot of leaves, broke the trunk lid off its hinges, and tore through ragged clothes that clouded with dust only to scrape the slivery boards beneath.

"Dirty! Dirty!" they sang as he gaped at them empty-handed. "Dirty! Dirty!" spreading their tongues, tossing their hips for insult.

"Dirty Bert in a dirty shirt.

"All he wants to do is flirt.

"Poke and stare, he don't care.

"Makes a mess in his underwear!"

Albert Barry winced. Now look at me, he muttered to himself. After twenty years of trying to grow up, I'm on my knees, playing in the mud.

Searching with blind hands, he finally grasped the smooth, firm thing. He laboured with it and the ground began to swell. He tightened his grip, drawing it out as earth heaved and split, releasing a foot-long human form: head, waist, legs, all clotted with muck. Not yet free. It was attached to something on a pole. He brought it all out steadily until it stuck again. Two more gentle tugs and the last part, the base, came out like a plug.

When he hosed it off, he found it wasn't gold at all, just some brassy electroplated thing, and rusty at that, though it seemed fairly well preserved.

Fool's gold, he told himself. I suppose that proves it was meant for me.

It had no wiring for a bulb, so he reasoned that it couldn't be a lamp. Still, it seemed to be domestic; some sort of 1930s misbegotten Greek-and-Roman-styled household thingamajig.

The statue on top intrigued him: a young woman with flowing hair holding a rainbow above her head. She was nearly naked except for folds of robe draping from her hips. Her face might once have gleamed, but it now was blank and pitted. He rubbed her flat belly and nipple-sized breasts, scraping the grit from a long lean leg. She stood upon a sphere that he imagined must represent the world; a very worn and tarnished world conveniently fastened to a stand.

An ashtray stand, he thought. That's what it is and the statue is its decorative handle. Amazing. Absurd. And somehow awfully wrong.

The tin ashtray crumbled in his hand. He broke off the base where the decay had eaten through and the statue was left standing on a simple iron pole. Holding it at arm's length, he wondered how it came to be buried outside his back door. There were too many previous owners of his house to guess who might have put it there. It hadn't been merely dumped; he was certain of that. The garbage cans were only steps away and it would have been snatched up in those back lanes where the garbage crews could never stay ahead of the North End foragers and gatherers.

He wondered, Perhaps whoever owned it didn't want to let it go. Too out of fashion to keep but with too much residue of value to toss away. It may have been stored near the back porch and forgotten as the dirt piled up—a prize for future archaeologists. Or was there a deeper intention to its being buried here? Was it meant to protect the place from evil spirits? Those old country immigrants, they've got superstitions that haunt their every move.

Mrs. Slawik returned with a pruning knife. Barry watched her ease her way into her willow bush and cut curved branches of pussy willows, musty with pollen. The blade flashed as she paused, noticing the statue in his hand.

"What you got there, Mr. Barry? Something your students made for you?"

He broke into a grin and held it high. "I teach music, Mrs. Slawik, not metal work. This is a lawn ornament that I bought downtown, in Eaton's basement. I was looking for a plaster elf like Mrs. McKay has on her lawn, but they were all sold out. So I picked this up instead. How do you like her?"

She snorted, not taken in for a moment. "It's time you find a girl-friend, Mr. Barry. That one won't keep you warm."

"I've got no luck with real girls, Mrs. Slawik. Besides, I think she's kind of pretty."

"Too skinny. Not enough meat."

"Not even for a poor vegetable gardener?"

Mrs. Slawik studied the maiden with a sideways stare. For a moment, she was thoughtful among her branches, her fingers rubbing at the glowing bark, the moist wind whispering through her hair. "Mr. Barry," she said, "you stick her by the gate where you plant your beans. Don't wait until tomorrow. You put her there tonight. Then later, some bean plants, they'll climb up. She might be a good thing for your garden."

He nodded respectfully and they both turned away.

There is something about the first warm night in May with the air so moist and yeasty. It would not let Albert Barry fall asleep. He'd wanted to sleep so he could dream, but he couldn't keep his eyes shut. He'd felt whispers up his back and such a hunger in his arms that he spoke his thought aloud. "I've been alone too long." And the four years he had shared with Lydia suddenly felt like the loneliest time of all.

There was something else that he was missing, something in the garden. So Albert Barry came out of doors again. He heard night noises all around: a siren wailing down Inkster Boulevard, that wild red-haired Riley boy playing tin-can soccer down the lane, the hollow roar of Main Street's traffic, and some TV somewhere chattering out the late-night news.

Yet his garden seemed separate from all of that and he listened for its slow cooking of a thousand seeds underneath the ground. Still, that wasn't why he'd brought his dusty bottle of red Italian wine.

It's for my lady, he decided. Because I've been so out of touch and out of tune and I never really knew it before she came.

The statue stood in front of its grove of broomsticks and galvanized pipes; all of them stuck in the ground and tied with string to hold a future crop of beans. Her arms were held high as if to draw down rain and call up seeds and greet anyone who called to her, even those who didn't know her name. The statue was not nearly high enough to be a bean pole, but Albert Barry was keeping that a secret between Mrs. Slawik and himself.

"Our gardening secret," he murmured to himself.

He took a full deep drink and gave one to the statue, the red stream splashing on its feet and rusty globe, running down the pole into the upturned earth. The garden got the next one in a circle poured around them both. Then assuring himself that he wasn't yet a total fool, he finished off the rest.

When he felt the magic growing in his guts, he looked to Mrs. Slawik's window. He had an impulse to invite her to a polka around the pole, yearning to see her years fall off with every circle round until she turned into a maiden once again. But he knew that the old woman was probably snoring in her bed with enough dreams of her own.

Looking past her window, he imagined a row of windows, Lydia's first and then those few other women whom he had known before her, every window blank, reflecting a barren sky.

"Don't look," Barry told himself, half remembering some fear, childish or primitive, of losing one's self to an empty mirror.

He concentrated on the earth instead and began to hum some ancient tune whose name he didn't know, a tune that played him high and low until he began to shuffle, then to sway and kick at dirt. The rhythm took him around the pole in a dance as out of fashion and peculiar as any Art Deco pseudo-Roman-Greco female ashtray ornament. A tune got him spinning, slipped him out of his slippers, lifted up his head, and waved his arms, with his blood pumping faster and fuller, and his chest heaving, bellowing the night air in and out as if it were going to inflate him larger than his life had ever been. It even managed to squeeze out a couple of hurrahs before his knees finally bowed him out and Albert Barry collapsed in front of the statue. Where he sat to find his breath and then to brood.

Until he was graced by a full white moon that floated free of laundry lines, telephone lines, and TV antennae to hang above the statue's upraised arms. It was then he felt the moonlight soak the earth and heard seeds breaking open under him as if they were sprouting in a maze. As if they were moving under the fence and across the lane with roots stretching east to the Red River and north past Stein's Style Shoppe, City Butchers, past the movie house, and on till Main Street turned to highway and its ways were free of curbs and shops. Roots running west past Salter, MacGregor, McPhillips, King Edward Avenues to tie friendship knots with prairie grasses. Roots that would rumble south to break the walls of City Hall, to crack the Royal, the Imperial Bank of Commerce, and then the bars of the city zoo, and on to the swimming pools and patios of Tuxedo.

His ears were ready to hear the crack and split. His moist eyes were ready to see the sun wind up the world for one more turn. Albert Barry was ready for the most golden light to flow through the maiden's arms, opening every crusted heart, beginning with his own.

And for Old Man Werner's fence posts to come alive again and sprout young leaves; and Mrs. Klatt's sickly pigeons, bright as flames, to weave laurels above the street lamp; and pale Mrs. Nojuk's withered apple tree to bear children, who would dangle from every branch, their mouths singing out golden clouds of pollen.

But most of all, Albert Barry was ready for the young bean plants to climb up to the maiden whose pole had taken root so firmly in the earth.

THE GREEN INSECT

JOHN Steffler

I had a green insect, a kind that had never before
been seen,
descendant of an ancient nation, regal, rigid in ritual.

It would sun itself on my windowsill, stretching its legs
one by one, its hinged joints, its swivel joints, its
claws,
unfolding and folding its Swiss army knife implements.
It was ready for a landing on the moon.

Around my page it marched itself like a colour guard.
It halted, and its segments fell into place, jolting all
down the line.

It uncased its wings which glistened the way sometimes
very old things glisten: tortoiseshell fans, black veils,
lantern glass.

It was a plant with a will, an independent plant, an early
invention wiser than what we've arrived at now.
It was a brain coiled in amulets for whom nature is all
hieroglyphs.

People gawked, and a woman pointed a camera, and I
hesitated, but—I did—I held the insect up by its
long back legs like a badge, like my accomplishment,
and the air flashed, and the insect twisted and fought,
breaking its legs in my fingertips, and hung

lunging, fettered with stems of grass,

and I laid it gently down on a clean page,
but it wanted no convalescence,
it ripped up reality, it flung away time and space,

I couldn't believe the strength it had,

it unwound its history, ran out its spring in kicks and
rage, denied itself, denied me and my ownership,
fizzed, shrank, took off in wave after wave of murder,
and left nothing but this page faintly stained with
green.

REASONS FOR WINTER

NAOMI *Guttman*

I. PERSEPHONE

Mother, it's not as they say:
while your back was turned I prayed
for the ground to open
and the arm that took me down

was solid. The fruit his wet hand slit
—those tart red bombs he fed me—
converted me, their intelligence
so palpable I felt the sun in my throat.

II. DEMETER

After you vanished the sky
stayed blue, the fields unaltered,
but my mouth was a husk, my hands
a fever. Sheaf within my sheaf,
my single blond kernel, my skin
is helpless without you.

O earth, once teeming in my care, somewhere
you opened your muddy lips and drank her.
Until I know that chimney of loss
I will not trust you anywhere.

SLEEPING FIGURES

This is no trompe l'oeil, bronze-cast
couple on a crafted bench. No, this
is Venice Beach: he sleeps, stretched out—
she's slouched over, shell-bent, holding
his head in her lap. They are hatted,
scarved, ragged, and out cold this warm
spring afternoon. What faith in the world

or lack of it has led them here
to be watched over by the hawkers, gapers
kaleidoscope of skaters, crystal-readers, and
miraculous limbless dancers? And hours after
the last refugee brings down his stall,
packs away the final Chinese kite or pair
of espadrilles, will they be woken then
by headlights, hunger, or the cooling air?

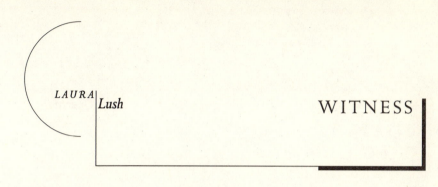

LAURA Lush

WITNESS

My father at 61
clings to this farm
like blood to an accident.
How for thirteen years he's tried
to make it work.
I watch his geese bobbing behind him,
the water balloons of their bodies
splashing forward, their necks
loose white springs.
Watch him chase his heifers
across the fields, his legs
graceful as a hockey player's.
And I watch him drive the tractor back
to the barn at night, hunched over,
the porch blossoming with moths.
But mostly I watch him watch
other farmers falling.
Their big hands
fold over their faces while
the earth tightens.

GIVING
SHAPE
TO GRIEF

SINA Queyras

#4

When I am afraid of solitude, I know it's time to be alone. Surrounded by chattering friends, muscles slacken. Discontentment is everywhere.

Instead of enjoying the magpies dancing under lodgepoles, I am desperate to share this with you. Listen. If suddenly you see a wing, listen.

Sometimes, when I sing, I think I have not loved enough. I long for prairie grass waving, a heart that huge, that open. Can it be like that for us?

If the eyes are the window to the soul, the feet are the porthole to the heart. Oil eucalyptus, cream: the heel is where the poem is.

I tell you, when I am older I will have a kayak and trace the coastline of my beloved, follow the whale's song, and become a rock to rub on.

#5

She has prairie grass in her hair, distant volcano mouth, ice receding from the
explosion of her heart. Traces of silt under her nails, smell of baked shark

in the softest consonants, in the skin and cells. She conjugates verbs, a desire
to connect selected historiography. Collage. A bruise of memory.

In my dream, I see her arc moonward, sorrow jet fuel, stardust, the afterburn
a trail of pastel flowers. And I know that memory is not a template.

Sometimes love is too complicated for wine-drinking or lovemaking. It is
best spent on hitchhikers and gardens full of beans and day lilies. Maybe

the trick is knowing what kind of love you have, what kind of wine to serve
with it, what kind of stranger you should offer your palms to. Or not.

#6

France, I have not seen your scar, only the fold in your shirt where
there was once flesh. Yet I feel it in my own breast, sudden and sharp.

I understand why you have let your hair grow. Celebrate and celebrate
the length of it. Let it go, grow luscious and wild. Uncontained.

My story of you has been so restrictive. Even in my encouraging,
I had a shape for you to grow into. O but to love, just to love, just to love

as you are. And I cannot look at knives now. Nor can I cut away a knot,
must undo and undo and undo till my fingers numb, heart is aching, heavy.

What does a breast weigh? Do you feel it there still? Or dream it
somewhere frozen and erect, lonely breasts, needing to be touched.

WHO SAYS
LOVE ISN'T
LOVE

WE DROVE OUT TO GLADYS AND LAL'S farm where Bess, of course, waited in the car. Must've got hot in there by three or so—there's no air conditioning in the old black Ford, and in the house we were sweltering even in front of the fan. But Bessie can sit out there for hours on end. She always does, with her tin of Almond Roca and her bag of crocheting and her women's magazine with its needlepoint patterns. You'd think she was an old lady. Someday, she explains if you ask her (if there's anyone left who hasn't asked her), she is going to learn needlework, and she has to find just the right thing to begin with. She sits there staring at those pictures for who knows how long, turning those curled pages. It'd take more than browsing through that one old magazine over and over again, if you ask me. But I wouldn't say that to her. Not on your life.

Why do you sit out there? I asked, exasperated.

Because I want to, she said.

Why do you want to? I said.

I don't have to justify my likes and dislikes to you, she said, all icicles and elocution. Now do I?

Nope, I said. Just curious.

Because I like to. That's all there is to it, she said. Promise.

I used to try to lure her out of the car when we went visiting. Nothing worked. Not a batch of new kittens. Not the smell of a saskatoon pie. Not the sight of the ice-cream churn. Not me with my pants down and my dick sticking right out with wanting. You name it, it wouldn't work. I got sick of the game. Even got peeved for a while before I got it through my thick skull that what I felt didn't make a difference to what she did. But it troubles me every time. What a thing, when my own wife won't visit with my sister. Downright awkward when family won't get along.

She's just selfish, said my sister Gladys. Never thinks of you; only thinks of herself. She's always been like that.

Don't you talk that way about Bess, I said. But in private I do wonder sometimes.

People are welcome to go out to Bess, welcome to get into our old black Ford, but they've mostly stopped doing that. She's holding her goddamn court again, Gladys says. To heck with that. My kitchen or parlour not good enough, to heck with her. Let her rot.

Bess sees herself as some kind of enigma, Lal says, when really she's just a big pain in the you-know-where.

In the ass, says Gladys. Right in the big fat ass.

Well, I didn't want to say that, says Lal, with a giggle.

I'll say it for you. We can all see it, says Gladys, who isn't exactly tiny herself. It's not anything that isn't true.

Hey, you two, I said, indignant. It is *not* a big fat ass.

Depends on what you like, I suppose, brother dear, says Gladys.

Well, what the hell else should it depend upon? Hm?

Rolling their eyes in tandem, the two of them say, Oh, Clare. Have another cookie.

Eventually, they got air conditioning out at the farmhouse, but Gladys and Lal didn't have even the idea of it that day. How to tell they're not your real farmers, but gentleman farmers, gentle*woman* farmers, I suppose is what you'd call them, although gentle ain't always the word for either one of them, particularly my sister Gladys. And not a hired man in sight. I suppose they might have a hired woman, if they could find one. Those two do everything, and I mean everything, public and private, by themselves. If you know what I mean. I'm not a one to go into details, you'll find.

So Bess was sitting out there in the car steaming like a Chinese pork bun. Some might call it stewing in her own juice. Could be that, too. Dumplings in a chicken stew. One heck of a cook she is when she wants to be, but don't count on it. She has subscribed to this *Gourmet* magazine for as long as I've known her, but if you go and count on sampling those fancy recipes, or make the mistake of picking out a picture and saying, How's about this one? you'll be getting macaroni and cheese before you know it. Hold off on the comments and she'll gourmand you to bursting with Cornish hens in raspberry what's-it-sauce and green beans armadillo like you never et in your life before. That's the way she is. Everything's got to be her idea even if it ain't. Makes for a somewhat precarious life sometimes, let me tell you. It's hard not to count on things when it's in your bottom nature to do so and you like a bit of security now and again. Makes me wonder how on God's green earth I ever allowed myself to get permanently tangled up with her. If I had a choice, that is. Which is another good question that's not likely to get answered.

I'll never forget the day—in Winnipeg, where I met her—that she took my two hands and placed them on her bosom. My face could've started a forest fire. One hand on each full, warm breast. I lost my balance and just about fell over when my knees buckled. Don't be such a chicken, she whispered, yanking me upwards by my wrists. Bock. Bock, she whispered, teasing. Chicky-chicky-bock-bock. Knead me, chook chook, she whispered. Knead me, you old rooster, you old cock, you old cock-a-doodle-do. I do, I said, gasping for air and shaking like crazy. That's not what I mean, she whispered, thrusting harder against me.

Oh, Bessie. Won't you please get out of that car?

So on this day, I sat inside with Gladys and Lal—they offered me the parlour, I said the kitchen's just dandy—we'd fall down dead if we didn't have this exchange every visit—and into the kitchen we go, where Lal has covered up the Arborite table with a clean terry cloth. Big pink and purple flowers on the one for today, and a couple of cigarette burns right where you can't cover them up with a doily without it looking peculiar, from when Gladys used to smoke and drink simultaneously. Nowadays, she won't touch either. And she's set the table for our tea. Lal's also not smoking today, I notice. The place smells different without it. Clean. Hopeful. Lal is getting a little paunchy, I see, but then hell, I've got a bit more around my middle now than I did when I was twenty, too. Bess, well, when I met Bess she had a stomach hard as rock from pushing her old man around in that wheelchair day after day, and she's always been one for sit-ups. Until recently, she'd tuck her toes up under the blue chesterfield in the bedroom and hoist herself up twenty, thirty times a day. With some things, she's like clockwork. With others, the mainspring is long gone and you can't hear a tick for love nor money.

There's always a teacup and a bread-and-butter plate laid for Bess, though the last time she set foot inside the house is anybody's guess. It was Bess who pointed out to me about those cups. Me, I wouldn't notice unless I got no cup at all, and even then it might take me a minute or two. Bess told me that Lal chooses the cups real carefully, that you don't need to read tea leaves to know what that little woman's thinking of you. You can tell from the cup in a second. Don't ask me how she figured all that out, but something tells me it figures in why she sticks to the car now. Bess told me, You can rest easy if Lal gives you the one with the little purple violets. You can expect to take some chewing out and up if you see the one with the Egyptian design round the top get set in front of you. Plain ochre's a snub, and look out for the navy cup with the blood-red trim and no flower. That's big trouble. That's mine, Bess said with a laugh. Tell her you want a different one then, I said. It doesn't work that way, said Bess. I don't know; I can't figure it out.

Lal and Gladys get ticked off about Bess's sitting in the car. Gladys did go out there once, and after a while we could hear her hollering through the glass of the window Bess had rolled up tight. Gladys was furious at being ignored. I thought she would bust the glass. I waved at her, said Bess on the way home, a little indignant. And smiled, sort of. I only started ignoring her when she wouldn't go away.

And today, Bess'll be interested to hear, everyone's cup is the same; it's their good china, with the garlands of fruit around the edges. Ain't Christmas, or Easter, or Thanksgiving. Everyone with the same cup, and the cream and sugar to match. What's this world coming to? And Christmas cake, even though it's mid-July, cut all nice and arranged so pretty on a serving plate that matches. I'm rattled by the sight, let me tell you. The layout reminds me of those tea parties people give after funerals. But I go along. Act calm, like there's nothing unusual. I'm wishing Bess was with me, I don't mind saying. Just to balance things a little. In the end, I act the way I do with one of Bess's escapades. Wait and see but don't take your shoes off and be prepared to bolt, because this may be the best time you ever had, or the worst.

Gladys and Lal aren't exactly sisters, or cousins, though they're closer than most of the ones I've ever known. Haven't had one without the other since they started to play in the dust when our families lived next door to one another after my dad came here looking for work and got some on the Macintosh farm. Lal's family was working there, too. Siamese twins, our mothers used to call the two little girls, though they hardly resembled each other. Have you seen the twins? one mother would call across the yard to the other. Where have those Siamese sisters got to? And then maybe someone would hear a giggle, and some little kitty mews, and out the two of them would crawl from someplace dusty and dirty, count on it. Here they are! Here they are!

Those two. They shared candies one of them had already sucked, licorice ropes, bottles of pop, you name it. Even gum one of them had already chewed—darn near made you gag to watch them pull the wet, gooey gob from one mouth and then stretch it into two pieces and pop the half of it into each of their mouths with their grubby fingers. And then off they'd go, grinning and chewing. Nothing ever belonged to just the one.

Funny, but sometimes they seem old, and other times they seem so young it's hard to believe. Easy as pie I can peg them as two old spinster ladies and next thing you know it's like they're eight years old, all surprised and thrilled with something silly. Come look, Gladys! Lal might call in from outside. Come see this ladybug! And Gladys will drop everything and go look, and the two of them will share the peering at this bug like it's the best thing that happened to them all day.

Gladys and Lal never really got a handle on Bessie, though to be fair, maybe no one could. And Lal and Gladys have been wrapped up in each other so tight from day one they've seldom had much use for anyone else their whole lives long anyhoodle. That isn't to say that they don't make time for family, don't make time for regular visits, and for helping out when they're needed. It's just that they prefer each other's company. And because Bess didn't come from around here—well, that always makes a difference, doesn't it? Did I say I met Bessie in Winnipeg? The finest woman

I ever set eyes on. I was a farm boy back then. Back then, I didn't know how to act proper in the town right near us, let alone in a big city like Winnipeg. "Hick" is what Bessie's father called me, right off. What's a hick like you doing in town? he asked, leaning forward so's Bessie could light his cigarette. Buying hayseed? he asked. Then he tried to laugh and commenced into choking. I never had no use for that man, I'll admit.

Bessie and I have attended just two funerals together. The first was his. He passed on a few years ago now, but his passing was a gift from heaven, as far as I'm concerned. Gifts come in strange packages sometimes, but I recognized that one right off. Though Bess didn't.

The aide the old man hired after Bessie wouldn't give me up for him (though she still spent most of her time over there) had wheeled him down to the duck pond before she left for the day. Parked him facing the water, beside the picnic table. He had a little dish of pebbles in his lap— he liked to tease the ducks, fool them into believing he was feeding them, and he'd laugh and hack when they'd dive for the bits of what they thought was bread. The old bastard tipped over when he was reaching for his cigarettes on the picnic table and went face first into the muck and stayed there. The neighbour found him, Player's packet floating a little ways off, him all covered in mud and duckshit, wheelchair on its side. Who lugged him up to the house and cleaned him off a little before Bess got there, I don't know. I never asked. Some things it's hard to care about. Some people are hard to care about when all they do is cause someone you care about endless grief. I knew right off Bessie would feel guilty about being with me—for not being there with the old man to pass him his goddamn cigarettes—until the day she died, even if I told her a million times what happened weren't her fault.

Bess is a gift, too, I've decided, though there's been plenty of times I'd have denied it. Gifts may not always be what you expect, or what you asked for, but who are you to say no thank you? It seems to me that there might be big trouble if you turn a gift away. Take them as they come, even when they're dressed up more like Trouble at first. They can turn out to be the best damn thing in your life, and then your biggest fear starts to be that someone might take that gift away.

She bought a gold chain with her inheritance, and she never takes that heavy bugger off. Spent everything he left her—which wasn't one whole hell of a lot—on that gold chain and six pairs of socks for me. I told her I wasn't interested in anything that came from him, no offence intended, him being her father and all, but that I hadn't had much use for him when he was living, so it wouldn't be right to change my tune now. If I spent it *all* on just me, I couldn't stand myself, she said when she handed me the six pairs of McGregor Happy Feet in six different colours. Now I can walk on that son-of-a-bitch *and* his grave, was the first thought that crossed my mind.

On this particular day, it's news that Gladys and Lal are wanting to share.

You tell him, says Gladys, after pouring the tea. She is breaking a piece of Christmas cake into little bits. Making a little pile of the nuts on her plate. Popping the bits of red cherry into her mouth. It was your idea.

You, says Lal, trying to keep her hands steady enough to get her teacup to her lips but spilling tea all over her hands and the tablecloth onto the sugar she already spilt. You're better at telling. And he's your brother.

No, you.

Somebody cough up the info, I say, giving my older brother cough. Get a move on, girls. Haven't got all day.

We intend to get married, says Lal.

Married!

Well, that threw me for a loop, let me tell you. I mean, we all know their ... what do you call it, situation, but I thought we were dealing with it the best we could already—being polite, making no big public mind or notice of it, that's for sure. And they weren't exactly all huggy and kissy in broad daylight on the main street, and they didn't wear funny clothes and hairdos the way those ones in the cities do, the ones you see on the TV. What's the word I'm hunting? Bess would know. Discreet. That's it. They were discreet so's that no one who didn't know them would know, and no one who did had to. Most liked to think of Gladys and Lal as real close friends, a couple of unmarried, almost middle-aged ladies sharing a house, that's all. Unlucky in love, or the right fellas just hadn't come along. And some folks still thought of them as the twins. There was lots who still called them the twins, me included. And Bess, too, though she had other names for them as well.

And what is wrong with the current way of life? I ask, as calm and casual as I can. Just why do you feel the need for public display? I'm not sure it's wise, I say. For you two. Right now. These days.

We love each other.

Well, I know that. Anybody with half a brain knows that.

We love each other like married folk love each other.

Well, I wouldn't know about that.

No, I expect you wouldn't, says Gladys looking me in the eye.

Lal nods, eyes cast down like some magazine blushing bride.

I'm not with Gladys because I couldn't get a man, says Lal in her small strong voice, her little hands all knotted together. But that's what people think. And I won't have them thinking like that if there's anything I can do about it. We're here because I love Gladys and Gladys loves me, and be damned anyone who says love isn't love unless there's opposites involved.

This time it's Gladys who nods, but her eyes look right at me. Be damned, she says.

Look, you two, I say, still trying to find the right position to take on this issue. People get married to have children. You're too old to have kids, even if you could figure out how to do it.

And you're getting too old for your own good, Clare, says Gladys, and Lal tee-hees in the background. You sound more like Daddy than you. "People get married to have children." Like you and Bessie, I suppose? You're a fine one to talk about kids. You and Bessie have had a whole flock now, haven't you?

Touché, I say.

Leave him alone now, says Lal. Don't go too far.

And anyway, who's to say we're too old to have children, says Gladys, softer now. That just might be in our plans too, if you must know.

As you can see, Gladys can be a little starkers with the truth. But she did let several years pass before she asked why Bess and I weren't reproducing. I told her about Bessie's visits to the city, to the specialist, after her father died. The doctor couldn't find nothing physical wrong. Figured it may be something psychological. But worrying would only make things worse, she said. Trying too hard could cause trouble between Bess and me. Try to find fulfillment in some other way, she said. Those were the very words.

You must be forty! I say. Next thing you'll be telling me you want a veil and Kleenex pompoms on the car and a reception where you tink the glasses with your fork and kiss every two seconds.

So what if we do?

I want a wedding dress, offers Lal.

So do I, says Gladys. They exchange looks.

We want *two* wedding dresses, says Gladys, and they start into laughing as though it's the funniest thing on earth. Both of them have to put down their teacups. The sides of my mouth start to twitch. The two of them all got up like they're playing dress up. I could picture that.

White?

That sends them into gales, and they carry me along with them. In a flash of sadness, I wish for Bess. She should be in here with us.

Whatever goddamn colour we want, with or without sequins and tassels, and whatever the hell else we feel like having, says Lal, barely breathing, tears rolling down her face.

This is unlike Lal, I should say. She isn't usually such a laugher. Never has been. And she's never been much of a one for mouthing off, neither. When we were kids, she was the one squatted in the dust watching the ants walk by. Gladys was the one squashing them.

You going to invite the whole town? I ask, doubtful. I'd hate to have their feelings hurt, but I can imagine what some of the neighbours might say, guests or not. Not everyone's aware of proper guestly behaviour, not when there's a chance for gossip. And this'd be a doozy of an occasion.

This time Lal does the squashing. Let 'em come and gawk, let 'em stay away, makes no mind to us, she says. We'll be doing the neighbourly thing and asking them; they can do the unneighbourly thing and decline the invite if they so choose. But our love, she said dramatically, won't be hidden no more.

And neither, adds Gladys, will our desire for a child.

Marriage? Children? What in the world had been going on around here? I stand up and go to the window. The car looks empty from here, though I know she's inside. I sit back down, eat another piece of cake.

If you don't mind my saying so, I offer, dusting cake crumbs off my hands and onto my plate, trying to stay calm, and act casual, there are some biological complications you need to consider before you attempt to have a child.

The two of them exchange a mischievous look and then Gladys says, We're already pregnant, if you really must know.

You might even say, smirks Lal, and they both giggle, that we *have* to get married. It's going to be a shotgun wedding. You got one you could loan us?

I don't know whose belly to glance at. This is too much for me. I go back to the window. This time I can see Bessie's white hand. She's holding up her thermometer.

This is one of the many interesting and unusual things about my Bessie. She carries that blamed thermometer with her wherever she goes. When I go out to the car to drive home, she'll tell me, It was ninety-seven degrees in here! Ninety-seven, Clare! And when we go in our front door, she'll set it on the mail table, say hello to Banana, our dog, come back, and tell me, It's seventy in here now, Clare. It was sixty-five when we went out. She has packed the thermometer around as long as I've known her.

When we went on the honeymoon, I knew it was seventy-four in the bedroom, eighty-five by the pool, and seventy-one in the restaurant. Our moonlight walk registered seventy-four. And three a.m. in our bedroom? Well. I tried to get her to rest the thermometer on her chest, but she wouldn't have none of it. You'll have to just guess how hot I am there, she said. And there. And there. About 180, I'd say, I whispered.

There we are, lying on our backs, sheers fluttering through the open French doors. Moonlight beaming. Us beaming. Thermometer rising. Me rising. What a night.

Oh, Bess.

I suppose you each have a baby in your belly, too? I say.

You're getting personal now, Clare, says Lal. Watch your tongue.

But what's the *answer?* I say. Who's carrying the little critter?

Wait and see, winks Gladys.

Time will tell, says Lal.

They exchange one of those looks full of love. Downright shining, they are, like Bess and me on our honeymoon. You know, it never ceases to amaze me how one look at Lal can soften that granite face of Gladys's and make it look almost human.

You just give it a rest, brother dear, says Gladys, and kisses me.

All this real-life family drama, and Bessie sitting out there with that tin of Almond Roca and a Thermos of lukewarm tea and probably sweating to death with the windows rolled up tight and her wearing black like she's more and more prone to do these days, even in this heat of summer. Ladies don't sweat, Bess would say if she heard me say that. All right, then, Bess. You're out there *glowing* all over, from armpit to thigh to crotch. And thumbing through that same old magazine for the umpteenth time while at home are stacks of brand new magazines she hasn't even touched. Oh, it's beyond me why she does that thumbing. Depresses me. I haven't told Lal and Gladys that Bess ain't feeling herself lately. Gets chills. Goes from hot to cold in no time at all.

Which reminds me of something. One August we had this fire at our place. That fire swept through our front hill and scared the bejesus out of us both and damn near took us and our house with it. What I'm getting at here is that that summer was followed by a brass monkey cold winter, and our house froze over. Froze solid while we were down at the coast visiting Marl and Byron. We came home to an ice palace, Bess called it, all the plants frozen solid and all the pipes burst, ice in the strangest shapes. Some like sculptures. The fish bowl, the fish, the shampoo, the bleach, and the strawberry liqueur in the liquor cabinet—you name it, it was froze. I built a big fire in the fireplace right off and that warmed things up in the living room. Bess sat in front of the fire on the hearth rug with a chopstick in one hand, the strawberry liqueur bottle in the other, digging out chunks of iced, pink liquor like a bear digging ants from a log. All bundled up with the car rug, and stark naked underneath. That way I couldn't ask her to help me with anything, was my guess for why she'd stripped off in thirty-three below. How can I help you when I'm in my altogether? You want me to freeze to death? You do, don't you?

Oh, yes. We know a thing or two about hot and cold, Bess and I do. In and out of her altogether.

Place and memory get stuck together sometimes, don't they? One calls forth the other and they mix into a round piece of experience you can hold in your hand like a small bird, or a little ball of wool. Time gets all jumbled.

Gladys had an illegitimate child when she was seventeen. Now that was a jumbled time. Gladys and Lal broke up—the only time they had a serious quarrel, and it lasted almost a year. Over the stupidest thing, least-ways in my opinion, and I'm not alone. The two of them were at the fall fair, and Gladys wanted to go up in the ferris wheel. Now Lal hates heights, and Gladys knows that better than I do. But something in her likes to try to make people do things they don't want to. Especially Lal. Nope, we're not going up in that, said Lal flatly. And Lal didn't want Gladys going up in it alone because she didn't want to be left on her own on the ground craning her neck to see Gladys sailing through the air in those big revolutions. But Gladys wanted to go, Gladys wanted to go. Kept hounding Lal, trying to ply her with cotton candy and hot dogs and more nickels for the digger machine, but Lal would have none of it. Nice, quiet, but No.

In the end, while Lal was visiting the ladies' room, Gladys walked up to two perfect strangers and asked if one of them would go up with her in the ferris wheel while the other one waited below with Lal. Lal was some mad when she came out and saw Gladys with those boys. Stood there burning while she was told what had been decided and arranged, and as soon as Gladys and the one fella were in the seat and the bar had been snapped into place in front of them and the fella had his arm across the back of the car, Lal took off. Went home, and wouldn't have nothing more to do with Gladys. Gladys stayed stubborn, too, and ended up getting in thick with this fella—to irritate Lal further is my best guess—and what happened next is as common as scarlet runner beans, so it don't need expounding upon. She stayed at home while the baby grew inside her, and right next door Lal fooled around by herself and kept on going to high school. She got good grades, spending all that time alone with nothing much to do but study. There's a good side to everything, if you can just figure out what it is. After the child was born, it was put up for adoption and the afternoon of the day she signed the paper, Gladys and Lal were out walking together again, arm in arm, Gladys walking a little slow because of the stitches she had someplace female, and little Lal seeming to offer her support.

Well, goodbye, Gladys, Lal. Best of luck, and thanks for the tea.

I get in the car and unroll all the windows so's I can breathe a little. As we pull away, I say to Bess, Well, Gladys and Lal had some big news.

Oh? said Bess, putting down her magazine and stretching her legs out in front of her. I don't need to look in the rear-view mirror to know what's she's doing. She's putting away that magazine, sweeping crumbs off her lap, checking her thermometer one more time. Next, she'll lean forward and rest her head on the back of the front seat. If she's missed me, she'll run a finger across the back of my neck and around my ear and I'll know what we'll be up to as soon as we get home.

Clare, guess what the temperature is?

I don't know what it is, Bessie, but listen to this. We're out of the driveway now, and heading down the road.

It's ninety-three in here, Clare. Or it was until you got in.

Bess. I got some news. But first I'm going to say right off, and I know you aren't going to like it, that you should have been in there to hear this. Those two are your family, like it or not, because they're my family, and what I'm going to tell you is family news. It pained me that you weren't in there to hear. Gladys is real important to me. You know that.

I hear you, Clare.

Now, here's the news. Gladys and Lal are going to be married.

Married? says Bess, sitting forward just like I knew she would. I smile to myself.

Married? To whom? Clare? Whom to?

Each other, I say. Don't that beat all?

Doesn't that beat all.

That too, I says. And *that* ain't all.

Isn't.

One of them's got a bun in the oven.

A *what?*

Maybe both of them, for all I know. Knocked up. You know. Pregnant.

In the old days, Bess would be hitching up her dress and climbing into the front seat to hear me better. But she just leans more forward.

A *baby?* Which one of those dykes would sleep with a man, do you suppose?

My Bess may be feeling poorly these days, but she still has her tongue, by God.

They're not divulging that part. But, Bess—how the hell would they have wangled it?

I can see Bess's face without even looking. That's one of the good parts about being with someone so long, getting to know them so well. Almost makes me want to pull over by the side of the road and watch her precious face as she turns the question over in her mind like it's a chunk of conglomerate rock.

Maybe a turkey baster. I've heard they use those. But whose?

Whose what? Turkey baster? For what?

Oh, Clare. Dear. Sometimes you are so very dense.

And now her finger traces my collar, and I start to feel real good. I press down on the accelerator.

Well, I guess you want to know what happened in the end, don't you? You want to know was there a wedding, and so on. Well, yes there was. Some folks came, and some folks didn't, as could be expected. Gladys and Lal had to bring in a special preacher all the way from Vancouver, but he seemed a nice enough fella. And who was pregnant? Well, it *was* both of them, though the Lord only knows how they did it. They'll be having them any day now.

In the end, it was Bessie and our car that wore the white, not the two brides, in their magenta and their turquoise. In fact, I can picture the wedding as I sit here waiting on Bess—she wants me to take her into town, and I'm happy to oblige. She hasn't been too well lately.

Bess has me buy yards of white netting, and yards of white satin—and I can't figure out what the hell she's up to. The night before the wedding, she's up half the night—she decks our black car out in a big white hat, with netting over the whole goddamn thing like its face, and you have to lift this enormous veil to get inside. We drive at about five miles an hour, like we were a hearse, not part of a wedding party, all the way to the park, where the wedding is held. Bess gets me to pull right up close to the gate, near the garden. So's she can come in if she should so desire, I figure, hope springing eternal. But it's a pretty small trickle after all this time, let me tell you.

I leave her in the car, and join everybody else, and start doing my best man bit. We're about smack in the middle of the ceremony when out of the corner of my eye I see the car door open, and my heart leaps like a trout. Can't believe I'm right for once. Can't believe that miracles *do* happen. I'm the only one who sees, and I tell you, it's the happiest day of my life. I see Bessie get out, climb into Gladys and Lal's old station wagon, start it up, and drive out of the park. I see her take off the JUST MARRIED sign and put it on our car, and park it where the wagon was, for the newlyweds to get into when they leave the garden.

What a gal. Who'd dare to call her selfish now?

Then Bess damn near floats over to the high bank of rhododendrons, the ones the colour of orange sherbet, and stands there, by herself. You'd think she'd chosen her lipstick especially; it goes so well with the flowers. And I can see how the heavy leaves cast shadows on her pretty face when she moves farther into the foliage and crouches down, in her white silk shift with its long slit up the side. That thick gold chain disappears between those satin breasts. She almost looks as though she's peeing, but she ain't; she's just resting.

I'm still the only one who notices her. My Bessie's a knockout, and my eyes are drawn back to her again and again. I can see her now, in fact, as I sit here alone. In that bank of big orange blossoms and the big green leaves. I see her standing there until the service is over, and the confetti's flying, and then I see her motion, with her long sherbet fingers and lips, and her precious silken hips, for me to join her. And you can bet I oblige.

CHETAN *Rajani*

THE
SACRIFICE

For beyond time he dwells in these bodies, though these bodies have an end in their time; but he remains immeasurable, immortal. Therefore, great warrior, carry on thy fight.

—KRISHNA TO ARJUNA, *The Bhagavad Gita*

WHO KNEW WHERE IT CAME FROM, the rock that broke the wheel?

One minute Arjuna was jogging through the *maidan*, hauling the rattling, jouncing rickshaw over damp, rutted grass—carefully, because the woman in back, his wife, was pregnant. He was hauling, his face grimaced against the fine sharp rain, squinting through the morning gloom at the blurred horizon of the city beyond the field. He was picturing the havoc that rain would play on their shack in the shantytown, how leaks in the new, corrugated-iron roof he'd recently scavenged would allow the rain to soak through their meagre bedrolls.

Then up ahead, he saw the great white tent, rising.

And even as he slowed, surprised, and swerved—he had expected something more permanent, a brick building at least, and Krishna, the friend and fellow *rickshaw-walla* who had told him of the organ-donor clinic had made no mention of a *tent*—even as he glanced back at Puja, bouncing on the cracked leather seat in the stiff, prayer-like pose suggested by her name, and even as he took in her distended belly—that constant foreground in his mind these days—and altered his course, there came a soft explosion and the singing sound of metal against stone, and he knew the wheel was broken.

He felt himself thrown, dragged up and away. But somehow, with the instinct that daily saved him from mishap on the streets, with the iron legs and back and arms he'd earned from ten long years plying his trade over the length and breadth of the city, he righted and stopped the lurching vehicle.

Panting, Arjuna looked over his shoulder, stared dumbly at the sharp, wet grey protrusion in the grass—where had *that* come from? He could have sworn he was looking ...

Wincing, he stared at the wheel—aluminum rim bent beyond repair, spokes snapped and twisted, tire shredded. A soft moan broke in his throat as he mentally calculated the cost of this ... this ... *calamity*, and he cursed silently.

It was an omen.

He should never have listened to Krishna. Krishna with his crazy schemes to break free of the chiselling rickshaw company and the shanty-town by selling stolen watches, dropping parcels for men of dubious character. Selling his own body parts! He was a fool for having allowed himself to be seduced by Krishna's fantasies, by his visions of a life free from the daily, drenching grind of hauling fat merchants and their spoilt children up hills and down. How could he have been so stupid as to dream that just once at day's end, just once, his cold enamel bowl might contain beside a heap of rice and *dahl* perhaps a few curls of meat?

He cursed Krishna—in spite of his name. *That* Krishna, who had assumed it his *duty* to instruct him on matters great and small ever since he discovered the divine coincidence of their names, that Krishna was no god. Arjuna remembered how he had stood in the company lot the week after his operation, shaking, his scaly dark hand pressing the bloodstained bandage at his side even as he urged him, Arjuna, to follow his path: "Anything they want, you give them, *yaar*—except your heart, ha-ha—just take the money and run, away from this fucking exile. Go back to your *gaam* and buy a bit of land, and you and yours can loaf and work in the fields forever."

As for that *other* Krishna, that great blue-skinned lord and charioteer, that preacher of duty and *karma* who had forsaken him so long ago ...

He thought of turning back, then he glanced at Puja, sitting anxiously with a hand on her belly, and he began unharnessing himself. Slowly, he shrugged off the damp straps that were cutting into his lean, hard sides, and let down his yoke.

Puja, his constant curse and complaint, his sole consolation and companion these days, sat mute, as was her way, awaiting instructions. A bitterness rose from his stomach. Looking away, toward the broken wheel, he snarled, "Get down, *na!* Don't understand anything? Wheel is broke! Have to walk now!"

Then, watching as she struggled to stand, as she rearranged the shoulder-fold of her faded green *sari* and tentatively poked her head out the black shell of the rickshaw's canopy—only to be rudely spattered on the face by a drop of rain and to retreat, frowning and confused—he sighed. "Head cover, *na*—raining out," he said, a little less gruffly, as he watched her step carefully down from the awkwardly leaning vehicle, and walk up to him.

As they left the broken rickshaw behind and began walking, trudging through the slippery grass, Arjuna suddenly became aware of the presence of others in the rain-misted field, ghostly men and women and children in varied states of dereliction converging upon the great white tent. This is a dream, he thought, this field, these people, the tent—an endlessly familiar dream. Crowding with the others at the damp slit of the tent entrance— Krishna had said *nothing* about a tent—Arjuna realized that it was *this* that had caused the wheel to break, this sight of something from his past that had made him look up from the ground before him. But even as he pondered this, they were inside, and suddenly, as though the entrance were a great sieve, the chaos of their arrival was strained into order. White-clothed men and women, dazzling among their ragged clients, bustled about, barking orders: "Donors in this line for forms! Everyone else wait *there!* Donors, *this* line!"

Arjuna gestured for Puja to follow the people shuffling toward the waiting area. Inhaling sharp, tinctured air and sawdust, he glanced at the shadows on the canvas walls cast by the passage of donors moving against the temporary lights mounted on low stands, how the effect it created was that of multitudes waiting in the tent. Then he joined the staggering line of donors that ended at a low, stage-like platform where more white-clad men and women stood before folding tables, offering pens, and forms mounted on boards.

Waiting, he slipped into his road trance—the sight of his feet, the packed-dirt floor, everything else a blur around him. Hardly a minute seemed to pass before he was standing at a table, a moon-faced woman breathlessly explaining it all to him: what he could expect for which organ; what he was required to do—check-ups, tests—the nature of the surgery. He realized that as she spoke, she was quickly, matter-of-factly, appraising his body with her large kohl-lined eyes. And he noticed how, for an instant, those eyes held on to his powerfully chorded legs, and he felt a smile crack his face. Then he became aware of the rain-chill shaking his body, and that old pain in the groin muscles beneath his *dhoti*, and he looked away. And like a wealthy hostess in a film passing a plate of sweetmeats to a guest, the woman held out a form and pen.

"Quite easy," she said, pointing to some lines on the bottom of the page. "If you still want, then sign right there."

Just then there was a commotion up ahead. Behind him, Arjuna sensed the line of shuffling donors freeze, hush. The murmuring waiters also ceased. He looked up. At the head of the line was a plump dark man in a white suit with a stethoscope dangling from his neck. The man was howling at an orderly standing with his head cast down: "*Arré saala duffor!* How many time I have to tell you! One at a time. *One – at – a – time!* What, you think I have four hands?"

Pen in hand, nib hovering tremulously over the various lines and amounts on the release form, Arjuna numbly wondered how it would feel to go under the knife. He glanced again at the fat man, noting his thick glaring spectacles, his flushed cheeks, and fallen forelock, the sheer, unremitting indignation on his face. He knew the type well—always late, always in a hurry, mean tippers. That kind. Pious, educated bastards. He heard the moon-faced woman sigh, but he could not stop staring—there was something about this man, something very familiar, only he could not recall what.

And then, suddenly, he could: a night long ago when he was a child, the night of the Monkey Boy and the full moon. And, for a moment, he was there, standing—another field, another tent. Waiting.

It began like every other night.

They reached the new place, a little town named Lokh, just before sundown. As usual, Balraj, his mother's lover, drove the decrepit, farting truck fast around the town square, with Ghomti, his mother, bouncing in the cab beside him. Arjuna, eight then, and the long-haired man he knew as Rishi, stood in back amid their tent gear and folding chairs, clinging to the guard rails for dear life, shouting "Secrets of Immortality! Secrets of Immortality! Come see!" as they searched for—and soon found—a likely field in which to pitch their tent for the show tonight.

The town folk, mostly men, began trickling in soon after, drawn across the fields to the large tent by the kerosene lamps Arjuna and Rishi had mounted on the entrance poles. Each was greeted warmly by Balraj— Arjuna and the others out of sight now as instructed—and quickly seated inside. The Monkey Boy, giggling, riding on the shoulders of his fat father who was jiggling and panting from the jog across the *maidan*, was the last to arrive.

Arjuna, crouched out of sight in the truck, watched with fascination the antics of the Monkey Boy as the father tried to lower him to the ground: he was squealing and squirming, snagging his little slippered feet in his father's billowing, white silk *kurtha-pyjamas*. "Come down, you little monkey!" the bespectacled Brahmin said, mock sternly, "Come down, you!"

But the Monkey Boy gurgled, "No! *No!*"

Balraj, who had been changing behind the tent, rushed out, impatiently buttoning his shirt to conceal the welted scars on his torso. "*Arré sahib*, what are you doing? This is no place for young ones!" he hissed. But the father brushed past him, the Monkey Boy now clinging to his side, and strode into the murmuring tent.

"You know best, motherfucker," Balraj said under his breath as he hurried over to check on Arjuna. "*Aai!* Ready?" he asked, leaning over the guard rails and smacking Arjuna across the head. As usual, Arjuna noticed that Balraj had quickly looked about to ensure his mother was not around to witness this act. Balraj had instituted this precaution after Ghomti once caught him calling Arjuna a bastard, and made him sleep in back with Rishi for an entire week. Since then, his usual swearing and cursing had escalated to randomly administered, unprovoked attacks—stolen slaps, pinches, and shoves, accompanied by threats of graver consequences if Arjuna dared squeal.

Arjuna reacted appropriately: nodding eagerly, and whispering smartly, "Yes, Balraj Uncle!"

He began unbuttoning his frayed, torn shirt as Balraj's thin shadow of a body disappeared around the tent. Then he climbed out of the truck and ran over the dry, cracking grass to the entrance, and stripped off his pants. From the familiar, anticipatory hush that had muffled the audience of humble and guileless peasants inside, Arjuna could tell that things were going according to plan. He balled up his clothes, shoved them under the tent, and quickly drew the stiff and mouldy, dirt-reddened entrance flap around his bare body—to conceal his shame, to protect himself from the cool night breeze.

Always, he saw the show's opening through the audience's eyes, and tonight it was no different, at least at the start.

At first, there was only a solitary figure standing on the right side of the low, dimly lit, makeshift stage on the tent floor: an old-looking man in a white *dhoti* and waistcoat, with short hair and lensless black spectacles, all of which, from a distance, created an image subtly reminiscent of the great *Mahatma*. In his right hand, the man held a gleaming copper pot. With dramatic solemnity, he strode to the centre of the stage, where a large white circle was crudely painted on the boards, and began pacing its circumference. After three slow rounds, he dipped the fingertips of his left hand into the pot and began flicking water and rose petals into the circle.

A low, wailing, Sanskrit incantation rose from stage right and climaxed with an "Ommm." Then, on a second, piously intoned "Ommmm," a new man appeared on stage. He was dressed in a voluminous saffron-coloured robe, long oiled hair hanging loose. Except for a pencil-line moustache above his thick, red-stained lips, he looked every bit the holy man. This man walked slowly to stage right and stood there, quietly facing the audience. Suddenly his eyeballs rolled upward, until only the bulging whites of the orbs were visible, and his long-lashed eyelids commenced to flutter. The first murmur that always—momentarily—broke Arjuna's trance, slid through the small audience like a snake. Arjuna shivered and looked over his shoulder, across the dark *maidan* to the luminous white circle of the moon in the blue evening sky. Always, he saw something new etched on its gleaming grey-white belly—a coveted toy car, coloured chalk and slate, candy. This time, it was a red bicycle of the sort he had seen under a town boy earlier. Arjuna returned his gaze into the tent, stage left, toward the kerosene lamp hanging from a supporting post. The wick, as usual, was set low, and the moths were out around it. He saw them as the peasants might—patterns of white dots floating through the dim light, randomly colliding against the lamp in odd concert with the breathing of the tent sides in evening breeze. The mosquitoes, too, were out now, inciting the peasants to abruptly slap their heads and faces and bodies as they watched the stage, rapt, their breathing shallow with anticipation.

Now a woman in a widow's white cotton *sari* demurely entered the scene from stage right, her shoulder-fold modestly covering her head, though leaving visible a glistening, taut, honey-gold midriff that immediately drew all eyes across the dark space. She paused by the circle, hesitated, then eased into it sideways, and positioned herself to face the audience, knees drawn up, covered legs spread apart.

The old man, looking quietly on now, absently adjusted his *dhoti*, and, seemingly by accident, flashed his strong, dark, oiled thighs. He eased a foot beneath the woman's *sari* and slowly raised the hem.

A short, sudden moan escaped the collective mouth of the audience. Rusty folding metal chairs scraped, as heads collided, vying for an unobstructed view of the dark triangle between the woman's legs before the old man stepped closer and obscured it.

Abruptly, he dropped to his knees, a thud rattling the loosely secured wood planks and pipe scaffolding that formed the stage, and held the woman in a slow, leaning embrace.

A commotion jostled the audience, as it always did at this point in the show. Stage left, saffron robe's eyes began fluttering even more wildly, the white orbs struggling against their natural inclination to lower. Arjuna searched for the source of the disturbance: the white-suited man with the Monkey Boy on his lap. Monkey Boy's father, an odd frown now fighting the smug expression on his face, was attempting to rise from his seat in the middle row, but his neighbours on all sides were shushing and cursing and jerking him back into place.

The old-looking man paused in his embrace to glare over his shoulder. Arjuna caught the movement and swallowed: he had missed his cues—

both of them. He ran down the side aisle in a panic, and jumped on the stage, and faced the crowd. On the floor beside him, the couple's embrace was reaching an intensity rarely attained at this point in the show. The woman's face, as always, was averted from him. Arjuna felt desperate. He looked at the audience again, and as he had done countless times before—as he'd been trained to do, over and over again—he searched for that one simple, credulous face upon which to focus. But the only faces he could fix upon were that of the fat father with the wild, unravelled expression, and the Monkey Boy, red-faced, squirming. Arjuna was fascinated by the father's strained determination to hold his son in place, to lock his flailing arms between his elbows, and block the boy's ears and mouth and eyes.

Arjuna remembered the early days in the *e-school* he had attended once, long ago, before his own father disappeared mysteriously and Balraj arrived and talked his mother into joining the show. He remembered the chalk-dusted grey stone statue of three squatting monkeys on the pedestal beside the blackboard, one covering its eyes, the second its ears, and the third its mouth.

"Start or I'll skin you alive!" he heard Balraj hiss.

Arjuna gulped a breath and brought his palms together in the air above him, hard, for the sharp, resounding clap that always smarted for hours afterward. He aimed for his best voice—that eerie, sepulchral tone Balraj had taught him to use, only to croak his opening line: "I am the magic child whom this holy couple will conceive ... "

Chuckles and laughter that were not supposed to be there—*never* supposed to be there—rippled through the crowd. Arjuna lost control over the next part of his act. Words whose meaning he'd never understood to begin with, words whose sounds he would never have produced at all but for Balraj's and Rishi's coaching, and all those dramatic gestures he was only just beginning to refine, all emerged jumbled.

"I will not grow up happy like you on a farm but suffer great ... great hardship! In the great city—alone! One day ... I will a holy man meet ... teach me spells—meditations and chants that I will p–p–practise by the river until I can turn my eyes deeply inward and find inside me the seed of the light of God! I will blow on this light, no: I will, this ... this light will suddenly become very big and I will have freed the yoke—no, broken the yoke of human ... I will have powers unlimited, ov–ver death! Even over death!"

He tried to ignore the laughter—it was never like this, it was *not* supposed to happen. He became aware of the couple in the circle who were now entering the furious, quivering stage of their embrace, the one they were not supposed to reach until much later, until after the moths.

The moths. He looked toward Rishi in his orange robe. The crowd was restless now, their laughter mixed with menacing murmurs, a few shouts. Just then, he heard his mother emit a long shuddering moan, the kind she only used when things were going astray in the show. And Arjuna knew they were close to the sort of trouble Balraj always cited when admonishing him over some error in their rehearsals, the nasty kind of trouble a crowd could bring when little boys made stupid mistakes. Another moan broke free from his mother's mouth; the boards rocked furiously, the way the truck always rocked nights as he was trying to find sleep.

Unbelievably, the crowd quieted, eyes returned to the stage—all except the fat father's, whose face was averted now, and the Monkey Boy's, whose eyes and mouth and ears were all successfully blocked. Out the side of his eyes, Arjuna noticed that Rishi was moving forward now.

Instead of holding the crowd with his eyes, as he was supposed to, instead of preparing for his next lines, Arjuna watched. He could not help it.

Rishi stepped out of the halo of light cast by the moth lamp. His eyes ceased fluttering and his eyeballs returned to their normal position. Then, dramatically, he thrust out his fists, and his robe was all aglow. Quickly, he pointed to the lamp. All eyes followed. The other hand slowly dropped to his side, slid behind his back. The moths, chaotically swirling about the lamp, merged into a rough formation and flew toward Rishi's finger.

The crowd was rapt again—every one except the Brahmin and the Monkey Boy. Arjuna even noticed some mouths hanging open. He stared at the father, whose head was hanging low now, resting against his son's cheek.

Then Rishi snapped his fingers and the moths dropped dead to the stage. The crowd gasped. Rishi brought his hands together in a loud clap and the lantern guttered. Then, like the glow in his robe, it too was extinguished, leaving the tent in darkness. A moment later, the lamp burned anew, but now Rishi was gone, an iridescent afterimage hovering in the place he had stood moments ago.

The two in the circle abruptly ceased their thrashing. Arjuna heard Balraj's whisper, "End, you bastard! And don't ruin this time!"

Arjuna passed over the introduction to Rishi's lecture on the secret teachings and went directly to the ending he had been taught to use if things went wrong: "Now I have been conceived by this holy couple. I will grow up unfortunate, but it will not matter because my sorrow will become my path to powers beyond belief, power over death itself. Anyone doubts the truth of this prophecy, can leave now. Those who are ready for the secret benediction that will start them on this holy path also, stand now, and bow your heads! The Holy Mother and Father will bless you on the way out!"

Arjuna watched now as the Holy Mother and Father stood, and quickly straightened their clothes—slapping off dust and rose petals—and dashed past him to the entrance flap. The crowd, miraculously, exhibited a range of reactions not much different from other nights: a few seemed offended or disgruntled, but most were already reaching into their pockets.

"It's a good show—something for everybody. No matter which part they like, something always goes into Holy Mother's pot. Right, Holy Mother?" Balraj always said each night after the show, and always, he was right. Relieved, Arjuna jumped off the stage and ran across the tent to a place where there was a tear in the canvas through which he could exit, ahead of the crowd.

Outside, he hid by the truck and waited for a glimpse of the Monkey Boy and his father in the dispersing crowd. When he saw them, he noticed that the Monkey Boy, being dragged along by his father, was softly crying. Away from the crowd, the fat man paused. He stooped and said something into the boy's ears. The Monkey Boy nodded. And the father gently picked him up and sat him on his shoulders again. The Monkey Boy, knuckling his eyes dry, ceased his crying and heaving; and as they set off across the field into the cricket-punctured darkness, he looked up and pointed at the moon.

Arjuna, too, stared at the moon. Then Rishi appeared beside him, attempting to remove from his fingers the last tangled strands of the black string with which he accomplished his feats on the stage. And when he was done—shaking them off impatiently—Arjuna felt a heavy hand clamping down on his shoulder. He allowed the big man to jerk him around and haul him away to the entrance, where the other two now stood, swirling the copper pot around and around and staring into its dark mouth as though it already contained the *dahl* and rice they would not have until they were well beyond the limits of the town and, possibly, the local constabulary.

Meanwhile, there was much dismantling to do, and quickly.

But there was also just enough time for a beating.

And such a beating it was!

Kicks, punches, slaps, and pinches, all delivered with grunting vehemence and curses. And when his mother seemed to remember that she was his mother, and intervened, she got it, too, worse than he did.

The only thing that kept his pain bearable was the sight of the moon—for the first time, without a picture—the moon shining like a tarnished silver coin in the sky, and the hope that in the next town it would be the old moon again.

Towns came and went, but the moon was never the same.

Beatings, too, came more frequently, but each time his mother intervened, and each time she took the brunt of it. Now, standing in the great white tent, Arjuna remembered her final night, a night a few years after the Monkey Boy: he, Arjuna, standing over a ditch on a stretch of moonlit road; his mother in the ditch, round-bellied and bleeding; the truck roaring off into the horizon. He remembered other shows, other Balrajs and Rishis, other cities—all different yet all the same. He remembered other mothers. And all those people seemed to teem within him, a grotesque, convulsing monster, driven by some unseen necessity, rushing heedlessly toward some unnameable end. And Arjuna felt something rising inside him, rushing to spew out through his mouth.

Again the moon-faced woman cleared her throat. Arjuna looked at the fat doctor, who was quiet now, inhaling deeply and staring defiantly back at the watchers. And he thought about leaving, about getting the rickshaw to the company repairshop, but all he could think of was the time it would take to pay off the broken wheel, and what he would have to look forward to after that: years and years of carrying fat, *ghee*-fed people on his back, hauling them to the very ends of the earth for his living. Again, he thought of the knife, how it would feel to go under it, to have them cut a slit in his side; how it would feel to walk about with something missing inside. And he wanted to hurl the form at the moon-faced woman. But somewhere, in the back of his mind, Krishna's voice was saying *Give it to them, yaar, what does it matter?* and his mother's moan, *No! Don't! Stop! Don't hit anymore!* And he remembered Puja and turned toward her. She was staring at him with those cow-like eyes, hands bracing her back the way she had taken to doing after she felt something move inside. And he thought about the child within, squirming as though he couldn't get out into the world fast enough, get out and roar into his life like an out-of-control truck, like some calamity he would be helpless to stop.

He remembered the boy on the red bicycle, the little town with the letter writer under the tree in the square, and the way the fields and the river looked with the moon rising, and he wondered what it would be like to live in such a quiet and gentle place.

His fingers, gripping the pen—that unfamiliar object—felt numb. He swallowed, then carefully signed his name on the line beside the largest amount, and handed the board and pen back to the woman. Immediately, he felt lighter—the ache in his leg, aches everywhere, were gone. And he felt buoyed by this. It felt the way it did at suppertime, with his sore and aching back pressed against some smooth cool wall, the sights and sounds and smells of the shantytown a distant, gentle murmur around him. It felt like the end of a long hard day, only better.

LIZ *Ukrainetz*

LOWER CASE (ALPHA)

AT THE BEGINNING OF THE ARC, where the teacher places the fat pink chalk on the unerasable lines drawn just-so and just so high on the chalk board, a quiver runs through our collected bodies. This is the beginning. My own tongue, sitting loose in my mouth, curls thick at the back of my throat, hooked somehow, along with the *a* she is about to draw. My tongue is also hooked on her fingers, her hand folded around the chalk, the dusty anticipation of show and tell. The back of my tongue catches like choking and my eyes are too wide, waiting for her to begin.

Then she does it, her hand uncurls, the tail of *a*, and my own tongue releases the sound as she speaks, drawing dust on the shine-black surface. The classroom is just me and her then; all the other children disappear, as I struggle to understand. My ears are filled with her sound, her mouth; and her hand is far away on the board, her eyes indicating something in the draw and drawing—a circle and a stick—that will make me know what is most important to her; more important than this sound we both know and share, this *aaaaaa*, broken away from the flow of talk-talk. She indicates what she needs from me and I watch, so eager for her sight that the stick and circle drift away, drift right out of the room.

The articulation that arcs and gathers the point of the tongue against the top edge of teeth. How the sounds, in the linguistic textbook, begin to make it clear: Why is a vowel a vowel? Who in what classroom of which school building designated the *a–e–i–o–u* of letters to be placed aside, separated off, learned on their own away from the consonants? I thought it was their roundness (you can always roll a vowel, even the *i* has its dot), their smallness, and I couldn't tell why they were scattered across the alphabet with no discernible pattern. Why not group them together, at the beginning, the middle, or the end, so they can be apart within? Why separate them out to be grouped together and alone at the side board of the classroom where they can learn to be identified on sight.

soft *c*, hard *c*

the evocative and usable *s*

the simplicity of the small *l*

the almost sacrilegious *t*

Twenty years later, I find it is the toothless, lipless, almost tongueless vowel set aside—an inherent, maybe arbitrary, segregation—for the thick root of muscle at the back of the throat.

Teacher points the yellow rubber-tipped pointer at the pink chalk shapes, this failure of a drawing which is not a picture of anything, not a house or a cat or a hat. Then she breaks a sound away from speech. She willingly takes the world apart, piece by piece, making a tool of everything she can lay her mind on. Teaching me how. I mimic and I try to understand what she needs, but, more deeply, I understand that the effort is hopeless. My eyes that reach her eyes across the room, encourage her to try, try harder, to make me understand what it is that could be more important than she and I, here in the same room, speaking fluently the same language, already engaged in the unspoken conversations of emotion.

BUILDING MARRAKESH

LAURA IS STILL A YOUNG WOMAN when she arrives in Marrakesh, well into the evening, in the longest light of spring. Just beyond the town limits, she pulls off the road onto the wide shoulder, grinds the stiff gear into park. Stretching, yawning, she loosens the scarf from her sticky hair and takes inventory. Gasoline receipts. The shoes on her feet, unlaced. A cedar-lined trunk containing clothes and some books and a pocket knife still in its box. These are her possessions now.

Seven kilometres from Marrakesh, on the road to Taroudannt.

Down the road, headlights flare then disappear, and for an instant, from all directions, hers is the only car. She lifts the latch, presses the door open, ducks her head outside. The freshly paved road is a flawless black cord uncoiling into the middle distance. She rubs her eyes, checks her watch: seven forty-five. The luminous second hand performs a full revolution as she steps out of the battered borrowed car and pauses, her body and breath suspended in the levelling light.

The sky is ablaze as the sun sets, browed by the Atlas Mountains.

She stands there for a long while, as insects metal-blue and gauze melt into the dusk, and here or there the sky reaches back for a misplaced shard of light. She watches, listens, feeling for the pulse of this place. To the east, the crowded rivers; to the west, the scalloped hills. Above her, a wide copper sky, exhausted in recent days by hard heavy rain. Everywhere the cormorants, smooth-diving black chevrons. She can smell the sumac, hear the offbeat clatter of mountain goats, feel the sedimented soils beneath her feet, steeped in spice and ancient bodies, and maps long ago torn up.

Behind her in the shadows, through a path in the slumping grasses, someone's radio begins to play hot music, headlines, traffic bulletins, still-warm images of home. A newswoman breathlessly announces a tumbling Dow index; a weatherman forecasts night upon night of sea-borne storms.

Outside the ochre ramparts, the rhythm is broken, the colours change.

"Where will I take you?" Peter Michael asked her once. He smiled rivetingly, and offered the words with that look and that tone that meant, I will take you anywhere.

Marrakesh, Laura thought then, Marrakesh! But she told him that he needn't do that for her. And later she grew to understand that his offer, like her demurral, had its terms.

"Well, I'm free now," she says aloud. "Out of reach. I'm out of reach!"

The city shunts off its slumber. Just as it has done for more than 800 years. The morning call of the muezzin going out from the 70-metre-high Koutoubia, the spiritual beacon of Marrakesh.

The night ripens, heavy and hanging and almost too rich—the air seems to thicken and bend. She leans back against the hood of the car, hands along the fender, blending its warmth with the heat of emergence, impatient for the new sun; no need for sleep's unravellings, waiting on daybreak, in Marrakesh.

They do not try to follow when they discover she has gone. They have things to do and mouths to feed and lives to moisten, and they like it here, where they are. But when her first communication arrives, in the short hot spring of 1971, the whole family assembles. Thirty-odd people, from barely born to ninety years of age, sit restless in Aunt Cath's living room, munching and sucking on biscuits, drinking hand-squeezed lemonade.

Aunt Cath herself stands immobile in the centre of the room, tall and composed, in a closely fitted camel skirt and jacket. In her hand is the postcard that came in the mail only that morning, a photograph of a shell-white city surrounded by receding dunes. The buildings are squat and

crumbly like blocks of shortbread, with round holes cut for doorways—
they don't look anything like real homes. In the distance stands a cluster
of humped shapes that Bea feels sure are camels and Aunt Patti argues are
sand-doused rocks. At the bottom right of the card, an exotic look-at-me
script announces *Marrakesh.*

Marrakesh—what a word! What a strange word! They have never
been there, can't think of anyone who has grown or lived or died there.
Marrakesh. A foreign land, with who knows what currency or religion or
wandering savages! Marrakesh, goodness, what a word!

"It's her," Roger says, in a voice more tin than silver. "No doubt."

He points to the back of the card; a white wall vined with writing:

*As eternal as the snows on the highest peaks, as impressive as the Atlas moun-
tains, as entrenched in history as the palm trees are rooted in the earth, Marrakesh
stands as the finishing touch to a picture of timeless beauty. The mightiest kings fought
for it; dynasties inherited it; craftsmen, architects, painters, and sculptors in all ages
built magnificent palaces, mosques, and gardens. Marrakesh, the imperial city which,
at the dawn of its history, gave Morocco its name.* A cheery postscript frills the
stampless stamp box: *Every imaginable commodity abounds: palaces, hotels,
restaurants, golf courses—even a casino!*

No matter how hard her parents, Bea and Roger, or her husband,
Peter Michael, search, there is nothing more written in the red-bordered
space. No tears, no traps, no clues. There is nothing of her there to cling
to. Nothing of her eyes (which are green), nothing of her voice (which is
firm though not loud), nothing even of her gentle tapered hands that give
the children chocolates in lavender foil wrappers and birthday presents
twice a year. There is only silence, and then some crying, and no one knows
the time.

Roger re-knots his chequered tie and vows to fly out there, and Bea
wonders what passes for police in Maahrra-Kaahsh. Peter Michael stands
with two fingers absently polishing the piano and for the thousandth time
thinks over the four years he meant to love her. Aunt Cath waits patiently
for the postcard to return from its hand-the-hand. Then she clears her
throat and says: "It is getting on lunchtime. The little ones will be terribly
hungry ... "

So they gather round the old oak table and say a few easeful prayers.
Then sandwiches are served, tuna salad on enriched white bread buttered
to the edges, and the Lazy Susan is loaded up with cold cuts and relishes

and hard-boiled eggs. There is plenty of everything left over. Roger unravels a celery spear. Peter Michael sheds a hair into his milk and swears. Bea hasn't an appetite.

They want to talk about her, but it takes some doing.

Grandpa Evans recounts how as a girl she devoured mystery stories, anything in paperback, and even read from them at the table, and read the end first, spoiling it for everybody else.

Roger remembers that she always loved horses—

"Ponies," corrects Bea.

—but wasn't able to have a real one, on account of allergies, so he'd made a swing from a log, attached to a chain with bolts at both ends, glued on swatches of broom for a mane and tail, bottle-glass for eyes, a bicycle seat for a saddle—

"He even made legs for it," adds Bea. "Out of that old canary kitchen chair. Canary-yellow legs, on a horse. Can you imagine?"

—and after all his hard work, she had preferred to gallop about on an old driftwood cane—

"Making those awful noises," Bea says. "Neigh." She makes a pursy-mouth, pushes out a harsh, high noise. "Like that, sort of," she says, and looks to Roger.

"Horse noises," Roger clarifies. He shakes his head. "After all that work." He means to say something else, but a quietness comes upon him.

They want to talk about her, in a way they aren't used to.

"It's just a notion," Aunt Patti says. "We all get them. Some more than most," she chuckles, as one who in her day was known to entertain alarming notions.

One of the modern nieces has heard that Morocco is very much a hot spot. Cousin David snorts, and says if that's the case, he hopes she's had her shots.

They want to talk about her, but they aren't sure how.

"It's the sun, isn't it?" Uncle Bernie says. "She wants to be where the sun is. What do you call them? Snowbirds. I would bet on it," he adds. "I am that sure."

Then Grandpa Evans offers a packet of chewing gum to the boy or girl who finds his glasses, and Bea points out that at least the children needn't suffer, and somehow discovers her appetite.

Aunt Cath excuses herself, hinting at indigestion, and goes upstairs, and locks the door, and slides down the wall in the drifting murk of noise and laughter, and weeps the colour from her cheeks and the burnish from her hair, and is brave, all things considered.

At summer's end another postcard arrives. Aunt Cath brings it in, on a tray, almost as an afterthought, with Sunday dinner.

"I thought you might all take a peek," she says, then quickly sets down the potatoes that threaten to sear her bare palms. "These will need to cool," she says. "That is the trouble with doing them scalloped."

The card looks homemade. Two images are set on a rectangle of stiff cardboard the colour of sand. In the first, three men each sit astride a sleek tall horse, holding rifles. The men wear white loose clothes and fabric wrapped about their heads; the horses a rich brocade that masks their eyes and scarves their necks. The second picture is a building with thin stone pillars green and grooved as sucked peppermints, and a curved slate roof. Above this picture appears a legend; numbers penned neatly in the margins correspond to text on verso. One, *The Badhi Palace*. Two, *Dar Si Said*.

The sun bathes Marrakesh in light. Its rays show up the pink marble of the fountains, spread across the tiled courtyards, are reflected, and then bring warmth to the turquoise, greens, and whites of the mosaic, finally to be lost amid the stucco of the Dar Si Said, now a museum housing the finest masterpieces of Moroccan art. This same sun illuminates the remains of the Badhi Palace, where a shimmering mirage reveals the wonder of former glories to the dazzled visitor; the gold, the marble, and the onyx traded for their weight in sugar by the most celebrated Saadian ruler, Ahmed el Mansour (1578–1603). Again, there is a postscript: *(The perfect proportions of the Ménara pavilion may be contemplated at leisure, mirrored in the quiet, still waters that stand before it.)*

Cousin David wants to know what goddamned pavilion?—excuse his French—and mutters a little more, in French.

Just as before, there is no return address, no stamps.

"Collector's privilege," Aunt Cath says, and blushes at their fond bland looks. "Though, you know, they're *funny* stamps—"

Then there is a telephone call for Peter Michael; a baby starts to storm. Slowly, randomly, like dried leaves dropping, they all fall their own ways home.

How can they explain her? Driving to and from hockey practice, in the bar of the Curling Club, over the phone, they try. Grandpa Evans catalogues her every childhood lie, confirming his conviction that character is formed early. A few of her friends, some baffled, some hurt, send cards or weepy letters. Jen from work calls about forwarding mail and Em from next door about pricing that antique harpsichord, just in case. How can they explain her? It isn't easy.

Aunt Patti thinks it might be genetic, a brain malfunction perhaps, that makes a person act badly. Cousin David figures a heart that will wander will just damned well wander, and there's no telling why. One of the modern nieces blames the town's lack of options and amenities, though certainly the new arena has turned out pretty well, and now there's that Thai restaurant run by real Thais. Bea takes to saying that she blames herself. Everyone else says it is just ridiculous for Bea to be so hard on herself like that—she ought to get out now and again, get her mind off things, have a little fun.

There is no single answer that satisfies everyone, though most agree that the symptoms have been there from the start, in that dark streak she kept carefully hidden but is now so obvious: her generosity that (upon reflection) seems more like bribery; her penchant for time alone, with (it is apparent now) its buried sting of deliberate snub; her shyness (with hindsight) revealed as self-absorption. It is acknowledged that she has made a life of being irresponsible, uncaring, cold. Great-Great-Aunt Dorothy dies (of heartbreak?) believing just this. At her funeral, no one mentions postcards from the East.

By now a sense of resignation has replaced the hope that she will return. Aunt Cath still sets a place for her on Sundays, but no longer fills the glass. Peter Michael is mostly seen alone now, or in the brisk thrall of Mona, his executive assistant, who has always managed his jam-packed schedule and now the rest of his life as well.

At Christmas. Mona forgets to tag the presents she alone has selected and wrapped, and poor Peter Michael has no idea which package is for whom. He stands there by the coughing fire, shaking slightly, in a jumble of wrapping and Scotch Tape and toy reindeer, squinting and sizing up and allocating. Seven gifts are opened in her name. She sends nothing.

In March, an envelope arrives from Marrakesh, addressed to ten-year-old Warren Steven, once her favourite nephew. Warren feels funny reading it out loud, so Uncle Dillon, a lawyer from Sydney with two German cars, does the honours.

He slits the envelope very slowly, as though a serpent were snuggled within. Inside is a loose charcoal sketch. Unfolded, it is a smudged palm print. Aunt Patti thinks it a good likeness of Warren, but with the Smithson, not the Evans nose. Cousin David pronounces it disgusting and awfully unkind. Four-year-old Kenny brings the picture to his face, fascinated by the dark powder settled there. Wetting his finger, he draws circles in his ash-marbled flesh before the mirror. The other children lick their fingers and surround the drawing with new interest. Inside the envelope is flower-folded a second, thinner sheet of paper, without signature or watermark.

Sunrise over Marrakesh. The dawn adds a note of accentuated contrast to the imperious splendour of the Saadian tombs. Below, a multicoloured crowd invades the winding streets of the medina. Groups of men jostle toward the Ben Youssef mosque, nestling against the Medersa, the vast and superb Koranic school founded by the Mérinide sultan Abou el-Hassan (1331–1349) and one of Marrakesh's most remark-able monuments. Your carriage awaits for the Palmerie.

Once again, her parents can find no hidden messages. No teary after-word, no solemn pleas of regret. No signature, no embedded kiss. Has she forgotten her upbringing? Her conscience? Is there a law against conscience in Marrakesh?

Bea reads it a second and a third time, one black licorice fingernail propping up the words.

"I don't know," she says. "What am I to do with this?"

One of the modern nieces, who had taken a psychology course at university, thinks it isn't quite normal to send letters like this. It implies alienation.

"Well, alienation is what you get," remarks Cousin David, "when you just up and bugger off."

At this time two stories are told. Roger tells how he went to the police station and joshed with all the officers he'd vaccinated for mumps and polio and rubella twenty years before, and filed a missing-persons.

Under "physical description," he wrote "big-boned." Then he thought for a bit, and crossed it out, and started over. After he had started over six-odd times, he gave up. "I was worried," says Roger, "that people might see 'big-boned,' and get the impression she was fat."

Bea recounts a dream in which her daughter lies in a basin of soft ice, wearing a childhood sweater with a clock sewn into the front. In the dream Bea watches, powerless to do more than wonder at the sweater, gone so long without mending, and now its clock, tick-ticking away on the body setting like candied lemon into the jammy ice. Bea says she hopes this dream isn't prophetic, and one of the modern nieces notes that prophesy and symbol are, rather unfortunately, often confused.

"Actually, I didn't have that dream," Bea says. "I'm not sure why I said I did."

And perhaps it is at that point that they no longer want to talk about her.

"It is odd, about the stamps—" Aunt Cath begins, but no one pays attention.

So Aunt Cath stands near the window, listens to the sea roaring along the docks below, imagines the sands whirling and rising free below the foam, settling calmly to the bottom, now lazily changing shape—

Finally it is suppertime, and as plates and cutlery clatter across the table, Aunt Cath thinks to herself, *If only.*

Then she says, to no one in particular, "Will that be enough pumpkin squash? I can never remember who eats it … "

After supper, she quietly slips the letter and drawing into her pocket and out of their minds. It will not be spoken of. Instead, plans are made for the summer. The family will gather at Cedars Island, Aunt Cath's inheritance. They will lumberjack in the tilting mossy birches, and paint the shutters forest-green, and fish, and leave tempting nectars on the wharf in the hopes of pelicans. They will bring the children. They will not think of Marrakesh. They will play sand games and refresh themselves at twilight. The horseflies will stay away. The mosquitoes will drown in the silver evening rains. Peter Michael will throw the football, straight and on target, every time. Bea will make wild blueberry bounce. Roger will barbecue his famous double-garlic steaks. They will all pitch in where needed. They will have a wonderful time.

Aunt Cath hugs the door of her bedroom, wrapped in an old emerald nightgown. Some minutes ago, she climbed from bed to ease her bladder, but now finds herself unable to walk any farther.

I will move soon enough, it's only a cramp. I will just wait awhile, she tells herself, but she is anxious all the same. *I have carried them for so long. Too long. I can hardly imagine a life apart.* Once again, she imagines fused ocean and desert, bright sea and spun sand.

Still she cannot move. A shudder traces rapidly up her right side, a mean streak of pain. She feels, then doesn't feel, her right leg seize, then her thigh, hip, stomach, chest, arm, hand, head. Faces stretch past, out of focus, mouths open. Hands grip her skin, sowing rough red bubbles. She sees many, many shadows: of torsos, of windmills, of cats she has known. The room widens, narrows, widens again. She is spinning, somehow, against her wishes, guided against her will. Through the swim of noise and angles, she hears a voice, thin and damp and brisk as a water-reed: "Cath? Cath, you sleepyhead! Do you have five dollars for doughnuts?"

She crumbles, mouth twisted, silent, shaking, knowing.

It has been three months since Aunt Cath's stroke, and they are cautious that Thanksgiving. Even the children nudge each other to calmer states. Aunt Cath sits at the table's head. Her right arm and leg ripple occasionally, nerves sending dead letters. Behind her voice, not quite masked by it, her larynx skips and rasps and her words come slowly, molasses dredged through a straw. A pretty gilt napkin tucked under her chin catches the saliva that descends in rungs from her seized, split lips.

"Bless you, bless you," they say, and look away. The children are instructed not to hug too hard, and when she automatically rises to serve them, Uncle Bernie proffers a restraining arm.

"Not too much. Remember doctor's orders. Just one plate at a time, Cath. One thing at a time."

No one speaks of Marrakesh. She has forgotten them and so must be forgotten. Her place is long since filled. Other chairs lie empty. Death has claimed Dorothy, Miami Beach has claimed Aunt Patti, and Peter Michael is essentially elsewhere; board meetings, business guilds, Venezuela in a week, and what if Mona is pregnant—

Roger and Bea sit at the far end, arms linked in a modest show of force. They arrived in silence and will leave in silence—if they can get the car started.

"Oh, but we'll have to get a new one," Bea says. "Just ask Rog. Goodness, the windows were stuck shut tonight, not a crack of fresh air—that old beater!"

Roger nods vaguely, spaghettis his arm still more tightly through hers. They travel together in that way, in a car without windows or horizon, in short culs-de-sac. But when they go out, they link arms.

Aunt Cath sees it all, is overcome suddenly by the stiffness that lingers in her right side from eyebrow to ankle, thinks of the stamps, and promises herself, *Soon, very soon.*

She goes upstairs then, pleading fatigue, and they watch her gravely, with the expectant boldness of young grackles at feeding time. She refuses the listless arms they offer her. Alone, her door shut and bolted, Cath hears the ragged white hum of the stereo tuner scanning stations, the shudder of low notes of pop music. Feet move, run, scrape, change direction. Relieved of the burden of respect, the family grows fluid once more.

Cath tunes her hearing to a pitch above the noise, sits carefully on her settle, tumbles out the postcards, chooses one, reads it with a growing hunger:

Time has passed you by. In the copper souk, perhaps, where the metal is worked by craftsmen following age-old traditions, their faces set in profound concentration. Or perhaps it was in the Langhzal Souk, home of the wool merchants. Or in el Btana, with its sheepskins. Or in the hubbub of the Zarbia Souk, where carpets and caftans are sold to the highest bidder.

You are in another world. Where the smell of saffron, cumin, black pepper, ginger, verbena, cloves, and orange flower enchant the nostrils. Among sacks of almonds, ground nuts, and chickpeas piled high like mountains, with baskets of dates, casks of olives, and, on the apothecaries' shelves, pots of henna, flasks of rose extract, jasmine, mint, kohl, pieces of amber and musk. For all the beauty gathered here, for the sheer joy of the senses, you cannot miss the souks of Marrakesh—

Cath breaks off, unwillingly. There is too much to read, if she starts now. She will be here all day. She will always be here.

The old house is freshly cleaned, and quiet. Aunt Cath's three leather cases are packed and stand side by side, an ordered procession waiting only on a signal, a signal that she herself will give, any time now. She will tell them she received the news through government authority, on the municipal level. She will show them the card and the limpid blue wild-flowers, wired all the way from Marrakesh, their wavy roots tipped with dark sand and algae, as though just moments ago plucked from the sea with an upward thrust and a tourniquet applied to clot the wound. They will live for a week or more, and everyone will say how appropriate they were, how exotic but how familiar.

Aunt Cath has worked it out with all the patience of a lifetime of service. She sees that the path most attractive to her is, for once, the path she will choose.

Dragging her suitcases out of sight, checking the oil and windshield fluid in the car, Aunt Cath readies herself. She lets the curtains down in all of the bedrooms, taking care to leave two fingers of light. Her mail will be forwarded to a post office box near enough to drive to. There are too few jewels left to sell. Finally, she lifts the telephone, picks out the rounds of numbers.

It is a low day, charcoal grey, the sun seeping out beneath an overhang of clouds. The family gathers once more in Aunt Cath's living room. The children are peevish, the adults hushed and tense. Everyone waits without complaint.

Watching Aunt Cath, they feel her sadness. That Christmas Uncle Bernie will break down, shockingly, while carving white meat, and recall that he saw then in Aunt Cath what he had seen in *her*, just before *she* left; *seen* it, *known* it—

But then, they suspect nothing. All they see is sadness. It is strange that when Aunt Cath speaks, she does not cry.

"I have a letter, from friends of hers, in Marrakesh. She died there, last week, at peace and happy. It was cancer, you see, but she—she did not wish it made public."

Cancer. That's it, that's why, they think. That is the answer. Now they understand. Who wouldn't have done as she had done? Moved away in her pain like an injured wolf from its pack, wanting to spare them her weird disintegration, the slow, certain loaming of her tissues and marrow.

Cancer—it is the key they need. They explain her to each other in light of this revelation. They recall how kind and unstinting she had always been. How generous, giving what she could while she still had time. How tactful, keeping it to herself, never losing her dignity. How quietly courageous, to the very end refusing to be a burden. Cancer—how terrible!—and yet it relieves them, it fills in gaps.

"Upon her wishes, she was cremated. Her ashes will go to Cedars Island. She was loved, well loved. She was well loved, and though we all will miss her, we will remember that she was loved."

There is no more. There could not have been.

Many conversations follow the hush, but none will be remembered.

Catherine is nearly sixty when she arrives in the place she knows as Marrakesh, well into the evening, in the longest light of spring. She pulls into the driveway, drops her good hand over and grinds the stiff gear into park. Stepping out of her car, she walks the path to the small stone house, continues around it.

The sound of the wind in the foliage, chirping birds, the heady odours of jasmine and honeysuckle and the persistent perfume of the famous Marrakesh roses, saffron, poppies, antimony for black, the trees weighed down in their abundance.

In the garden she finds flagstones painted with images of the desert: a sun red-gold as a baking apple over plumes of blown white sand. Wiry cacti, fragile dusty cities. To her left, a skeletal greenhouse rises. To her right, a fluting hand-stitched canopy. A roof, she thinks. A roof, for the souks of Marrakesh.

Carts overflowing with oranges and roasted grains, storytellers, musicians, public scribes with their black umbrellas, fortune-tellers, potion vendors, and healers all contribute to the unreal spectacle.

Under the canopy, racks of driftwood, scaled and woolly with seaweed and dried sponge, are piled high with trinkets collected from the beaches, nubbed wrinkled starfish, silver dollars, spooning aluminum cans. Sea-glass by the barrel, all speckled and smooth, old coins mixed and matched to fill hope chests for those on a budget. So many treasures, so many left to build. Cath is pleased, she is glad: Marrakesh seems more and more as she dreamed it.

East of Marrakesh, water, water, everywhere!

Cath can't stop smiling—it must be the air, the strong sea air. She walks into the house, parts the heavy bead curtains, skirts sculptures and huge prints of meringue-peaked mountains, steps between terra cotta pots. She touches everything, the shining, oiled wooden walls, the kites that hang from the wicker furniture, the slender pewter table ornamented with a furious patch of hand-blown glass, bright and creamy as fresh marzipan, turned in the shape of a hummingbird. Over the door, a sign made from the unbound leaves of a travel brochure: Marrakesh, City of Fascination.

On a pewter table Cath tumbles out the postcards from Marrakesh, postmarked from Scrimms, Nova Scotia, a mere hundred miles from the family seat, where she is now, where she will remain. Then she tilts her good ear toward the back of the house, says gently:

"Laura—don't be afraid. I've come to help you finish it. I belong here too."

The halting reply, the rummaging for words, the simple response:

"Hello, Catherine. Welcome to Marrakesh."

Later, as the land hums with the rosiny songs of insects, they make plans. It isn't easy to build a city. They will need to keep track. Deluxe White Alkyd, $32 per gallon. Chicken wire, $66 per bale. Dry sand, fine grade, $18 per 40-kg sack. The house with its hoopy skirting, bending like a bustle across the cliff's lip. The windows, storm-shuttered against the near sea. Virgin palms, all-weather, $130 with root ball. It will take wit and industry to build a city. It will take time.

In the morning, they sit in the garden and begin the perimeter wall. Laura spades a furrow for the foundation, lining up with stake-and-string sightlines. Cath trowels sand into concrete, pauses, listening for the propeller cries of the fishing boats, and suddenly she is crying, barely believing:

"O Laura, Laura, Laura—I am finally out of *reach*—"

She has never returned, Aunt Cath, and her house was eventually sold, her share kept in trust for the children. They speak of her often, and with love. She was well loved here, and she will be missed, but they will always remember that she was loved. They wish her luck and wisdom in the wilds of Marrakesh. But they will not try to follow; they have things to do and mouths to feed and new lives to moisten, and they like here, where they are, where they were born.

CHRIS Collins

UTOPIA MUST BE HERE—
SO WHERE ARE THE JOBS?

Utopia must be here
since our postman asks
"any trouble with the French Surrealists?"
while handing over bills and coupons

a bus driver with Junior Mints and Thucydides
on the dash
Debussy in a Walkman

and at Safeway a boy bags groceries
while quoting a Stoic philosopher
"adapt yourself to the environment in which
your lot has been cast and show true love
to the fellow mortals with whom
destiny has surrounded you"
with that voice's profile, Marcus Aurelius
tattooed on a forearm flying over broccoli
two thousand years dead and orating above my Oreos
competing with the beep and computer-monotone
of the talking register

"Utopia must be here," I remark at Ultracuts
and she responds, blow-drying with a degree in sociology
"Oh, let's do a study. Trim the sideburns?"

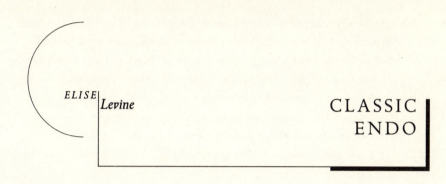

CLASSIC ENDO

ONE DAY IN THE SWIMMING POOL, I spoke in tongues. The pink parts of my bathing suit began to glow: that's what the witnesses said. They also said my hair—which I've worn stylishly, brutally short for years—grew into long tresses like tentacles, but here the disputes begin. Some claimed my feet grew fins, amphibian green, flecked with gold. Others swore my arms and legs glistened silver like scales catching sunlight. Still others muttered about eyes like polished abalone, lips viridian o's of astonishment.

How I must have looked! They carried me out on a stretcher, but not before a lifeguard dragged my limp body to the edge of the shallow end, rolled me up out of the pool, and tried to resuscitate me exactly, I suppose, as she had been taught in Bronze class. I opened my eyes, looked directly at her, and she blushed.

Thank you, I said. I must have dozed off.

In her nineteen-year-old's gaze, the cruellest presentiment: I was conscious but I couldn't move; I didn't want a fuss made; I was embarrassed—a newly middle-aged woman whose body had given out in the pool, knowing what old age would feel like.

Daddy used to say, Young lady—you're out of control, as if describing an irrefutable fact.

I was always his young lady.

One dark Sunday afternoon when I was five, Daddy and I sat in the kitchen of our Moore Park house eating corn chowder, thick as mucus. I crumbled milk biscuits into it until it was thick as stew and drank Orange Crush, my orange moustache annoying Daddy a little. He moved his unused butter knife half an inch to the right over the table, then back again. He cleared his throat. I continued to eat. The muscles in his jaw clenched. I put my spoon down.

Light bends when it passes through a medium, he said. This is calculable. Light passing through the eye creates sight. There is a code that will tell you everything. When you grow up.

My mother had died a year earlier, from diabetes. I remembered her only as a thing roundishly hard as the Royal Doulton figurine in the living room: her glazed eyes, my mother's broody trance.

Put out your big paw, Daddy said to me through an afternoon sky silky with snow at my mother's burial in the Necropolis, three rows away, he pointed out, from William Lyon Mackenzie's resting place. The other mourners—a progenitor or two, a colleague from the university, eyes flitting like birds behind thick glasses—had left. Holding my left hand in his, Daddy wiped melting flakes from my face. His hat furred white as he leaned toward me.

He said, We're in this together now.

In the spring, melting snow leaked through our house's broken Italian tile roof. At night, my room brimmed with small swimming things while sly electrical storms gambolled on the lawn; the wainscotting inside the window rattled miserably through my sleep. Uncertainty festooned my waking hours: walking to the bus stop on my way to school each morning, I thought buttresses on the nearby cathedral flew like rainbows; timbrels clanged in the sky.

Between lunchtime bites of toasted tomato sandwich (I was a girl with a stomach for a head), I'd repeat after Daddy: light as the source of all colour, all colours travel at the same speed in a vacuum.

He'd pat my hand. He looked after me well.

On my way back to school, only the grappling hooks of Daddy's pure science seized buildings as they threatened to lean, dissolve in something much like madness, like slicks leaking out.

Takes after her mother.

My aunt's voice thumped from the living room on one of her rare visits. I was thirteen, gobbling cupcakes in the pantry. I stopped chewing: What had she meant?

A sharp rap, probably Daddy's knuckles on the mahogany end table, made me gag on a lick of vanilla icing.

Evelyn, he said. I believe she knows better.

I did know. At Havergal College for Girls, I performed admirably: by fifteen, I could binge and purge with the best of them. Waiting for the five o'clock bus each day after school, my high math scores blossomed on my lisping breath, constellations in the already dark winter sky. But I was coming to know something else, as well: not for me the usual achy doldrums of being fifteen with no place to go but home, where I sputtered into clarity only under Daddy's gaze. In our house, I shrank—from his hands on his hips, his stares; my growing body, hips loosening into adolescence. I was mute as my mother's figurine, boxed, in storage.

After school one cold day in January, snow squeaked like Styrofoam beneath my boots. Behind me the tower and turret, the leaded-glass windows and grey winter ivy of Havergal College collapsed sullenly and sank into early night. A Land Rover carried off the last of my languishing classmates, waving weakly at me through fogged glass.

Cars hummed exhaust over icy Avenue Road, their interiors glowing faintly, and I imagined all the car radios in the world turned on and crackling, static flocking like crows above my head. If I listened carefully, turned a corner, and my ears popped—if I listened sideways somehow—I would hear them, ghostly emissaries singing, tremulous at first, then jangly: destiny, aliens, something out there.

Barring that, somewhere else I could be.

I remember the summer I turned seventeen. The fast car I stepped into. I'd become a fast girl with good hands, the boy breathless next to me, mouth slightly agape, braces glinting in moonlight. I couldn't chart that, make velocity-time graphs of the million stars at night above the fields of uncut hay.

I'd sneak home after midnight through the neighbour's garden so Daddy wouldn't hear the car engine. Pat Jimmy, the neighbour's boxer who slept outside in summer.

She'll break your heart some day, the brittle aunt told Daddy years before.

By my thirty-ninth birthday—in the end it was the aunt who moved in to take care of him—I suppose it was true.

When Daddy died, I joined the central YMCA and learned how to swim. Day after day, I lay on my back in the beginners' lane and fluttered up and down. The skylights were what I imagined cancer cells would look like under Daddy's microscope, puffy marshmallows poised to yield their geometric niceties. I gave up swimming and joined the beginner fitness class instead.

Three days a week at noon I leave my St. Charles Street office to walk past the shimmer of Yonge Street clothing stores, jammed with what I gave up wearing years ago, having entered the twilit zone of an uncertain age: no hard abs here. Hence, once inside the coolly sequestered foyer of the YMCA, the following elegant formula: grey unitard, black oversized T-shirt. Join the procession up the stairs from the change room to music swirling like mist. Twitch to Madonna's latest immaculately happy beat, until the instructor puts on a low-impact tape. Merengue like crazy.

See the two new girls, blonde, athletic—next time they'll take their lithe spandex-clad bodies to the intermediate class for a real workout—

giggle as the every-Tuesday man rolls his eyes, sticks his tongue out in concentration, spittle flossing the grey stubble on his chin.

Shudder into an unconvincing semblance of Latin excitement past the pillowy mother who—free for two hours, three times a week from the spongy machinations of her one-year-old twins—mutters, If I wanted to merengue I'd take the fucking dance class.

Stretch. Curse. What works, works.

Imagine a rose clenched dangerously between my teeth, my eyes like daggers, my heart a dark mystery.

My clients—architects for whom I'm a public relations consultant—approve of this building.

Like Philip, in black. We meet for lunch at the restaurant upstairs.

A polyphonic discourse between a socio-economic dialectic and an essential, infrangible otherness, he might say of this building, probing his Belgian endive drizzled with walnut dressing. He is famous for this, duelling to the death those other clients of mine more thoughtful of the structure's neo-classical humanist contextures, its schematic reification of the non-heroic modality. Each encomium pins the utterer to a rabidly guarded theoretical camp, like an insect specimen jabbed through the thorax to a dusty case in a museum few would willingly visit.

Here you are, Philip says when I join him. He's already ordered. I nod: here I am. There is no arguing with Philip.

Well, he says, before I've opened my menu. Kira almost had a breakdown when I told her Jon was mounting Graeme's next show. Silly bitch. What did she expect? He's not fucking *her* anymore.

At a single table nearby sits a famous abortionist, taking time out from the firebombings. Other celebrities frequent the place, too, from the CBC national treasure to the elegantly appointed diplomat-turned-publisher to the only slightly tarnished civil-rights saint—usually on Mondays, the YMCA is crowded with those desperate to expiate the sins of weekend excess.

The doctor seems ravenous, devouring his black bean soup and apricot-oatmeal muffin. He licks the crumbs from the side of his mouth and with his fingers grooms the table for extras.

I eye Philip's leftover terrine with raspberry coulis.

Ken and Tony split up again, he says. *And* I hear from reliable sources Marta'll get fired.

Philip veers across the table, chin grazing his former appetizer. His voice drops, thick brows lean. He carefully mouths each word. Like my father, Philip fears I might miss something.

You know. *The Holbein disaster.*

The coulis, I determine, is delicious.

And. Amy wants you to come for dinner next Saturday. We'll do Thai, all right? Found a fabulous new source for lemon grass.

The skin around my mouth, eyes, tightens. My hand drags across the table like a dead thing. With superhuman effort, I successfully negotiate my fettucine, loading up on carbohydrates limpid in low-fat sauce.

Philip pushes back from the table, elbows cocked. About Amy, he says. His wrists bend unnaturally. The man is all angles, like his old apartment, ten years ago, on Shuter Street, a monochromatic enclosure of limited edition chairs, a Philippe Starck table or two. The expert collection of toys in aid of the studied deviance on the futon, underneath the Mapplethorpe.

Lacking talent myself (a fact I admitted long ago with only a few tears shed), I made a point of bedding brilliance. Though it was easier then: risk was the rage, every sexual act a code of transgression, a deconstruction of the ganglia of desire.

I was young then.

Like Amy. Philip's—impossibly—young concubine. Her fasts, *detoxification rituals.* High priestess of high colonics, she'll probably live forever; Philip, too, having found the fountain of youth in an enema bag.

Don't people just fuck anymore?

The waiter materializes with a flourish. The good doctor has vanished from the single table. Philip turns down the usual latte and orders another mineral water.

About Amy, he says again, and blinks at his paper-pale hands.

She's pregnant. Thought you should know.

From the restaurant, I wander to the pool viewing area, three storeys above a bleary grotto of water.

Here I am. Below, the lifeguards change shifts. Across from me, the director of memberships sales quietly eats her lunch. Light aches through glass to this lull in the ordinary day: a hole in solid unimpeachable space to fall into.

A miracle.

Which is what I need. To be not what I am: doomed—to a small waist and large hips, a short torso, and a round belly that will never ripple with the obscene number of sit-ups I force it through daily (at home, in private).

No escape. Your body, yourself, every micro-DNA impulse (I'd make Daddy proud!) drives you to the gym, the fitness rooms; to the squash courts, couples locked in an algebra of mortal combat, the rubber ball angled just so under the harsh white glare; to the dance studio, the stretching rooms.

Chunky with muscle, mesomorphs eschew the Nautilus machines on the second floor for the free-weight room on the top floor: fetishists with leather weightbelts, gloves, purists pumping 200-pound bars.

Ectomorphs—ropy sinew twisting with each step—ascend to the roof to lope around a track, giddy with height and fumes from the congested streets below.

Endomorphs (that's me) swim to support an irreparable deficit of muscle tone; exiled to the subterranean depths, they suffer the briefest flash of exposure (though a plain black Speedo offers excellent thigh-slimming coverage) to become mere flickers, shadow creatures garlanded by curlicues of cellulite like speleothems gone berserk.

Realize your potential. Be the best possible you.

Be who you are.

This cave has been here a long time, Daddy said. Long before you or me. And it'll be here long after your children and their children.

We were in Texas, touring a cave after a conference Daddy attended. I was eight, on summer vacation, squirmy with white runners and white socks, white heat, humidity.

I pondered his pronouncement as long as I thought necessary to appease him. I looked over at the other children on the tour, skipping about our guide; maybe their names, strange ones like Bubba and Cleta June, made them invulnerable to the heat.

This cave, the guide said, then paused and smiled, as if she had a secret— even at that age, I found her annoying—this cave is ninety-five per cent active. It's growing all around us.

She pointed to a toad lodged in a crevice.

We think he's been here twenty years. Probably hopped in when this was the only entrance for the surveyors. He eats bugs that fall in through the opening.

The other children crowded toward the toad, infinitely more interesting than clammy rock, and knelt in dust beneath a jumble of stone hammered by light from an opening above.

He can't get out again, the guide said.

Daddy held my shoulders. We gazed at the ceiling, the walls where the guide shone her flashlight at fossils, clay banks, places turning black and greasy from people's touch. In the close air of the cave, a clutter of elderly women, amateur speleologists from the Cleveland Second Mile Club, smelled of old lady sweat. Though they *did* know about caves, answering in unison when the guide said, What's the difference between a stalactite and a stalagmite? Showing off to each other, saying, Eileen, look at that, and Eileen saying, Oh, I've seen plenty of *that* before, up in Sweetwater. Flesh hung in strips along their swollen calves and ankles, crinkly, unsmooth as old wallpaper.

The other children crouched beneath the opening, light from above carving their faces. I turned to face Daddy.

Can I play with the toad? I said.

He shrugged his hands from the nape of my neck, as if I had failed him.

By the end of the tour I was tired and thirsty. In the souvenir shop half a mile above, they sold grape Sno-cones and plastic paperweights you could shake to make snow fall on a Texas Ranger, in unabashed defiance of climatic laws. But returning to our starting point, the guide fussily assembled our group, pursing her lips until all stragglers arrived. A clammy breeze, Daddy's hot breath, rummaged my hair. Suddenly, darkness. A man's voice rose.

God creates mysteries. God creates order.

The ceiling smudged blue; a creeping rose latticed the bumpy walls. Listening to the recording, I rested against Daddy. He pushed his hip against me, put his arm across my chest, and pressed.

What I remember feeling next: Daddy and, despite him, something— myself—grown lopsided amid a shakiness of breathing rock, spores of pinky light; a chatter of wind through limestone like the rustle of wings through an as-yet undiscovered corridor.

Marvel, children of God, as you behold His house, the recorded voice serenely urged.

My head felt hot, then coolly hollow as blown glass, the sound of the voice slivering it until a shock of whispers seemed to shiver from my feet and rustle my skin.

Somewhere in there, the dark-cave heart of things, something I will always know: a father holds his hand out to his little girl and waits for her—a woman with a hole for a head.

Below me in the pool the swimmers looked hazy, indistinct beneath the membrane of water. Their small bodies looked like crazy fish pulling them-selves up the length, along the veinous thread of black line on aqua tile. From above, everything seemed so slow: the lifeguards, legs floating over the arms of their high towers and every now and then a twitch of the foot, up and down, a briefly perceptible impatience punctuating the afternoon's *longueur* only to lapse again into nothing.

Nothing goes fast. Like waking slowly from a long dream. Like pulling yourself out of the pool, having swum a slow pumping mile: that heaviness in the legs, feeling your heart lurch like a bear greeting spring. So slow it hurts.

I always waited. Something rich, something strange.

Nothing happened.

Only this: my body—classic endo, irreducible though lovers and diets come and go—and the face I watch collapse with age, sucked inward, downward by this relentless science Daddy never mentioned: this catastrophe called gravity.

In the change room, I stashed my DKNY dress in a locker. Removed my Bakelite bangles. Stripped to my lumpen mass. My afternoon calls could wait.

In the pool, I licked the dusty insides of my goggles—unused a year in my tote—then pulled them on and tested the seal. One, up; two, down. Eventually, five and six. Finally, nine, where I touched the edge of the deep end and pushed off again, chest tightening like a drying plaster cast.

Heaving past the muscled legs of the lifeguard I conjured ten, the water's glazed surface hard as porcelain; summoning eleven, the heavy water held only an overtonal blast of bubbles trumpeting from my marbling lips— and this single viscous thought: *I'm going to drown.* Twelve, thirteen, unbearable fourteen. Being forty-two. Trapped in my ribs.

Then I felt light, unbelievably light, and fast. The water held me up; I could almost breathe it in.

Then the water closed over me. Dark.

Chain chain chain—I'm running in a circle, flapping my arms like an ungainly bird—*chain of fools.*

I work those glutes (fabulous glutes!), the Raylettes (so sweet! so beguiling!) teasing Ray: *Baby shake that thing.*

Stretch it out, the instructor says later, during the mat work.

Grunting deliriously, chin yearning impossibly toward my left kneecap, I can't fully recall the time I fell asleep and dreamed strange dreams. When black wings—black as the black lines that tell you which lane you're supposed to swim in—pulled me up out of the pool, and I forgot my name and where I was. I woke laughing, drowning, my blood pumping chlorine. Angels, everything, last Thursday.

Reach up, the instructor says. Let yourself fall.

CAROLINE Adderson

THE
CHMARNYK

IN 1906, AFTER SCORCHING THE DAKOTA SKY, an asteroid fell to Earth and struck and killed a dog. Only a mutt, but Baba said, "Omen." It was her dog. They crossed the border into safety, into Canada. But the next spring was strange in Manitoba, alternating spells of heat and cold. One bright day, Mama went to town, stood before a shop window admiring yard goods, swaddled infant in her arms. From the eaves above, a long glimmering icicle gave up its hold, dropped like a shining spear. The baby was impaled.

These misfortunes occurred before I was born. I learned them from tongues, in awe, as warnings. My brother Teo said, "Every great change is wrought in the sky."

Grieving, they fled Manitoba, just another cursed place. Open wagon, mattresses baled, copper pots clanking. Around the neck of the wall-eyed horse, two things: cardboard picture of the Sacred Heart; cotton strip torn from Baba's knickers. Every morning as she knotted the cloth, she whispered in the twitching ear, "As drawers cover buttocks, cover those evil eyes!" Thus protected, that old horse carried them right across Saskatchewan. In Alberta, it fell down dead.

So they had to put voice to what they had feared all along: the land wasn't cursed, they were. More exactly, Papa. A reasonable man most of the time, he had these spells, these ups and downs. Up, he could throw off his clothes and tread a circular path around the house knee-deep through snow. Or he would claim to be speaking English when, in fact, he was speaking in tongues. "English, the language of angels!" but no one understood him. Down, he lay on the hearth, deathly mute, Baba spoon-feeding him, Teo and Mama saying the rosary. I was just a baby when he died.

But this is a story about Teo, dead so many years. I remember him stocky and energetic, his streaky blond hair. If they had stayed in Galicia, he would have been a *chmarnyk*, a rain-man. In the Bible, Pharaoh had a dream that seven gaunt cows came out of the river to feed on cattails. He dreamed of seven ears of corn on a single stalk, withered and blighted by east wind. But Teo never relied on the auguries of sleep. He could read the sky.

"Rain on Easter Day and the whole summer is wet. If you see stars in the morning from one to three, the price of wheat rises."

He told me this in a field still bound by old snow. He had stood out there the whole night and I was calling him to Easter Mass, 1929. "What'll it be this year then, smartie?"

"Drought." He pronounced the word like he was already thirsty. "Little sister, listen. The sky is only as high as the horizon is far."

"Well, la-di-da."

Teo was nineteen, I twelve, and the skin of my own dry lips cracked as I echoed: "drought." All that spring, smoke rose straight out of chimneys and every evening the sky flared. "That's dust in the air already. That's dry weather," he said.

Always reading, he got an idea about the cattail. "Ten times more edible tubers per acre than a crop of potatoes."

"Just before a storm," he said, "you can see the farthest."

Since the price of wheat was not going to rise, Teo sold our farm and bought the store in town. There I learned our other names: "bohunk" and "garlic-eater." People didn't like owing us money, but the fact that they did never stopped them writing in the newspaper that we couldn't be loyal subjects of the British Empire. That we would never learn to put saucers under our cups. I refused to wear my embroidered blouses and sometimes even turned to the wall the cardboard picture of the Sacred Heart. It embarrassed me the way Our Saviour bared his sweet breast, as if he didn't care what people thought of him.

Teo was unperturbed. There was work to be done and I could be his little helper. At Mud Lake, by then half-receded, ringed by white alkali scum, he asked me to remove my clothes. Covering my breasts with spread-open hands, I waded in, then clung to a snag slippery with algae while Teo, on shore, named clouds.

"Cumulus. Cumulus. Cumulus."

"Why me?" I shouted.

"Needs a virgin," he called. "A smooth thigh."

I came out festooned with leeches—arms, legs, shoulder even. He chose the halest one and burned the rest off with his cigarette. All the way home, I wore that guzzling leech sheltered in a wet handkerchief. Like a doting mother I nursed it. Then we put it in a Mason jar with water and a little stick.

"Leech barometer," Teo said. "Fair weather when the leech stays in the water. Unless the leech is dead."

The next year, Mud Lake had disappeared. Rising out of what once was water—a secret charnel-house. Old glowing buffalo bones.

Already farms were being seized. Some families had been paying us in chits since 1929. To one farmer, Teo made a gift—an idea expressed to hide the giving. "If he wanted, a man might collect and sell those bones as fertilizer." We saw the farmer working every day. On first sight of the bones, his horse had spooked. Now, it had to be blindfolded—led like a reluctant bride through the sweltering town, an antimacassar the veil on its head. It strained with the cart, load white and rattling. Vertebrae fell in puffs of dust on the road, provoking feud among the forsaken dogs.

I never knew there could be so much death in one place or that the labour of removing it could be so gruelling. Finally, all the bones in a dry heap at the train station, ready to be loaded. Women could go down and have their photograph taken with a huge skull in their lap. Boys swung at each other with the leg bones.

Strangest railway robbery anybody had ever heard of. Overnight, it all vanished. Not even a tooth left on the platform. The exhausted farmer lost his remuneration. After that, he posted himself in front of the store warning those who entered that Teo was not as stupid as he looked. Declaring revenge was a man's right when he thirsted for justice. He spat so often on our window, I made a routine of cleaning it off. The pattern of saliva on the dusty glass was like cloudburst.

It was so dry in the Palliser Triangle dunes of dust stopped the trains. We tucked rags around doors and windowsills, blew black when we blew into our handkerchiefs. In Galicia, Teo would have been a *chmarnyk*, a rain-man. He took me with him, driving where roads were passable, farm to farm. Waiting in the car, I watched him point at the sky. Children circled, staring in at me. They thumbed their noses and wrote "garlic" in the dust on the windscreen. I kept my gaze on Teo as he exhorted skeletal-faced farmers to send their wives and daughters into the fields. Send them into the fields on Sunday morning and have them urinate, for a woman's urine has power to cause rain.

Brandishing brooms, they drove him off their porches. They kicked him in the seat of the pants.

"Why are we doing this?" I cried. His every good deed bred animosity.

Teo said, "They didn't know Our Saviour either." To give me faith, he made a drop of water appear at the end of his nose, glistening like a glass rosary bead. "That's without even trying," he said.

Nobody went into the fields, of course. Just Mama and Baba. And me, squatting, skirts hoisted. I saw my urine pool in the dust, ground too parched to drink. High in a tree, a crow was watching me. It shouted down that rain comes at a cost, and even then might not come for good.

In the Bible, Pharaoh dreamed of seven gaunt cows. By 1932, I must have seen 700 so much worse than gaunt. Angular with starvation or dead and bloated, legs straight up in the air.

"Ten times more edible tubers per acre in a crop of cattails than a crop of potatoes!"

"Who told you that?"

"And the fluff! That's good insulation! Mattress stuffing, quilt batting! From the stalks, wallboard and paper! The leaves—baskets, clothing!"

I laughed. Who would wear a cattail? "How come nobody ever thought of this before, smartie?"

"Lots nobody ever thought of! Every great change is wrought in the sky! God made the cattail!" His tongue raced, arms circled in the air.

But the big idea was cheap cattle feed, deliverance from famine. Teo the Deliverer. "Is a cow going to eat a cattail root?" I wanted to know.

"Cows eating pieces off tractors! Cows eating gate latches!" Hardware disease.

And the next morning, he drove away from the Palliser Triangle, northward, looking for a cattail slough. I waited. Baba sucked on her bare gums all day, as if that way she could wet her throat. Mama—always the same stories. "Dakota. 1906. A good doggie." She raised one fist in the air, swept it down with a loud smack into her outstretched palm. Weeping, she mimed the baby in her arms. That lance of ice, it dropped right out of heaven.

Then this, another sorrow: how Papa died. As a child, I thought he'd been plucked from the plow and raptured straight on high. Mama used to tell how she had clutched his ankle and dangled in mid-air trying to hold him back. Nothing could be further from the truth. He threw himself on a pitchfork. So much blood, it was like when they killed a pig. This she confessed in the back room of the store as I sat on a lard pail. Suicide triples a curse.

On a red background I appliquéd a cattail. The words: THE EVERYTHING PLANT. For batting, I planned to use the brown-and-gold pollen of the cattail flower. We were going to string it across the back of the car when we, brother and sister, did our tour of the drought towns, made our presentation at the feed stores. We were going to sleep under it at night. I was Teo's little helper.

In the corner of every eye, a plug of dust. I was afraid of crying, of someone licking the water off my face.

I urinated again in a field.

There were no clouds to name.

Now they said we were worse than Jews, almost as bad as Chinamen. I had never seen either. On the counter, they scattered handfuls of raisins, railing "Stones! Stones!" as if they actually paid us. What could we do about fly-infested flour, rancid bacon, the desiccated mouse in the sugar? When the cash register opened, chits flew out like a hundred moths. On all these accusing faces, the dirty lines were a map of the roads Teo had gone away on.

Now we wanted Teo to take us away. Baba said she could smell hatred. It smelled like gunpowder.

In Galicia, Mama said, Drought is a beautiful woman. She persuades a young peasant to carry her on his back. Wherever he goes, crops wither and die, ponds evaporate, birds, songs stuck in their throats, drop out of trees. Horrified, he struggles to loosen the cinch of her legs round his waist, her grappling hands at his neck. In the end, to be rid of his burden, he leaps from a bridge. Drought dries up the river instantly and, crashing on the rocks below, our young peasant breaks open his head.

Finally, a package. Inside, a big tuberous finger, hairy and gnarled. We marvelled it was still wet.

"What is it?" Mama asked.

"A cattail root."

When Baba touched it, she started to cry. What did it mean? Would Teo come for us? Alive, it was holding the rain. That night, to keep it moist, I brought it to bed and put it inside me.

To cure fever, drink whisky with ground garlic. Eat bread wrapped in cobwebs. But I did not think it was fever. Overnight, my hair had curled like vetch tendrils and my head throbbed where a horse had kicked me seven years before. Beside my bed, the leech barometer. So many years in the jar, I had thought the leech was dead. Now it shimmied out of the water and halfway up the stick.

Mama said, looking over the town, "Smoke from all these chimneys curling down." When I would not take the bread and whisky, she pulled my hair.

Just before a storm, you can see the farthest. We saw you coming miles away. Dust-maker, you were weaving all over the road, horn pressed. By the time we got Baba down the stairs and into the street, a crowd had gathered round the car. You were standing on the hood, almost naked, wet skirt of cattail leaves pasted to your thighs.

Mama gasped, "Teo has his father's curse."

The sere voice of a crow: *Rain costs.*

And I was part to blame. I had given my innocence to a cattail root while you held its power.

From the beating part of your chest, your brow, water had begun to trickle, ribboning downward, the sheen of moisture all across you. Motionless, arms open, fingers spread and dripping—you were sowing rain. We were sweating, too, the day dry and searing, but soon you were dissolving, hair saturated, nostrils and eyes streaming culverts. Then you turned, spun round, and spattered the silent crowd. Turned again, kept spinning, faster. Whirling, whirling on the slippery hood, you drenched and astounded us, became a living fountain. And then, amazing! A nimbus, seven-coloured, shimmering all around you.

In Galicia, when thunder sounds, prostrate yourself to save your soul. That day thunder discharged, a firearm, reverberating. Mama and Baba dropped to the ground. A dark curtain was drawn across the Palliser Triangle. Black geyser sky.

You bowed forward and vomited a river.

The crowd fell back. They had never seen a *chmarnyk.*

After Teo made it rain, the whole town was filled with steam, water evaporating off the streets and the wet backs of the men who carried Teo's body away. Dogs staggered out of cover to drink from temporary puddles. And in all the fields, green shoots reared, only to wither later in the reborn drought.

They carried Teo's body away and wouldn't let us see him. "Struck by lightning," they said. How could we argue? I was only fifteen and neither Mama nor Baba could speak English. The moment he was taken, we had been rolling on the ground. But I remember clearly the presence of that farmer, the one robbed of his charnel-house, his smile like lightning. The English word "shotgun" never had a place on my tongue.

Years later, Teo came to Mama in a dream. In the dream, he had a hole in his chest big enough to climb into, gory as the Sacred Heart. "I have seen the face of Our Saviour," he told her. "He lets me spit off the clouds."

As for me, two things at least I know. The cattail root holds more than water. Every great change is wrought in the sky.

MARC
ANDRÉ *Brouillette*

TOMORROW
WE SHALL
DEPART

Demain nous quitterons Brigance,
comme le souvenir d'un pays étranger dont
on ne peut plus déjà se détacher. Nous
laisserons cette contrée de l'imaginaire
pour qu'elle recouvre le silence qui lui
appartient. Autrement et comme un geste
du vent, nous irons sur d'autres lointains
embrasser les territoires du temps.

Tomorrow we shall depart from Brigance. From now on, it will be no
more than the memory of a foreign country we once knew.

We will leave this imaginary place so that she may regain the silence
which is hers by right.

In another way and as the wind blows, we shall go on to other distant
lands and embrace at last the spaces of time.

Translated by Rachel Wyatt

AUTHOR BIOGRAPHIES

CAROLINE ADDERSON attended the May Writing Studio in 1987 and 1991, writing "The Chmarnyk" at Banff in 1991. The story was nominated for a National Magazine Award and was published in Adderson's first book, *Bad Imaginings* (Porcupine's Quill 1993). *Bad Imaginings* was nominated for a Governor General's Award and the Commonwealth Book Prize, and won the 1994 Ethel Wilson Prize. Adderson is now working on a novel, *A History of Forgetting.*

Writer and artist KELLEY AITKEN is the author of *Love in a Warm Climate* (Porcupine's Quill 1998), a story collection set in Ecuador. Her work has appeared in *Room of One's Own, Prism International, sub-TERRAIN, Grain,* and *Coming Attractions* (Oberon 1996). A participant in the 1995 Writing Studio, Aitken lives and works in Toronto as a freelance illustrator and ESL and art instructor.

PAUL ANDERSON'S writing has been published in Australia, Britain, Canada, and Mexico. "To Everything a Season" is an excerpt from *Hunger's Brides,* a novel-in-progress. At the 1996 Guadalajara International Book Fair, a stage adaptation of *Hunger's Brides* was presented by One Yellow Rabbit Performance Theatre. Anderson attended the 1995 and 1997 Writing Studios, where Edna Alford edited Books 1 and 2 of his work.

A participant in the 1997 Writing Studio, KEN BABSTOCK has been published in several Canadian quarterlies and anthologies and won gold in the 1997 National Magazine Awards. The sonnets in this anthology also appear in his first collection, *Mean* (Anansi 1999). Babstock lives in Toronto.

ROSEMARY BLAKE came to Canada from Australia in 1978, lived in Calgary, and now lives in Toronto. Her work has been published in the *Antigonish Review, The Fiddlehead, Ariel, blue buffalo, Dandelion, Waves,* and anthologies including the *Anthology of Magazine Verse and Yearbook of American Poetry* (Monitor Book Company 1997). Blake attended the 1992, 1995, and 1998 Writing Studios and recently completed a poetry collection about coming to Canada, *Heartwood* (Quarry forthcoming).

LESLEY-ANNE BOURNE published three books of poetry with Penumbra Press: *The Story of Pears* (1990), *Skinny Girls* (1993), and *Field Day* (1996). She also published a novel, *The Bubble Star* (Porcupine's Quill 1998). Bourne attended writing programs in 1985, 1986, 1987, 1990, and 1995. She worked with W.O. Mitchell, Don Coles, and Jane Urquhart. Bourne received the Bliss Carman Poetry Award in 1986 and the 1994 Air Canada/Canadian Authors' Association Award for a writer under thirty with outstanding promise. She now teaches at the University of Prince Edward Island.

MARC ANDRÉ BROUILLETTE'S work is published in many journals in Quebec and France. He has two collections of poems, *Les Champs marins* (Éditions du Noroît 1991) and *Carnets de Brigance* (Éditions du Noroît 1994), which won the Desjardins Prize in 1995. Brouillette is completing a Ph.D. on the space in contemporary poetry. He lives in Montreal.

CHRIS COLLINS has attended the Writing Studios twice, winning the Bliss Carman Poetry Award in 1984. His poetry has appeared in *Quarry, Freelance, Briarpatch, NeWest Review,* and *In the Clear: A Contemporary Canadian Poetry Anthology* (Thistledown). His first collection of poetry, *Earthworks* (Thistledown), was published in 1990. Collins currently teaches English in Hong Nong, a village on the east coast of South Korea.

MÉIRA COOK'S most recent book of poetry is *Toward a Catalogue of Falling* (Brick Books 1996) and her first novel is *The Blood Girls* (NeWest Press 1998). She worked with Don Coles and Edna Alford at the Writing Studio.

JOHN DONLAN is a poetry editor with Brick Books and a reference librarian at the Vancouver Public Library. Donlan attended the 1993 and 1995 Writing Studios. His poetry collections are *Domestic Economy* (Brick Books 1990 and 1997), *Baysville* (Anansi 1993), and *Green Man* (Ronsdale Press 1999).

At age forty, IRENE GUILFORD left a career in computers to write. A 1991 and 1995 Writing Studio participant, she has now been published in various journals and anthologies, and has been shortlisted in the CBC Literary Competition and the *Event* Creative Non-Fiction Contest. Guilford's first novel, *The Embrace*, is forthcoming (Guernica Editions). She lives in Rockwood, Ontario.

A participant in the 1989 May Writing Studio, NAOMI GUTTMAN won the Bliss Carman Award that year for the poem "Reasons for Winter," which was later published in her collection of the same title (Brick Books 1991). *Reasons for Winter* won the 1992 A.M. Klein Award for poetry from Quebec's Society for the Promotion of English Language Literature. Guttman teaches literature and creative writing at Hamilton College, New York.

STEVEN HEIGHTON has published three books of poetry, most recently the Governor General's Award finalist *The Ecstasy of Skeptics* (Anansi 1995). His two collections of stories are *Flight Paths of the Emperor* (Porcupine's Quill 1992; Granta 1997), which was a 1993 Trillium Award finalist and *On earth as it is* (Porcupine's Quill 1995; Granta 1997), which was chosen by the *Toronto Star* as one of the best books of 1995. Heighton's first novel, *The Shadow Boxer*, is forthcoming (Knopf Canada and Granta).

In 1977, BRUCE HUNTER was an equipment operator when he won a scholarship to attend the summer session of the Writing Studio. He returned to the program in 1978. Hunter attended York University (1980 to 1983), taught at Banff as an assistant instructor (1984), and participated in the 1985 and 1986 Writing Studios, working with Don Coles. His publications include three poetry collections: *Benchmark* (Thistledown 1982), *The Beekeeper's Daughter* (Thistledown 1986), and *Coming Home from Home* (Thistledown forthcoming); and a story collection,

Country Music Country (Thistledown 1996). Hunter has taught at Seneca College since 1986. He is now working on a novel.

Toronto poet MAUREEN HYNES participated in the 1993 and 1995 Writing Studios. Her work *Rough Skin* (Wolsak and Wynn 1995) received the League of Canadian Poets' Gerald Lampert Award for best first collection of poetry. Hynes has also written *Letters from China* (Women's Press 1981). "Harm's Way," the title poem from her current manuscript, is forthcoming in *Arc*.

Born in England in 1953, MICHAEL C. KENYON has lived on Canada's West Coast since 1967. At the Banff Centre, he attended the 1992 Dramatic Writing Workshop, the 1993 and 1996 Writing Studios, and the 1998 Radio Drama Workshop. He has published six books, most recently a work of short fiction, *Durable Tumblers* (Oolichan 1993), a very short novel, *Twig* (Outlaw Editions 1996), and a collection of poetry, *Winter Wedding* (Reference West 1998).

RICHARD LEMM attended the 1976 summer Writing Program, becoming a resident instructor in the program in 1977 and head of poetry in 1978. He then taught in the Writing Program through 1987. He has published three poetry collections: *Dancing in the Asylum* (Pottersfield 1982), *A Difficult Faith* (Pottersfield 1985), and *Prelude to the Bacchanal* (Ragweed 1990), which won the Canadian Authors' Association Award for poetry. His poems have won awards in the 1983 and 1992 CBC Radio

Literary Competition and the 1998 League of Canadian Poets National Poetry Contest. He is also the author of the biography *If You're Stronghearted: Milton Acorn, People's Poet* (Carleton University Press 1998). Lemm teaches at the University of Prince Edward Island.

JOHN LENT attended the 1993 Writing Studio and recently completed a novel, *Coyote Bridge*. His other books include *Monet's Garden* (Thistledown 1996), *The Face in the Garden* (Thistledown 1990), *Frieze* (Thistledown 1984), *Wood Lake Music* (Harbour 1982), and *A Solid Rock* (Dreadnaught 1978). For the past twenty years, Lent has taught creative writing and literature at Okanagan University-College.

ELISE LEVINE'S work has appeared in *The Malahat Review, Grain, Prism International, This magazine*, and *Quarry*, and has been anthologized in *Frictions II: Stories by Women Writers* (Second Story Press 1995), *Coming Attractions* (Oberon 1994), two editions of the *Journey Prize Anthology* (McClelland & Stewart 1995 and 1998), and *Concrete Forest: The New Fiction of Urban Canada* (McClelland & Stewart 1998). She worked with Edna Alford at the 1992 and 1994 Writing Studios. Levine is also the author of the short story collection *Driving Men Mad* (Porcupine's Quill 1995). Born in Toronto, Levine now lives in Chicago where she is working on a novel.

LAURA LUSH attended programs at the Banff Centre in 1986, 1987, and 1990. She was a guest reader at the 1994 Vancouver International Writers Festival. Her first book, *Hometown* (Véhicule Press 1991), was nominated for the 1992 Governor General's Award for poetry. Her other work includes *Fault Line* (Véhicule Press 1997). Lush holds an Honours BA from York University and an MA in English and creative writing from the University of Calgary.

Halifax poet SUE MACLEOD also works as a freelance writer and editor. She attended the last of the Banff May Studios in 1993, working with Don Coles. MacLeod placed third in the League of Canadian Poets National Poetry Contest in 1994. Her first book, *The Language of Rain* (Roseway 1995) was published the following year and was shortlisted for the Milton Acorn People's Poet Award. "A woman is making" appeared in *The Malahat Review* and is part of MacLeod's second manuscript, *Mercy Bay and other poems*.

Born in Vancouver and brought up in the West, RANDALL MAGGS is now at Sir Wilfred Grenfell College in Corner Brook, Newfoundland. He attended three sessions at Banff, working each time with Don Coles. His writing has won several prizes, including the Bliss Carman Award for Poetry. His poems have been published in literary magazines and anthologies, and in the collection *Timely Departures* (Breakwater Books 1994). Maggs received a Canada Council grant for his next project, a book of poems on the life and times of goaltender Terry Sawchuk.

RACHNA MARA (pseudonym for Rachna Gilmour), attended the 1991 Writing

Studio. "Asha's Gift" is part of a collection of interconnected stories, *Of Customs and Excise* (Second Story Press 1991), which was shortlisted for Best First Book, 1992 Commonwealth Book Awards (Canada and Caribbean Region), and the 1993 Ottawa-Carleton Book Award. The author has also published several works of children's fiction under the name Gilmour, including *Lights for Gita.*

Poet and singer-songwriter JOSEPH MAVIGLIA attended the Writing Studio from 1981 to 1983. As a musician and performer, he plays clubs and gives readings at venues at home and abroad. His most recent collection of poetry is *Winter Jazz* (Quarry Press 1998).

A participant in the 1996 Writing Studio, LORIE MISECK has been published in several journals, including *Prairie Fire, Grain, Contemporary Verse II*, and *Room of One's Own*. Her work has also been broadcast on the CBC and the Women's Television Network. Her book *the blue not seen* (Rowan Books 1997) was shortlisted for the 1998 Henry Kreisel Award for Best First Book. She lives in Edmonton.

LISA MOORE has written radio plays, art criticism, and a television script. Her stories have been published in journals across Canada and her work appeared in *Coming Attractions* (Oberon 1995) and *Extremities* (The Burning Rock). Moore's first collection of short stories is *Degrees of Nakedness* (Mercury Press 1996). She lives in St. John's, Newfoundland, and is currently working on a novel.

At Banff in 1980 and 1982, SHELDON OBERMAN learned he could be a writer. His ten books include *The Always Prayer Shawl* and *The White Stone in the Castle Wall*. He now writes for theatre, film, radio, and newspapers, as well as songs for seven of children's entertainer Fred Penner's albums. Oberman travels widely, storytelling and giving readings and workshops.

JOANNE PAGE lives in Kingston, where she has worked as a visual artist, mother, newspaper columnist, editor, and creative writing teacher. A participant in the 1995 and 1997 Writing Studios, Page edited the collected essays of Bronwen Wallace, *Arguments with the World* (Quarry Press 1992), and has published a collection of poems and drawings, *The River & the Lake* (Quarry Press 1993).

At the 1985 May Writing Studio public reading, HELEN PEREIRA read "Tangents," which later appeared in *Prairie Fire* and the fiction collection *The Home We Leave Behind* (Killick 1991). Pereira's other fiction collections with Killick Press include *Magpie in the Tower* (1990), *Wild Cotton* (1994), and *Birds of Paradise* (1997). Her stories have been published in the anthologies *Going Home* (Oberon 1995), *Great Canadian Murder Mysteries* (Quarry 1991), and *Selections from Canadian Forum* (1981). Pereira was born in Grand Forks, BC.

Writer SINA QUEYRAS currently lives in Toronto.

Born in Jinja, Uganda, CHETAN RAJANI
has lived in Ottawa since 1972. Rajani
studied English and psychology at
Carleton University, and worked as a
bookseller, story/script editor,
dramaturge, writing coach, and
freelance writer and editor. His stories
have been published in numerous
Canadian literary magazines. Three
stories, including "The Sacrifice," were
selected for *Best Canadian Stories*. Rajani is
now working on a short story collection
and a novel/script project for a
Hollywood producer.

A participant in the 1987 and 1994 Writing
Studios, J. JILL ROBINSON published
"Who Says Love Isn't Love?" in *The
Fiddlehead* and in her third collection of
stories, *Eggplant Wife* (Arsenal Pulp Press
1995). Robinson's work has been heard
on CBC's *Between the Covers* and has won
the *Prism International* fiction contest, the
Sterling Prize for fiction, the Alberta
Writers Guild Award for a short fiction
collection (1991), and she co-won the
Event Creative Non-Fiction Contest. She
holds an MA in English literature
(Calgary) and an MFA in creative writing
(Fairbanks, Alaska).

BARBARA SCOTT'S "Oranges" was aired
as part of CBC's *Alberta Anthology* and was
published in *Grain*. The story is also part
of a collection forthcoming from
Cormorant Books. A participant in the
1995 Writing Studio, Scott lives in
Calgary, where she teaches at the
Alberta College of Art and Design. Her
work has appeared in literary magazines
and in the anthologies *Due West*

(Coteau/NeWest/Turnstone 1996) and
Alberta Re/Bound (NeWest 1990).

ANNE SIMPSON attended the 1997
Writing Studio, where she worked with
Joan Clark and John Steffler. In 1997, she
was also one of two winners for the
Journey Prize for her short story
"Dreaming Snow," first published in *The
Fiddlehead*. Simpson has completed her
first novel, *Canterbury Beach*, and recently
assisted Rita MacNeil with her
autobiography. She lives in Antigonish,
Nova Scotia, where she coordinates the
Writing Centre at St. Francis Xavier
University.

Canadian writer STRUAN SINCLAIR is
currently based in South Wales, where
he is completing his Ph.D. at the Centre
for Critical and Cultural Theory, at
Cardiff University. "Building Marrakesh"
is from his first short story collection,
Strange Comforts (Gutter Press 1998).
Sinclair participated in the 1997 Writing
Studio.

DOROTHY SPEAK grew up in Southern
Ontario. She has published two short
story collections, *The Counsel of the Moon*
(Random House 1990) and *Object of Your
Love* (Somerville House 1996). The latter
was also released in China and the
United States. Her stories have appeared
in the *Journey Prize Anthology 6*
(McClelland & Stewart 1993) and the
*Penguin Anthology of Stories by Canadian
Women* (1997). A participant in the 1982
and 1995 Writing Studios, Speak now
lives in Ottawa, where she is writing a
novel.

JOHN STEFFLER participated in the 1984 Writing Studio. His poetry collections were published with McClelland & Stewart: *That Night We Were Ravenous* (1998), *The Wreckage of Play* (1988), and *The Grey Islands* (1985). His novel *The Afterlife of George Cartwright* (M&S 1992) won the 1992 Smithbooks/Books in Canada First Novel Award and the Thomas Raddall Atlantic Fiction Award. Steffler lives in Corner Brook, Newfoundland, and teaches English at Sir Wilfred Grenfell College.

Born in England's industrial "Black Country," ROY TESTER grew up in Birmingham, lived in Barcelona and Australia, and then came to Canada in 1979. His fiction has been published in *Quarry*, *Prism International*, *B&A New Fiction*, *Church-Wellesley Review*, the *Globe and Mail*, *Golden Horseshoe Anthology*, and *Broadway*. A participant in the 1996 Writing Studio, Tester recently completed a collection of twelve stories, *hands over the body*. "Crooked Hollow" first appeared in *B&A New Fiction* (December 1995) and won the 1996 Hamilton and Region Arts Council's Award for Fiction.

BARBARA TURNER-VESSELAGO attended the 1982 Writing Studio and is the author of *Freefall: Writing Without a Parachute* (Writing Space 1997) and *Skelton at Sixty* (Porcupine's Quill 1986). She is currently completing a novel about West Africa that won the Toronto Arts Council's Work-in-Progress Award. Turner-Vesselago teaches writing internationally. She was recently chosen as one of six "Voices of the Nineties" to lecture on creativity at the University of Western Ontario.

LIZ UKRAINETZ has published prose in various journals across Canada. Her novel *Minor Assumptions* (Exile Editions) was published in 1994. She lives, works, and writes in Toronto.

SUE WHEELER'S first book, *Solstice on the Anacortes Ferry* (Kalamalka Press 1995), won the Kalamalka New Writers Prize, and was shortlisted for both the Pat Lowther and the Gerald Lampert Memorial Awards. She published a chapbook, *Islands* (Reference West 1996), and won the Gwendolyn MacEwan Memorial Award (1998) and *The Malahat Review* Long Poem Prize (1994). Wheeler participated in the 1993 Writing Studio, working with Don Coles, and returned in 1995 to work with Don McKay.

ABOUT THE EDITORS

EDNA ALFORD Recipient of the Marian Engel Award and co-winner of the Gerald Lampert Award, Edna Alford has published two collections of short fiction, *A Sleep Full of Dreams* (Oolichan 1981) and *The Garden of Eloise Loon* (Oolichan 1986). Her work has appeared in numerous journals and anthologies. She was co-founder and co-editor (with Joan Clark) of *Dandelion Magazine* for five years and fiction editor of *Grain Magazine* for five years. She has served on the editorial board of Coteau Books since 1988 and has edited many short fiction collections as well as co-editing (with Claire Harris) the anthology *Kitchen Talk* (Red Deer College Press 1992). She is Associate Director of the Writing Studio at The Banff Centre for the Arts.

DON MCKAY Don McKay has published eight books of poetry, including *Birding, or desire* (McClelland & Stewart 1983); *Night Field* (McClelland & Stewart 1991), which received the Governor General's Award; and *Apparatus* (McClelland & Stewart 1997). His work has also received the National Magazine Award and the Canadian Authors Association Award. Since 1975 he has served as editor and publisher with Brick Books. He taught creative writing and English literature at the University of Western Ontario and the University of New Brunswick for twenty-seven years before resigning to write and edit poetry full time. From 1991 to 1996 he edited *The Fiddlehead* magazine, and he has also served as a faculty resource person at the Sage Hill Writing Experience and The Banff Centre for the Arts, where he currently holds the position of Senior Poetry Editor.

RHEA TREGEBOV Rhea Tregebov was born in Saskatoon, raised in Winnipeg, and now lives in Toronto. She has four collections of poetry: *Remembering History* (Guernica Press 1982), which won the 1983 League of Canadian Poets' Pat Lowther Award; *No One We Know* (Aya/Mercury Press 1986); *The Proving Grounds* (Véhicule Press 1991); and *Mapping the Chaos* (Véhicule Press 1995). She has also published four children's picture books and edited the anthologies *Frictions* (1989), *Frictions II* (1993), and *Sudden Miracles* (Second Story Press 1991). Tregebov was co-winner of *The Malahat Review* Long Poem Competition in 1994 and also received the 1993 Readers' Choice Award for Poetry from *Prairie Schooner* (Nebraska). She teaches creative writing for Ryerson's Continuing Education program and works as a freelance editor of adult and young adult fiction and poetry.

RACHEL WYATT Rachel Wyatt emigrated to Canada in 1957. Her four novels were published by The House of Anansi. Her most recent books are *The Day Marlene Dietrich Died* (Oolichan 1996) and *Mona Lisa Smiled a Little* (Oolichan 1999). Her stage plays include *Geometry*, *Chairs and Tables*, and *Crackpot*. She has written many radio dramas for the CBC and the BBC. She was on faculty at the Banff Writing Studio in 1993, 1994, and 1996 and is currently Director of the Writing Studio at The Banff Centre for the Arts.

PERMISSIONS

"The Chmarnyk," by Caroline Adderson, was previously published in *Bad Imaginings* (Porcupine's Quill 1993). Reprinted with permission of the publisher.

"Hatchetface," by Kelley Aitken, was previously published in *Love in a Warm Climate* (Porcupine's Quill 1998). Reprinted with permission of the publisher.

"First Lesson in Unpopular Mechanics" and "To a Sister, Wherever," by Ken Babstock, were previously published in *Mean* (Anansi 1999). Reprinted with permission of the publisher.

"Diving off the Wreck" and "After the Nightmare," by Rosemary Blake, were previously published in *The Fiddlehead* (No. 179, Winter 1994).

"Tomorrow We Shall Depart," by Marc André Brouillette, was previously published in *Carnet de Brigance* (Éditions du Noroît 1994). Reprinted with permission of the publisher.

"Utopia Must Be Here—So Where Are the Jobs?" by Chris Collins, was previously published in *Earthworks* (Thistledown Press 1990). Reprinted with permission of the publisher. This version is an abridgement of the original.

"String Quartet," by Méira Cook, was previously published in *Toward a Catalogue of Falling* (Brick Books 1996). Reprinted with permission of the publisher.

"Tilt" and "Coelacanth Clouds," by John Donlan, were previously published in *The Fiddlehead* and then in *Green Man* (Ronsdale Press 1999). Reprinted with permission of the publisher.

"No Vacancy," by Irene Guilford, was previously published in *Quarry*.

"Reasons for Winter," by Naomi Guttman, was previously published in *Reasons for Winter* (Brick Books 1991). Reprinted with permission of the publisher.

"To Everything a Season," by Steven Heighton, was previously published in *On earth as it is* (Porcupine's Quill 1995). Reprinted with permission of the publisher.

"Tidal Bells," by Bruce Hunter, was previously published in *The Beekeeper's Daughter* (Thistledown Press 1986). Reprinted with permission of the publisher.

"Precaution," by Maureen Hynes, was previously published in *Contemporary Verse 2* (Winter 1998).

"Frozen Carp," by Michael C. Kenyon, was previously published in *Prism International*.

"Love Poem on Pogey Cheque Night," by Richard Lemm, was first published in *Prelude to the Bacchanal* (Ragweed 1990).

"Roofs in the Morning," by John Lent, was previously published in *Event* (vol. 23/no.3, 1995) and then in *Monet's Garden* (Thistledown Press 1996). Reprinted with permission of the publisher.

"Classic Endo," by Elise Levine, was first published in *Grain* and then in *Driving Men Mad* (Porcupine's Quill 1995). Reprinted with permission of the publisher.

"Witness," by Laura Lush, was previously published in *Hometown* (Véhicule Press 1991).

"A woman is making," by Sue Macleod, was previously published in *The Malahat Review* (No. 27, Winter 1997).

"Fer de Lance," by Randall Maggs, was previously published in *Timely Departures* (Breakwater Books 1994). Reprinted with permission of the publisher.

"Asha's Gift," by Rachna Mara, was previously published in *Of Customs & Excise* (Second Story Press 1991). Reprinted with permission of the publisher.

"Nino's Work," by Joseph Maviglia, was previously published in *A God Hangs Upside Down* (Guernica Editions 1994). Reprinted with permission of the publisher.

"Dedication" by Lori Miseck was previously published in *the blue not seen* (Rowan Books 1997). Reprinted with permission of the publisher.

"Eating Watermelon" by Lisa Moore was previously published in *The Malahat Review* (Spring 1996).

"The Lady of the Bean Poles," by Sheldon Oberman, was first published in *New Quarterly* and then in *This Business with Elijah* (Turnstone Press 1993).

"Tangents," by Helen Pereira, was first published in *Prairie Fire* and then *The Home We Leave Behind* (Killick Press 1986). Reprinted with permission of the publisher.

"The Sacrifice," by Chetan Rajani, was previously published in *Best Canadian Stories*.

"Who Says Love Isn't Love?" by J. Jill Robinson, was first published in *The Fiddlehead* and then in *Eggplant Wife* (Arsenal Pulp Press 1995). Reprinted with permission of the publisher.

"Oranges," by Barbara Scott, was previously published in *Grain*.

"Building Marrakesh," by Struan Sinclair, was previously published in *Strange Comforts* (Gutter Press 1998).

"The Green Insect," by John Steffler, was first published in *Event* (vol. 25/no. 3, 1996/97) and then in *That Night We Were Ravenous* (M&S 1998). Reprinted with permission of the publisher.

"Crooked Hollow," by Royston Tester, was previously published in *B & A New Fiction* (December 1995).

"What'll You Have?" and "Their Futures Drift Like Ash Across the City (Triangle Shirtwaist Factory, New York, 1911)," by Sue Wheeler, were previously published in *Solstice on the Anacortes Ferry* (Kalamalka Press 1995). Reprinted with permission of the publisher.